…GE ON THE LEVELS

A gripping crime thriller full of suspense

DAVID HODGES

Detective Kate Hamblin Mystery Book 2

Originally published as *Requiem*

JOFFE BOOKS

Revised edition 2019
Joffe Books, London
www.joffebooks.com

First published in Great Britain in 2014
as *Requiem*

This paperback edition was first published
in Great Britain in 2022

ISBN: 978-1-80405-538-0

AUTHOR'S NOTE

Although the action of the novel takes place in the Avon & Somerset police area, the story itself and all the characters in it are entirely fictitious. Similarly, at the time of writing, there is *no* police station in Highbridge. This has been drawn entirely from the author's imagination to ensure no connection is made between any existing police station or personnel in the force and the content of the novel. I would also point out that I have used some poetic licence in relation to the local police structure and some of the specific procedures followed by the Avon & Somerset Constabulary in order to meet the requirements of the plot – for example, changing the name of the force's present road policing unit to that of traffic, which is a more traditional generic title, as well as referring to a police technical support unit to avoid any connection with the hi-tech crime unit currently operating within the force. Nevertheless, the policing background depicted in the novel is broadly in accord with the national picture and these little departures from fact will, hopefully, not spoil the reading enjoyment of serving or retired police officers for whom I have the utmost respect.

BEFORE THE FACT

Twister could hear the barking of the police dogs, see the blue lights flashing above the buildings behind him, illuminating the night sky with an ethereal ghostly brilliance. At least the moon had faded again, which gave him a chance, but the pain in his abdomen was tearing him apart and he could feel the blood soaking into his underclothes from the knife wound, despite the bandages he had so expertly applied.

His fevered thoughts burrowed through the fog clouding his brain, taking him back to another time and another place, where, as a member of an elite SAS unit and despite a nasty combat wound, he had been forced into a gruelling retreat through four miles of swamp to the helicopter RV. As he hallucinated, he could once more feel the sticky heat on his perspiring skin, taste the decaying stench of the mangroves as he waded through the tepid leech-infested lagoons, one hand pressed against the wound in his side from the guerrilla's bayonet. He had managed to survive the experience intact, despite loss of blood and a serious infection, but only because of his outstanding physical fitness. This time was different, however.

Although still fitter than most, age and drink had taken its toll on him and, after less than two miles, he knew he was about done. The street lamps were fuzzy white balls in his distorted vision, the sweat pouring down his face in rivulets and he could feel his heart thudding with the desperation of an over-taxed engine running out of oil. Ten minutes maximum, even with *his* state of fitness, and then his legs – already trembling fitfully – would buckle and he would hit the pavement. Finish.

But he couldn't let that happen, couldn't let Old Bill nail him and stick him in some shit-hole of a cell like before – this time to await a life sentence in stir for multiple murder. He had to make it to the address that had been imprinted on his memory for so long – the address his old mate, Louie the Dip had given him, the day before his release from Wandsworth, just in case he ever needed it. Well – bloody hell – he needed it now!

He found the alleyway, snaking off between the back gardens of a small development and then, as he emerged into a cul-de-sac, he saw the house, an old detached place set back among some trees in the far corner. Number 8, that was it. He made it to the front doorstep, feeling the blood squelching in his shoes, then collapsed with his hand on the bell.

Sunlight slanted in through the vertical blinds. A small, brightly painted bedroom with a couple of mobiles rotating gently in a cool breeze on hooks attached to the ceiling. Twister's gaze took in the bed – just like the sort they used in hospitals – and the tall stand by his head with a tube running from a plastic or nylon bag (who cared which?) suspended from the top of it to his bandaged wrist. A cable was taped to his naked chest and connected to what looked like a monitor on the wall and an ominous looking cylinder, with a face mask attached, stood beside it. Oxygen? Probably – thank the gods he didn't need it.

Raising the edge of the sheet which covered him to waist level, he examined his heavily bandaged abdomen, noting what looked like old bloodstains down one side and feeling sudden soreness from the catheter that had been inserted.

He felt sick and let the sheet fall back over him, closing his eyes tightly for a second to give his swimming senses time to stabilize.

He didn't hear the sound of the bedroom door, but jerked his eyes open when the voice spoke. 'Ah, back with the living now, I see.'

His visitor was short, plump and balding, with a pointed, black beard and moustache, like one of the Cavaliers from a Dumas novel, and his smile seemed to be a permanent fixture. 'Doctor Leasing,' he said, 'Hammond Leasing. You had a very nasty knife wound, but thankfully, there doesn't appear to be any serious damage to your internal organs.'

'How long have I been *here*?' Twister queried, tensing and glancing quickly towards the window at the sound of a distant siren.

'Just over a week.'

'A week?'

The doctor nodded. 'You had a nasty fever after I stitched you up and you've been out of it for several days.'

Twister let his head fall back on the pillow. 'And how long will I stay here?'

Leasing pursed his lips. 'I would think that a man as fit as you could be up and about in, say, a further two weeks.'

Twister nodded. 'Excellent. You've done a good job.'

The smile seemed to broaden. 'Nothing is too much for a friend of Louie's.'

Twister frowned. 'How do you know about Louie?'

'You told me while I was stitching you up – quite informative, you were.'

'How informative?'

Leasing sighed. 'Do you know, I've forgotten already,' he said meaningly.

Twister nodded his approval. 'Let's keep it that way,' he said, wondering why Leasing had been struck off by the GMC and reduced to looking after injured cons instead. Despite his curiosity, however, he decided it would be imprudent to ask under the circumstances.

Instead he said, 'I've a contact I need to ring, to fix up somewhere for me to lie low once I'm fit enough to travel.'

The little man pointed to a telephone on the bedside table. 'Yours to use whenever you want to. Be my guest. And after you've made your arrangements and are ready to leave, we can talk about my fee, eh?'

Twister studied him with a narrow smile of his own. Seeing as he didn't actually *have* any money to pay for his medical treatment, there wasn't very much they had to talk about. But that didn't really matter, for he had already planned to kill the nice doctor when the time came anyway. In fact, he was looking forward to the moment and, with what he was planning for the future, he couldn't afford to leave any loose ends behind anyway, could he?

CHAPTER 1

The man in the red Volvo spotted the girl when he turned the corner. She was standing under the same street lamp as the previous night, one foot up against the adjoining wall, her provocative silhouette partially wreathed in the smoky mist that had drifted into Bridgwater off the Somerset Levels. He braked gently, almost stalling the stolen Volvo's stammering engine, and pulled in closer to the kerb, flicking the switch of the front passenger window seconds before the car came to a stop. As the window slid down, the dank smell of the marshes that lay just beyond the town rolled into the car, awakening carefully stored memories and supercharging his adrenalin so that for a few seconds he could hardly breathe.

'You lookin' for some more business, love?' the young woman called, recognizing him and coming off the wall to peer in through the open window.

Once again an adrenalin surge hit him with painful force. Slim, in her mid-twenties, with a mass of auburn hair tumbling down to her shoulders, her resemblance to the young woman whose face had dominated his thoughts for so long was uncanny. Seeing her a second time was enough to confirm the assessment he had made the night before: she was ideal for his purposes.

He leaned across and threw open his door. 'Same terms then?' he queried, playing along with her, even though, for what he had in mind, the price was irrelevant.

'Told you before, depends what you want me to do,' she retorted and, settling into the front passenger seat beside him, pulled the door closed after her. 'I'll do any trick you like long as you pays the goin' rate.'

Her cheap perfume filled the car, obliterating even the dank smell of the mist. He smiled thinly in the gloom as he engaged gear and pulled away. 'Oh, I'm a very imaginative soul,' he murmured. 'I have no doubt that we can come up with something new this time.'

She lit a cigarette without asking. 'So where we going then? My flat again, is it?'

He glanced across at her, briefly noting the long legs and pelmet for a skirt as they passed through a pool of light created by another street lamp and thinking of the pert breasts and milky-white skin he had caressed just twenty-four hours ago. 'Not tonight,' he replied. 'There's a little place near here I thought we'd try.'

She shrugged. 'OK by me,' she said, 'but remember that me basic's fifty quid an hour – an' the clock's already tickin'.'

'Judging by your performance last night, I'm sure you'll be worth it,' he acknowledged. 'In fact, I *know* you will.'

Highbridge was out for the count – nothing moving along the Bridgwater road, save the fuzzy headlights of a lone articulated lorry heading back the way they had come. He swung left into a narrow side-street, then sharp right into a cul-de-sac, pulling up in front of a pair of wooden gates.

The girl peered past him through the driver's window, her uneasiness palpable. 'What *is* this place?' she queried.

He gave a short laugh and, climbing out of the car, went round to her door and jerked it open. 'You'll see in a minute,' he said, flashing a torch in her eyes. 'You coming?'

She slid one shapely leg out of the car, then stopped short. ''Ere, that sign there says Funeral Directors. That's undertakers, ain't it?'

He shrugged. 'Used to be. Business folded a couple of years ago, though. Just somewhere to doss now.'

She seemed unconvinced. 'Don't know about this,' she said. 'Place is kind of creepy. Why couldn't we have stuck to my flat?'

He sighed, his irritation showing. 'You can always walk back to Bridgwater,' he grated. 'Your choice.'

She pouted. Then, taking a deep breath, she stepped out of the car and, with obvious reluctance hobbled after him in her high-heels to the half-open double gates. Beyond, lay a concrete yard littered with rubbish. At the far end a long two-storey building, flanked on one side by what looked like a massive garage with steel doors, peered at them through the gloom.

She shivered as he prodded her forward with his torch, the beam then cutting a path ahead of them through the mist as he guided her across the yard by one elbow. 'What a crap-hole,' she breathed, lowering her voice. 'Gives me the jitters.'

He said nothing, but firmly steered her towards a door with a frosted glass pane. She heard the rattle of keys and waited while he reached past her to unlock it. 'Electric's off, I'm afraid,' he explained before ushering her through, then gave another short laugh. 'Still, maybe you'd prefer it in the dark this time, eh?'

A long hallway opened up before the beam of his torch. It was cold and smelled of damp and decay. She shivered again, suddenly wishing she was back on the streets of Bridgwater.

'In here,' he said, pushing open a pair of doors on their left.

Weak yellow light filtered into the hallway from the room inside, ghostly and uninviting. Once again she hesitated, a voice in her brain urging her not to go any further. But it was already too late, for he was now right behind her, firmly nudging her forward. The next instant she was over the threshold – and into a macabre ghoulish scene that might have been devised by the director of a Hollywood horror film.

The room was small and thickly carpeted, illuminated solely by flickering candlelight. A long table, covered by a cloth, stood in the centre, the tall candles in the multi-stemmed candelabra that lined each side licking at the rippling shadows pressing in on them with hungry smoky tongues.

It was not the table or the candles that held her startled gaze, however, rooting her to the spot with a kind of horrible fascination and starting the worm of fear crawling around inside her, but something that stood on the table between the candles.

The open wooden coffin was empty – she could see that much even in the gloom – its lid resting against a corner of the table, the brass handles glinting in the candlelight like slitted yellow eyes and its gaping maw grinning at her with cold mirth.

''Ere, what *is* this?' she demanded, her voice sounding strained and unnatural as she jerked round to face him.

'The old chapel of rest,' he replied. 'Now, take off your clothes.'

'What, in 'ere?' she exclaimed. 'You got to be jokin'.'

He smiled. 'You said you would do any trick,' he reminded her.

'Yeah, but not with that thing leerin' at me?' she said, nodding towards the coffin. 'What's it doin' 'ere anyway? You said noffin' about coffins.'

Twister kicked the door shut with the heel of his shoe and treated her to another smile. 'Why, it's for you, my dear,' he replied, 'just for you!'

And it was at that terrible moment that she knew she was dead.

CHAPTER 2

Blue lights pulsing in the winter murk, their intensity dimmed by a thickening mist, the metallic clatter of police in-car radios punctuating the still night air in sharp bursts of unintelligible conversation and a tiny knot of local residents, mostly still in their night clothes, gathered in the street nearby like inquisitive ghosts, bathed in the fuzzy light streaming from their homes.

Real life drama had come to Highbridge and it seemed to have drawn on the entire resources of the local police.

Two marked police patrol cars and several plain vehicles were drawn up untidily across the wide open gates accessing the rear yard of the building that occupied the corner of the cul-de-sac, a lone uniformed constable standing a little uncertainly in the opening, as if awaiting instructions, while behind the windows of the derelict property torches probed the shadows like mini searchlights.

Detective Inspector Ted Roscoe scowled and set his familiar pork pie hat more firmly on his bullet-shaped head before slipping a piece of chewing gum into his mouth. Called out in the middle of a late-night poker session from the back room of his local, he was far from happy about things, especially as he seemed to have copped a real bummer of a job this time.

The young woman lying in the open coffin seemed to have been specially prepared for viewing; her auburn hair combed back from her face and spread out carefully on the pillow, her hands crossed demurely over her breasts and the distinctive sleeveless, padded jacket, white shirt and black trousers arranged like the clothes on a shop mannequin. The flickering lights of the candles placed on either side of the coffin lent an unnatural surreal quality to the scene, casting sinister moving shadows up and down the walls and across the ceiling, imbuing the corpse with a new vitality – as if, like one of Dracula's undead, the eyes were about to pop open and the slender hands grip the sides of the coffin to raise itself up.

Roscoe's feet fidgeted uneasily in his blue plastic booties – which, like the rest of those present, he had been required to pull on over his suede shoes to protect the crime scene – paying little attention to the scenes-of-crime officers moving about the room in their white plastic overalls, like aliens from a *Doctor Who* episode, as they set up their cameras and lighting equipment.

'Who found her?' he snapped, apparently to anyone who happened to be listening.

The uniformed constable relegated to the doorway of the chapel of rest cleared his throat. 'Control got a call from some bloke saying he'd seen a man climbing over the wall at the back, sir. When Robbie Jones and me attended, there was no sign of any intruder, but we found her like that.'

Roscoe turned to face him. 'And who was this "bloke"?'

The constable shrugged. 'Dunno, sir. Said his name was Ron Smith, but when Control checked the address he gave, it turned out to be duff.'

'What about the phone number?'

'Nicked mobile apparently – already listed in Property Index.'

Roscoe thought about that for a moment or two, chewing furiously. 'What the hell are we dealing with here?' he said finally, as if someone else might have all the answers. 'In case no one happens to have noticed, she's wearing a bloody police uniform!'

'Yeah, but she's not "job",' responded a plainclothes officer standing behind him.

Roscoe wheeled on him. 'Is that so, Phil?' he barked. 'So exactly what *is* she then?'

Detective Sergeant Philip Sharp cleared his throat. 'Bridgwater tom, Guv,' he replied simply.

'A tom? And how do we know that?'

Sharp shrugged. 'We found a bundle of clothes and a handbag dumped in the corner of the room. Picture on the driving licence in the handbag matches her exactly. Seems her name is Jennifer Malone and a CRO check reveals she has a whole string of convictions for importuning.'

Roscoe chewed furiously again. 'Great. So we have a killer who picks up a prossie from Bridgwater and brings her all the way to a derelict Highbridge undertakers just to stiff her. Then he strips her and puts her in a police uniform – which, I suppose, he just happened to find hanging on a peg in Marks and Sparks – before sticking her in a conveniently abandoned coffin?' He snorted, adding with heavy sarcasm, 'What could be more straightforward?'

'It's probably not that complicated when you think about it, Guv,' Sharp suggested airily. 'For a start, it's easy enough to get hold of a police uniform these days. Plenty of military surplus stores have them in stock. And this place *was* once an undertaker's, so there's likely to be a coffin or three knocking around somewhere.'

Roscoe glared at him. 'Tell me something I don't already know,' he snarled. 'Like maybe *why* our friendly neighbourhood psycho chose tonight of all nights to shit on my winning poker hand?'

Sharp smiled faintly in the gloom. 'If you ask me,' he replied, 'we're dealing with some kind of authority freak who's into a bit of necrophilia on the side.'

Roscoe studied him. 'Is that right?' he retorted, in a tone of feigned amazement. 'Well, *Sherlock*, help me with one more thing, will you? Seeing as there are no obvious marks on the body and the Home Office pathologist is still en route, perhaps you could use your wonderful deductive powers to tell me,' and he raised his voice, '*how the little tart died*?'

'Her neck will have been broken,' another voice cut in before the embarrassed DS could think of a suitable answer. 'Just like before.'

Roscoe switched his gaze to the young woman in uniform standing beside Sharp, his body stiffening. 'What the hell are you saying, Kate?' he breathed, plainly shaken by her words.

Sergeant Kate Hamblin returned his stare without flinching, her eyes unnaturally bright in the candlelight. 'It's Twister,' she replied. 'He's come back for me and this is his way of letting me know.'

'Twister?' Sharp put in. 'And who the hell is Twister?'

'Larry Wadman,' Roscoe grated, his gaze remaining fixed on the policewoman. 'Used to be the funeral director here until he started doing the terminations himself – and she's talking bollocks.'

'Am I, sir?' Kate retorted grimly and, moving closer to the table, she held up some strands of her own shoulder-length auburn hair in the candlelight as she stared down at the coffin. 'Just think about it,' she said. 'She's the same build and has the same hair colour and style as me, she's been dumped in a coffin in Twister's old funeral parlour and she's been kitted out in a police sergeant's uniform. Furthermore, if you look closely at the epaulettes on her tunic, you'll see that she has the same shoulder numbers as me.'

'Meaning?' Roscoe snapped, angry with himself for not noticing the shoulder numbers and knowing what was now coming.

Kate took a deep breath. 'That this poor girl was specifically chosen because she looks like me,' she said, 'and she was dumped here like this to warn me that my days are numbered.' She shuddered. 'Twister's back all right and this is his calling card.'

Roscoe couldn't contain himself. 'Bloody Nora, Kate,' he threw back at her, 'it's almost two years since that Operation Firetrap business. Larry Wadman either finished up in a ditch somewhere or he simply scarpered abroad – end of.'

She shook her head. 'But we never found his corpse, did we, sir? And he could hardly have bought a ticket to Barbados after being stuck in the guts with a blade, could he?'

Roscoe blew a bubble with his gum and licked it back under his Stalin moustache, clearly out of his comfort zone. 'Probably just a copycat job,' he growled. 'Some psycho's idea of a sick joke.'

'A joke?' Kate released her breath in a sharp impatient hiss. 'And who else would have bothered to set up an elaborate scenario like this and why now, after all this time?'

Roscoe scowled again. 'How the hell should I know?' he snapped, his uneasiness now palpable. 'There are plenty of nutters around out there.' Then, cutting short any further discussion, he gesticulated with his torch. 'OK, people, everyone out. Time to let SOCO get on with their job.'

Leaving the uniformed patrolman just outside the doors to secure the crime scene, the DI accompanied Kate into the hallway.

'Bad dreams still a problem?' he asked bluntly.

Kate didn't reply, her thoughts pulling her back to that dark place in her subconscious where she had tried so hard to bury the whole thing.

Two years – it had to be all of that – since the confrontation with the psychotic killer in the hallway of this house of death and, even after all that time, there were still some nights when she lay awake shivering in her own perspiration, fancying she could again smell the stench of the undertaker's mortuary and hear the squeak of the gurney creeping towards her in the gloom as she waited for Twister's powerful hands to close around her throat.

With hindsight, maybe she should not have accepted promotion to uniformed sergeant at her home station in the first place, but requested a posting to the other side of the force area, which was the usual policy on achieving a higher rank. At least then she would have had more chance of putting the business behind her, instead of enduring the constant reminders that living and working in the same environment brought with it. But it was too late for regrets now and, with this grisly killing, the whole nightmare had been resurrected, allowing the awful spectre of Larry Wadman to stalk back into her life again. And she had the strangest feeling that he was not that far away, watching and waiting.

'I'd like you to take another look around,' Roscoe said, lighting a cigarette and coughing over the smoke. 'See if there's anything your plods may have missed. I've got an incident-room team to sort out.'

Kate nodded. 'Fine by me, sir. I'll let you know if I find anything.'

The DI grunted, then stopped with one hand on the handle of the back door. 'You sure you're up to this after all that happened here before?'

Kate glared at him, 'I'll pretend I didn't hear that, sir,' she said tightly.

Roscoe jerked open the door. 'I'll leave DS Sharp here to manage the crime scene, until the official crime-scene manager arrives,' he added. 'Liaise with him if you make any startling discoveries.'

Then he was gone, a heavy lumbering shape disappearing into the mist.

CHAPTER 3

For a moment Kate stood there, listening to the creak of the building around her, her skin crawling, her stomach twisting.

Then, turning her back on the uniformed policeman left to secure the murder scene, she directed her torch along the hallway, noting the half-open door a few feet away and remembering with surprising clarity the mortuary and embalming room that lay on the other side.

Drawn by a kind of morbid curiosity, she crossed the hall and stepped into the room, her torch immediately picking out the gleam of the stainless steel dissecting table straddling the gulley and drain in the centre of the tiled floor and the matching sink in the corner, then focusing on the three big refrigerators still standing against the far wall, two with their doors hanging open.

The floor seemed strangely gritty underfoot and something crunched beneath her heel. Directing the beam of her torch upwards, she trailed it along a pair of glass-fronted cabinets standing against the adjacent wall and saw at once the jagged fragments leaning half out of the lower frames of the doors. So the local vandals had been in then, she thought grimly, wondering what use the scalpels and other lethal surgical instruments that she knew had once been inside would be put to – or had already been put to – on the local streets.

Returning to the hallway, she checked to make sure the uniformed constable was still in position outside the chapel of rest and made her way slowly towards the staircase, every ounce of her being rebelling against the prospect of penetrating any further into this nightmare house, but knowing she had no choice.

Unsurprisingly, the grandfather clock she remembered seeing in the alcove at the bottom of the stairs the last time she had been in the building was gone, no doubt removed to the hall of some enterprising villain's home by now, and she guessed that anything else not securely fixed to the walls or bolted to the floor would also have 'walked' long ago.

The door at the top of the stairs was wide open and her torch beam touched a fire-damaged settee and a broken, overturned table as she stepped into the living-room of the little flat that occupied the upper floor. Then, crossing the room to another door on her left, she found herself in a narrow corridor with small windows on one side and more doors on the other.

A check revealed a galley kitchen, a bathroom and what seemed to be a study of some sort – all showing evidence of more vandalism, with wrecked furniture and crude slogans sprayed on walls that had had their fittings bodily ripped from them, but there was little else of real interest.

Approaching a door facing her at the very end of the corridor, she pushed it open on one finger, carefully probing the darkness beyond with her torch before entering. It appeared to have once served as a bedroom and again the room was a mess – the double bed had been ripped open to the springs; a dressing-table smashed and lying on its side and graffiti covering the walls, but there was plainly nothing of interest here either.

Returning to the corridor, she paused for a moment, listening to the groan of the old building's arthritic joints and the occasional sound of heavy footsteps and muffled voices in the hallway below as the police forensics team went about their business. The first strands of fragile grey light were now beginning to steal into the corridor through the window beside her, heralding a murky dawn, and, peering down into the street, she noted the group of fuzzy onlookers standing at the mouth of the cul-de-sac.

People should have better things to do with their time, she mused, and was about to turn away from the window and make her way back to the living-room when she froze, the fizz of a match in the patchy greyness drawing her attention towards the main Bridgwater Road. Then as the eddies of mist parted, she saw him – a figure, dressed in what looked like a long hooded coat, standing on the opposite side of the road, apparently studying the building.

For a good few seconds she simply stared down at the sinister watcher, her mouth dry and her senses swimming. And as she stood there, unable to take her eyes off him, he slowly raised a hand in mock salute before vanishing again, swallowed up in the mist like a smoky wraith.

Tearing herself away from the window, she slammed back against the wall on one side, her body rigid and her eyes tightly closed in a state of total shock.

It was *him* – Twister – she was certain of it; the archetypical Freddie Kruger, Michael Myers bogeyman of every childhood fantasy, who had haunted her every conscious moment for two long years and had now returned to exact his revenge.

Pulling herself together, she lurched off along the corridor at a stumbling run.

The policeman guarding the crime scene jumped when she materialized from the gloom with the suddenness of a monster emerging from an anomaly in the Primeval television series. 'Leave that,' she shouted. 'With me – now!'

The small crowd of onlookers shrank back as she raced from the yard into the cul-de-sac, picking up the bobby on the gates en route. But a few yards further on, she came to an abrupt halt, peering intently into the misty clouds drifting around her. 'He was here,' she exclaimed breathlessly.

'Who was here, Skipper?' one of the policemen queried, plainly bemused by it all.

She ignored him and strode back to the crowd of onlookers. 'Did you see that man?' she said to an elderly woman in a dressing-gown.

'What man, dear?' the woman replied.

'The one with the hooded coat. He was over there,' Kate said, waving an arm in the appropriate direction.

'Not me, love,' the woman replied. 'Dunno what you're on about.'

Suddenly Kate realized how it looked. Even her two colleagues were shuffling their feet uncomfortably in the background. Damn it, she was making a prize fool of herself. What if her bogeyman had been nothing more than a product of her own fertile imagination, induced by the atmosphere of the place and her previous association with it? What if there had been no one there at all and she was the victim of her own paranoia?

'OK, thank you,' she mumbled. 'Just … just forget it.'

Her face burning with embarrassment, she swung on her heel and headed back to the house, leaving the policeman covering the yard gates to return to his post, while the other officer followed her at a discreet distance in awkward silence.

That wasn't the end of her embarrassment either, for the moment she pushed through the back door she was confronted by an irate DS Sharp. 'What the hell's going on, Kate?' he exploded. 'And what do you mean by snatching my crime scene man to go careering off into the street, without so much as a word to anyone?'

Kate threw the constable a swift sidelong glance and, although she couldn't read his expression in the gloom, she was relieved to see him slink quietly back to his post, obviously determined to stay out of a potential spat between two supervisors.

'Sorry, Phil, false alarm,' she replied and pre-empted any further questions with a question of her own, 'Pathologist here yet?'

Sharp stiffened slightly, but the distraction tactic seemed to work, for he didn't pursue his original gripe. Instead, he waved an arm towards the now spot-lit and taped off chapel of rest and grunted. 'Doing his stuff in there as we speak.' His voice tailed off and he appeared to study Kate for a few moments before continuing. 'You were right, you know,' he said. 'Doc reckons she *did* die from a busted neck, just like you said – and if that doesn't make you a bloody clairvoyant, I don't know what else does.'

CHAPTER 4

The mist was still rolling across The Levels when Kate Hamblin signed off on the duty sheet at Highbridge police station at the end of her tour of duty and drove home through the awakening countryside.

All in all, it had been a busy, testing night shift. Following her stand-down from the murder scene, she and her team of two had had to deal with a nasty accident on the edge of Burnham-on-Sea, two house burglaries in the village of Mark and the theft of a car in Blackford before she was able to return to the station to tackle the mountain of routine paperwork piled up in the in-tray on her desk. It was at times like this that she missed CID, as if it were a lost relative, and she vowed to get back on to the department as soon as possible and by virtually any means she could manage.

A grey heron rose with a silent beat of its huge wings from a hidden rhyne – or drainage ditch – to her left as she steered the nose of her blue Mazda MX5 into a sharp bend some distance beyond the crossroads on Mark Causeway, remembering with a shiver that this was the exact spot where Twister's Land Rover had forced her off the road during that infamous Operation Firetrap investigation two years before, totalling her previous MX5 and nearly killing her.

Instinctively, she glanced in her rear-view mirror, half expecting to see a pair of powerful headlights bearing down on her, but there was nothing, just a shifting swirling greyness, like the inside of a smoky tomb. 'Get a grip, girl,' she muttered to herself. 'It's all in the mind.'

The Retreat was a 'chocolate box' thatched cottage in the little village of Burtle. It had been Kate's home for the past six months, since she had moved in with her detective boyfriend, Hayden Lewis, from her dismal flat in Bridgwater, and ten minutes later the security light above the front door snapped on in greeting as she swung into the driveway at the side of the cottage behind Lewis's prized MkII Jaguar.

'Hayden?' she called, as she turned her key in the front door and stepped into the empty living-room. There was no response. The dying fire glowed faintly in the grate and the bottle of wine they had both shared the previous night before she had gone on duty still stood on the coffee table beside two unwashed glasses, but there was no sign of her man.

She glanced at her wristwatch and frowned. Seven-fifteen? Hayden should have been up by now. He was rostered for early turn CID-cover this week, which for the detective branch meant being at work by 8.30 am instead of the 6.00 am start uniform had to put up with.

'Hayden?' she shouted again, but there was not so much as a grunt.

Tight-lipped, she slipped out of the anorak she was wearing over her uniform and dumped it on the settee, before heading for the stairs. Where was the lazy sod – not still in his pit surely?

The bedroom on the right of the landing was in darkness, but the landing globe had been left on and the spread of its light was sufficient to reveal that the double bed was unoccupied.

An icy finger traced a line down her backbone as she remembered that previous occasion when Twister had lain in wait for Hayden at the cottage.

She pushed the door open further and stepped into the room, fists clenched, heart pounding. 'Hayden!' she said in a hoarse whisper. There was still no answer, but the figure hiding behind the door moved swiftly – seizing her from behind in a bear hug. Then, as she thrashed wildly and futilely in her assailant's powerful grip, a hand slipped inside her shirt and under her bra.

'I've always fancied women in uniform,' Hayden Lewis's familiar voice said huskily. Then he released her and fell back against the wall, laughing hysterically.

Kate turned on him, her eyes blazing and the tears streaming down her cheeks. 'Not funny, Hayden!' she shouted, beating against his chest with her fists. 'Not bloody funny!'

Lewis grabbed her wrists and held them out at arm's length until he felt her arms relax. 'Hey, hey,' he said anxiously, 'no need for that. I was only playing about.'

The bedroom light snapped on and he stared at her wet face in astonishment. 'What on earth's the matter with you, old girl?' he went on, pulling out a handkerchief and trying to dry her eyes with one hand as he put his other arm around her shoulders.

She pulled away from him, hiccupping her sobs for a few seconds. 'Well, I'm not in the mood for stupid games,' she retorted, slumping on to the edge of the bed to finish the job of drying her eyes with his handkerchief herself. 'You scared the hell out of me.'

He sat down beside her, rubbing her arm with one hand. 'Whatever's happened to make you like this?' he soothed. 'It's not like the fearless Kate Hamblin who used to live here.'

She stared at him with a faint smile, her anger subsiding – as it always did when she was close to this lovable, eccentric man with his old-fashioned, public-school ways and inherent courtesy, so untypical of the average CID officer. She could never be mad at Hayden for long. The soft hazel eyes with their permanent little-boy-lost expression, the wide good-natured face and the mop of unruly flaxen hair that tumbled over his ears and forehead like an uncut hedge may not have assured him of sex symbol status, but with his rumpled suits, threadbare shirts and scuffed suede shoes that looked as though they might have come straight from a charity shop, he had the sort of persona that could only have failed to arouse the deepest maternal instincts in a woman who was emotionally dead.

'There's been a murder at Wadman's Funeral Directors,' she blurted finally. 'A young girl about my age.'

His eyes widened. 'Wadman's?' he echoed. 'No wonder you were upset. Being there again must have awakened some rotten memories.'

She shook her head. 'You don't understand. It wasn't just the murder. She was actually dumped in the chapel of rest in – in a bloody coffin.'

'Gordon Bennett!' he exclaimed, then stiffened, his eyes narrowing. 'But there's more, isn't there?'

She nodded. 'The girl was a local prostitute, obviously picked because she looked like me – same auburn hair, build and everything.'

He frowned. 'You can't know that for certain, old girl. It was probably just a coincidence—'

'Coincidence, my arse!' she cut in savagely. 'Hayden, she had been stripped and then dressed in a police uniform with my shoulder numbers on the epaulettes and someone had broken her neck.'

Lewis gaped at her. 'Strewth, what are you saying?' he breathed, knowing the answer even before she replied.

'It's Twister,' she said. 'He's back and he wants me to know it.'

For a moment there was absolute silence as Lewis tried to digest what she had said. Then he took a deep breath. 'Wow!' he said. 'It seems unbelievable – and why now, after all this time?'

'That's what the DI said.'

'Well, he's right. Maybe it's a copycat job?'

She gave a hard, humourless laugh. 'DI said that as well, but it's crap. This is Twister, no doubt about it.'

'So what about the uniform? I know it's not difficult getting hold of police kit from surplus outlets, but I mean, the right size and everything. That must have been an incredible stroke of luck.'

Kate stood up quickly. 'Luck doesn't enter into it,' she said grimly and jerked back the sliding door of the built-in wardrobe. The empty hangar that had once held a spare set of her uniform confirmed her worst suspicions and seemed to leer at her.

'He got the real thing,' she said. 'Hayden, the bastard's been in this house!'

Twister was in a good mood – a very good mood. In fact, he was grinning to himself as he parked his stolen Volvo in the big car park at Highbridge and walked to the bus stop in town. He knew Kate Hamblin had seen him waving at her in the mist. He had clocked her pale face at the window of his old undertaker's business as he stood there watching the police activity and having a quiet smoke. He had slipped away before she'd had the opportunity of coming after him, but it was easy to imagine her shock and sense of panic. Good on you, girl, he thought – and this is just the beginning.

Killing the prossie had been a necessary start to his little game, but it had also been fun. First getting her to strip naked in that cold, candle-lit room had given him a real buzz. Her slim pale body had looked excitingly vulnerable in the flickering glow, the gold stud in her navel glittering at him invitingly as she'd wriggled her toes and stared at him with big frightened eyes.

She had already sensed she was going to die and her fits of shivering had had nothing to do with the cold – just pure terror. Strange how people still complied with a killer's instructions, even though they knew what the outcome would be; he had seen it many times before in the army when he had made his victims kneel in front of him before slitting their throats or snapping their necks. Maybe it was a desperate attempt to please the man who was about to take their lives, in the hope that he would change his mind or even an attempt to delay the inevitable for as long as possible? Whatever the reason, it added a certain extra enjoyment to the experience, made it much more of a special occasion.

It had helped him a lot, too. Dressing a corpse was always a lot more difficult than getting the victim to dress themselves before being wasted, although this one had looked a little surprised, even a bit hopeful when he'd produced the police uniform and tossed it to her – probably thought that maybe she wasn't going to be killed after all, just asked to perform some sort of perverted sexual act involving the coffin. Poor deluded cow! He'd snapped her neck while pretending to adjust the collar of her blouse – quick, clean and, above all, professional, just like the old days. He couldn't have felt happier with the way it had all gone.

There were two old ladies waiting as he approached the bus stop and he courteously helped one of them with her small suitcase before boarding the bus, receiving a nice smile and a 'thank you' in return. A gentleman, they obviously thought. Had they but known.

It only took ten minutes to reach Bridgwater's outskirts and he got off the bus just before the town centre, walking briskly across the road to a large industrial development. The man behind the reception desk nodded in greeting, recognizing him at once. Twister had hired one of the firm's vans before to transport some special equipment he had purchased to his hideaway out on the Levels and 'Mr Dennis Prewitt' was now seen as a trusted customer. Producing the forged driving licence he had used on the previous occasion – courtesy of good friends in the Smoke – he was soon behind the wheel of a long-wheelbase Ford Transit on an extended hire and heading back to Highbridge.

But he didn't stop there. He intended to pick up the Volvo once he had dumped the Transit, and so instead, took the road out of the town, via the village of Watchfield and along Mark Causeway, before heading out on to the Levels. The cottage came into view very soon afterwards, a dismal looking place, enclosed by broken-down fencing in the middle of a field. It was empty and in an advanced state of dereliction, but he'd known that already, for this wasn't his first visit. As an old soldier, he had made sure he carried out a full reconnoitre of the place before making a decision about it.

Turning into the gateway giving access to the field, he jumped out of the vehicle, leaving the engine running, and unhooked the chain holding the five-barred gate shut. A quick glance around him to satisfy himself that no one was watching and he drove through, stopping only briefly to shut the gate behind him before taking the rutted track across the field towards the house. Instead of pulling up outside, however, he continued along the broken-down boundary fence, then turned sharp left down the side of the place, gripping the wheel tightly as the Transit bumped and slewed its way through the tufted grass to the rear of the property and a large barn like structure crouched in the corner of the field.

The barn doors were tightly closed and secured with a heavy padlock, but that didn't deter him, since he had put the padlock and hasp on the doors himself a few days before, and he soon had them open wide enough to drive the Transit through.

Another quick look round outside, shielding his eyes to study the road and the adjoining drove, but there was no sign of anyone. Hardly surprising in this remote spot, which was probably why the property had been left to decay since the demise of the last owner; no one had the slightest interest in buying it. Even the barn was in a state of near collapse, but it suited Twister's purpose well enough and he had already blocked up any gaps in the timber walls with pieces of hardboard and sacking, tacking them in place to reduce the risk of the light from the powerful battery-operated lamps he had rigged up inside being visible to anyone passing.

Closing the doors, he now turned on the lamps and smiled with the excitement of a child given the freedom of his father's workshop for the first time. He had certainly kitted the place out well, even if he did say so himself: workbench, metal shelving, even a butane gas stove – well, you needed a cuppa when you were working, didn't you? The shelves too were packed with a variety of tools and other equipment, including battery operated drills, chargers, screwdrivers, hammers and spanners, steel brackets and rolls of black tape – everything needed for a spot of DIY, in fact.

Yet there were some quite curious items as well. Three leather swivel chairs, still in their cardboard packaging, had been pushed into a corner and a new mountain bike – which he had stolen from outside a cycle shop in Bridgwater a couple of days before, knowing he would need to get back to the Volvo in Highbridge after leaving the Transit in the barn – stood against one wall. The workbench itself held two large boxes. According to their labels, they contained computer and camera equipment respectively – opened, but as yet unpacked – together with a reel of electrical cabling, while a pair of oblong signs, expertly hand-painted by a sign-writer engaged a fortnight before, stood face in against one wall, the lamplight bouncing off the strips of black polished metal.

And watching over it all, incongruous in such a setting and strangely sinister, were two clothed shop-type mannequins, seated on a straw bale in the corner, their heads and blank faces turned towards the door and tilted slightly on one side, as if listening.

Twister seemed to acknowledge their presence as he stripped off his coat and reached for a drill on one of the shelves. Inserting a bit in the chuck, he gave a hard metallic laugh.

'Soon be party time,' he said, pressing the trigger for a few seconds to listen to the scream of the motor, 'then we can give old Kate the send-off she deserves. Now won't that be fun?'

And only the mannequins and the birds nesting in the roof above his head were there to share his twisted humour.

CHAPTER 5

Kate felt as though she had been hit by a truck. Unable to sleep after Lewis had left for work – late as usual – she had jumped at every sound in the old cottage; the crack of timbers, the rustling of a small rodent or bird in the thatch and the sigh of the newly arisen breeze through the eaves.

A thorough check of the place had produced no clues whatsoever as to how their burglar could have got in – or when. All the windows seemed to be securely fastened, the French doors at the back were locked and bolted on the inside and the front door was fitted with a special security lock that engaged as soon as the door closed. Yet someone had still managed to gain entry without using any force and that left Kate with a creepy unsettled feeling. As a result, even after satisfying herself for the second time that the front door and the French windows were locked and bolted and that there was a long-bladed knife from the kitchen drawer under her pillow for protection, she had still not felt secure enough to close her eyes for longer than a few minutes at a time. When exhaustion finally did claim her, the shrill of the bedside telephone about three hours later put paid to any further sleep opportunities.

'Hope I didn't wake you,' DS Sharp chortled, obviously enjoying the moment, 'but Guv'nor wants you in at the 1400 hours briefing.'

Cursing the weasel-faced detective, she stumbled from the bed into the shower and stood there enjoying the caress of the hot spray for several minutes before reluctantly switching off and stepping out on to the rubber mat in front of the cubicle. Removing her shower cap, she shook her auburn hair out over her shoulders again and wiped the steam from the wash-hand basin mirror to study her reflection.

Twenty-eight, and she still had her youthful freckles, but the blue eyes that stared back at her from the pale drawn face – once so alive and full of mischief – were dull and haunted, with dark smudges under them, as if she had used too much eye-shadow. Even her hair seemed to have lost its vitality and she brushed it vigorously for several minutes, seemingly in an attempt to restore it to its former coppery lustre. She glared at herself angrily in the mirror. She was fast becoming a wreck, just like after the nightmare business two years before. She really had to get a grip.

Expertly pinning up her hair so that it would fit under her hat, she took time to apply her makeup before dressing in her number one uniform, determined to present herself in the best possible light.

'You'll do, girl,' she said to the mirror and forced a smile as she headed downstairs.

The police station's rear yard was packed with unfamiliar vehicles and she was forced to leave her car in one of the bays at the front, designated 'Visitors Only'. The incident-room at the top of the building was in full swing, with a bank of computers, a couple of photo copiers and white boards bearing scribbled notes and scenes of crime pictures, already in situ. A plainclothes officer standing by the coffee machine with a plastic cup in one hand gave her an appraising glance as she made her way to the senior investigator's office at the far end and his lecherous glance gave her a much needed boost. At least she hadn't lost her pulling power completely then?

There were three of them in the cramped room; Sharp hadn't been invited, it seemed. The DI, chewing as usual, leaned against one wall, jacketless, with part of his rumpled shirt hanging out over his trousers and one of his blue braces so badly twisted that Kate desperately wanted to straighten it for him. It was obvious from the look of him that he hadn't been to bed yet and his eyes were heavy and slightly bloodshot.

The second man, seated on the edge of the desk, swinging his legs, could not have been more different. In his late forties and smartly dressed in an expensive looking blue suit and highly polished black shoes, his dark saturnine face with its slightly lopsided mop of jet black hair reminded her of pictures she had seen of Adolf Hitler, minus the moustache. The dark eyes that studied her as she entered the room after a peremptory knock were penetrating and analytical and the brief smile that was directed towards her had about as much empathy as that of a stone statue.

'Ah, Sergeant Hamblin, I believe,' he said, pre-empting Roscoe's introduction and holding out a slim pale hand as he slid off the desk to greet her.

Kate took his hand warily, expecting the handshake to be limp and effeminate, but discovered that it was just the opposite and winced as it crushed her fingers in a vice-like grip.

'Detective Chief Inspector Raymond Ansell,' he said. 'I have been appointed 2 i/c in this case.'

She nodded, knowing the name immediately from the 'bush telegraph' that bandied the names of notable senior officers about regularly throughout the force. Ansell was a man to be reckoned with, she'd heard. A recent import from the Met, with a reputation as a ruthless, ambitious tactician, he was known to have the Chief Constable's ear and would, it was rumoured, cut his best friend's throat – if he had one – to get to the next rung on the ladder.

He now motioned towards the third man, a rotund red-faced individual with a bald freckled pate and restless blue eyes. 'Detective Superintendent Maurice Willoughby. Mr Willoughby will be – ah – leading the investigation as the senior investigating officer.'

Kate smiled faintly this time. She knew of Willoughby too. Newly appointed to CID from the Bristol area, his reputation as an indecisive and sycophantic grandee had earned him the nickname 'Ethelred' after the Saxon king, Ethelred the Unready. The way Ansell had introduced himself first, despite the other's senior rank, indicated that the DCI would be calling all the shots, with Willoughby rubber-stamping his decisions. The Detective Super was just along for the ride and, from his slightly pained expression, it was obvious that he knew it. They had to be short of detective superintendents, she mused, to have brought him out of the closet.

'Do sit down, Sergeant,' Willoughby said, speaking for the first time and colouring up as he did so, no doubt anxious to be seen to be leading the meeting, but feeling self-conscious and under-valued.

She nodded again and sat down in the chair he swung across the room towards her. 'Good afternoon, sir,' she replied politely. 'You wanted me at the 1400 hours briefing.'

Willoughby threw a quick glance at Ansell, then cleared his throat, obviously knowing very little about it. 'Ah, that,' he said. 'Yes, it would be most helpful, but I … er … *we* wanted to have a chat with you first, seeing as you seem to be linked into things.'

He looked at Ansell again. 'Perhaps Mr Ansell would—' he began, breaking off in mid-sentence and dropping into a nearby chair.

Ansell returned to his vantage point on the desk and stared down at her, mentally dismembering her like an assembled Lego model, while Roscoe, whose gum chewing had slowed appreciably, watched with narrowed eyes. 'Two years ago, you were a key player in Operation Firetrap, I believe?' the DCI said.

'Not exactly a key player, sir,' she said, 'but I was involved, yes.'

Ansell nodded. 'I think I already know most of the background from the file, but, since I only arrived in the force from the Met three months ago, it would be useful to hear about it from your perspective.'

She hesitated. 'You mean all of it?'

Another insipid smile and he held out a hand in an inviting gesture. 'In your own time, of course,' he replied.

She glanced quickly at Roscoe and, receiving a non-committal shrug in return, she moistened dry lips and cleared her throat. 'I was part of a three up surveillance team,' she began, 'keeping observation on the home of a suspected arsonist, Terry Duval, out on The Levels—' She broke off and he raised an interrogative eyebrow, encouraging her to continue.

'I had to go for a … a leak,' she went on, 'and, while I was away from the vehicle, a man, later found to be Larry Wadman—'

'Twister?' he interrupted.

'Twister,' she agreed, 'placed an explosive device on the side of the vehicle and blew the thing up, killing both my colleagues. One of them was DC Alf Cross and it turned out that Alf's own wife, Pauline, was behind the killings and had hired Twister for the purpose so that she could claim on his life insurance.'

'Nice lady,' Ansell observed drily. 'And I gather your surveillance target, Duval, was framed for the murders, and was subsequently shot dead by one of our ARV officers?'

Kate nodded, wondering why he was asking so many questions if he knew the answers already. 'Yes,' she confirmed, 'he had taken me as a hostage and the ARV officer thought he was armed.'

'Unfortunate,' Ansell commented with little sincerity. 'And this man, Twister, came after you, eh?'

Kate gave another nod. 'I was the only witness to the murders and he didn't know how much I had seen.'

'With the result that your twin sister, Linda, was murdered by mistake?'

Kate shuddered and swayed slightly in the chair, remembering the awful night she had found Linda's body trussed to a chair in her flat. 'He – he thought she was me,' she said in a strangled voice.

With a surprising sleight of hand, Ansell produced a glass of water from the desk and handed it to her. 'Nasty business,' he said and waited while Kate took a gulp from the glass. 'So how did you discover Twister's identity?'

Kate handed the glass back to him and took a deep breath. 'From a partial print on a tracking device he had put under my car. Because of his CRO record, I was able to trace him to his undertaking business.'

Ansell smiled approvingly. 'Where you evidently rescued your boyfriend, DC Lewis, who was being held by him as a bargaining counter, and came close to losing your own life as well. Excellent work by the sound of it.'

'The troops arrived at the right moment, sir,' she said modestly, 'but Twister escaped in the pandemonium.'

He grunted. 'With a knife wound to his gut, courtesy of his co-conspirator,' he rejoined, more as a statement than a question.

'They apparently fell out,' Kate explained, 'but Twister was – is – a powerful man and the wound was not enough to finish him. He killed Pauline before she could get away and we later discovered that he had put her body in one of his coffins, swapping her for another deceased woman whom he returned to the mortuary fridge.'

'And Pauline Cross ended up being cremated in her stead?'

Kate nodded yet again, tiring of the questioning and wondering what the point was to it all.

Ansell slid off the desk for a second time, bending to smooth the creases out of his trousers. 'And you think Twister has come back to finish the job on you, eh?' he said, looking up at her.

The way he said it seemed to suggest that she was simply being neurotic and she flushed.

'The girl in the coffin was obviously put there for a reason, sir,' she said tightly.

'Of course she was,' he agreed. 'She was dead.'

Kate shot to her feet, her eyes flashing dangerously. 'With respect, *sir*,' she said, 'this is not a joke.'

'Sergeant Hamblin!' Roscoe castigated.

Ansell waved him to silence and straightened up, studying her fixedly. 'No one is suggesting it is, young lady,' he replied quietly, 'but it does seem rather odd to me that a wanted criminal would choose to return to the scene of his crime and blatantly advertise the fact with a stunt like this. If he's after revenge, why not simply do the job, and quietly disappear again?'

Roscoe glared at Kate, indicating her chair with a flick of his eyes, and she reluctantly sat down again. 'He likes to play games, sir,' she said, then added, 'That girl was not just someone who happened to be in the wrong place at the wrong time. She was specifically chosen for her resemblance to me and you're forgetting she was dressed in a police uniform bearing my shoulder numbers.'

'*Your* shoulder numbers?' Ansell echoed sharply and gave Roscoe a hard searching glance.

The DI cleared his throat. 'Sorry, Guv,' he said, 'I should've told you about that.'

Ansell's face had noticeably darkened. 'Yes, you should, Detective Inspector,' he agreed tartly. 'Anything else you haven't told me?'

Roscoe moved from one foot to the other, like a nervous schoolboy about to admit to some heinous transgression. 'You had only just arrived and there wasn't time—' he began, but Ansell cut him off. 'So what else should I be aware of?'

But Kate got in first. 'I believe the uniform the girl was wearing belongs to me,' she said. 'One is missing from my wardrobe at home – the bastard even took a pair of my knickers, a bra, tights and a spare pair of my shoes.'

Roscoe nodded. 'DC Lewis reported the matter when he came on this morning,' he said.

'DC Lewis?' Ansell queried.

'I live with him,' Kate explained.

'Do you now?' Ansell replied. 'How nice for you.' Then he added, 'So we have a burglary as well as a murder then, do we? SOCO taken a look yet, have they?'

It was Kate's turn to feel uncomfortable again. 'No, sir. Well, there was no break-in as such that I could see.'

Ansell took a few moments to digest the information. 'No break-in, but a burglary nevertheless, eh?' he said. 'Bit of a contradiction in terms that, isn't it? So how did your burglar get in – climb down the chimney or did he have his own key?'

Kate shrugged. 'I don't know, sir, but my uniform is definitely missing.'

For the first time Ansell looked worried. 'If your assumptions are correct, Sergeant,' he said suddenly, 'you are in considerable danger. From now on you can't be allowed to patrol on your own, understood? You must always have someone with you.'

Kate was once more on her feet, this time flushed with indignation. 'Sorry, sir, but that's not on,' she snapped. 'I'm a bloody sergeant.'

'And I'm a bloody detective chief inspector,' he said, giving her a cynical smile. 'And that means you will do as I tell you, OK?'

'Quite so,' Willoughby agreed pompously. 'No argument.'

Kate clenched her fists tightly by her side, her mouth a hard line. 'Under protest, sir,' she said.

'Excellent,' Ansell replied and glanced at his watch. 'And I do believe it's time for the incident-room briefing.'

CHAPTER 6

'Mind if I join you?'

Kate glanced up from the swirling depths of her coffee and stared at Phil Sharp's grinning weasel face, for a moment, uncomprehending. 'What?' she said distantly.

'I said, mind if I join you?'

He sat down anyway, hugging a bottle of coke and dumping a folded newspaper on the table.

She shrugged, eyeing the greasy-haired detective with distaste. 'If you really must,' she replied.

The dig was lost on Highbridge's self-declared number one sleuth and his inane grin remained fixed, like a plaster cast.

The canteen was virtually empty following the briefing. Most of the troops, including Hayden whom she desperately wanted to talk to, were already out on their assigned 'actions', including house-to-house inquiries in the vicinity of the murder. She had been spared that onerous task, but after being put on the spot and subjected to a tense question and answer session on Twister – who at least now seemed to have been accepted by the hierarchy as the number one suspect – she felt even more drained than before.

She had chosen the corner table, partly hidden by an ornamental bamboo screen, so she could linger over her coffee in peace prior to heading home to bed before the night shift, but apparently it was not to be and she stared at Sharp with a sense of resignation.

'We made the front pages of the nationals then?' he said, tapping the newspaper with a forefinger. 'Nice pic of Wadman's place.' He turned the paper round, so she could see the headline. 'Murder At Death House,' he read. 'Dead dramatic, eh?'

He chuckled at his pun, took a swig from his coke bottle and burped. 'I hear you've been told to stay well away from the press? Willoughby's probably worried you might upstage him when he finally decides to call a press conference. You know old Willoughby, "yes, I will, no I won't".'

She ignored his derogatory remarks, instead commenting, 'I thought you'd have still been in your pit after your busy night.'

He shook his head. 'Not me. Got home at five and was up again at eight. I don't need much sleep, see. Over-active brain.'

She raised a tired eyebrow. 'Didn't know you had one of those,' she retorted. 'Must have been a recent acquisition.'

His grin faded for a second, then returned with a vengeance. 'What do you think of the boss?' he asked, keeping his voice low and glancing around him as if he were on the set of a spy thriller. 'Not Ethelred, of course – the real boss, Ansell?'

Kate shrugged. 'Seems OK to me. Why?'

'Ex-Met, you know,' he replied. 'Transferred to us on promotion to DCI. This is his first big case, so he needs a result.'

'Good for him.'

'Bit of a hatchet man by all accounts.'

'Well, they would say that, wouldn't they?'

'I'm just telling you what I've heard.'

She sighed and took a sip of her coffee. 'Well, I'm really not interested in canteen gossip,' she said. 'Nor should you be.'

But he wasn't listening. 'No sense of humour, did you notice that?' he went on, oblivious to her censure. 'They reckon he had a charisma bypass – only known to smile once as a baby and then it turned out to be just wind.'

He chuckled at his own joke, then stopped short under her sober gaze, his grin vanishing at the same time. 'Let's hope Ansell gets a better result than Callow did on your Operation Firetrap, eh?'

Kate flinched, remembering with a sense of revulsion her former CID boss, DCI Roz Callow, whose sexual predation had made her life a misery.

'I hear she had it in for you,' he went on with brutal directness. 'My source tells me she fancied you and you wouldn't give her one. That right?'

Kate refused to be drawn, staring into her coffee cup again and trying to think of other things, but Callow's hatchet face stared back at her from inside her head even as she tried to blank it out.

'Ended up having it off with Alf Cross's missus, didn't she?' Sharp persisted, then gave a short laugh. 'Only to find out her nice little Pauline was actually the one behind the murders. At least she got her comeuppance when they sacked her anyway.'

Kate studied him with contempt. 'She wasn't sacked actually. There was insufficient evidence of anything. She was retired on ill-health grounds,' she replied tersely, wondering why she was bothering to say anything in defence of the woman who had set out to destroy her. 'She badly injured her leg and hip in a fall at the undertaker's place when we nailed Twister.'

'Yeah, yeah, yeah.' he sneered. 'Fell down the stairs as she was running away, I hear.'

She glared at him. 'Whatever,' she rapped, tired of his constant probing. 'Anyway, I'm going home to bed.'

'With anyone I know,' he called after her as she headed for the door, but his chortle jammed in his throat when Detective Chief Inspector Ansell, who had apparently been sitting on the other side of the bamboo screen, stood up and threw him a hard penetrating glance before following Kate out.

Twister parked the Volvo in the small car park and made out he was reading the newspaper he had spread over the steering wheel. The man he had been discreetly tailing across the Levels for the past twenty minutes nodded to him as he got out of his old green Land Rover and walked past him to the gate, his binoculars swinging on the cord around his neck as he walked.

Twister waited until the other had disappeared through the gateway before leaving the vehicle and walking slowly after him. The sign beside the gate indicated that he was entering a wildlife reserve and he smiled as he pushed through. A twitcher's paradise, he thought and, removing the binoculars he had been using in the stake-out of his target's house from the pocket of his hooded coat, he hung them around his neck in a similar fashion to his quarry.

It was very cold and although the thick mist of the morning had largely gone, save for a few wispy spirals creeping across the track close to the ground, the faint glimmer of wintry sunshine made very little impression on the gloomy day. Not surprisingly on this grey afternoon, the reserve seemed to be otherwise deserted and, apart from occasional panicky flapping in the undergrowth as he walked past, the surrounding woodland remained a sodden, dead world, brooding and secretive.

He shivered and pulled his hood up over his head, unable to comprehend why anyone would want to spend time in such a wet miserable environment simply to watch the antics of a few ducks and swans, but there again, train-spotting was just as daft to him, yet plenty of people seemed to enjoy it. Maybe he was missing something somewhere? But even if he was, he wasn't about to lose sleep over it; all that mattered was the fact that twitching had given him the ideal opportunity to complete his next move in the game.

The man he was following was way ahead of him, moving briskly along the track, obviously unaware of his presence and knowing exactly where he was going, but Twister kept his distance; the last thing he needed was to be spotted and quizzed on the local birdlife and that was a fact.

In a couple of hundred yards the track forked both left and right and Twister hesitated. Which way now then? His man was out of sight, so he could have gone in either direction. Then he spotted the boardwalk and at the same moment there was a flurry of activity from alarmed birds away to his left and he smiled again. Brilliant. Those feathered sentinels were better than an electronic tracker.

His rubber-soled shoes made only a slight sound on the wooden planks as he stepped on to the boardwalk and, within a few yards, he reached a bend in the track and saw the low wooden building dead ahead.

The hide stood on stilts among a jungle of reeds, a ramp leading up from the boardwalk to the single door, which was closed.

He decided that the best strategy was a completely open approach and he deliberately coughed as he mounted the ramp and pulled open the door. He was greeted by a welcoming smile. 'Nice to have some company,' the man said, turning back on the bench seat to scrutinize the lake with his binoculars through one of the open hatches.

Flicking up the wooden snib to open another hatch, Twister made a show of following his example, noting with little real interest the lake stretching away into the distance, enclosed on all sides by reed beds, giving way to the familiar woodland. Bending his head, as if to familiarize himself with his location, he watched a flock of geese swoop in like a squadron of fighter aircraft, barely grazing the surface of the water as they landed, then raised his binoculars to study them more closely.

'Canada Geese,' the twitcher explained. 'Nothing special there, would you say?'

Twister grunted, then moved past him to the other end of the hide, opening another hatch, apparently studying a reed bed to his right. 'Something interesting in there, though,' he said and stood back as the other slid along the bench to have a look.

'Sorry, what did you see?' the man queried.

'Nothing much really,' Twister replied and, seizing his head from behind in a vice-like grip, jerked it sharply to one side, then back again snapping his spine with a sickening crunching sound.

For a moment the killer stood there breathing heavily, as his victim pitched off the seat on to the floor, then he reached forward to pick up a greaseproof packet of sandwiches lying beside a flask on the sill that ran the length of the hide under the hatches. He opened the greaseproof paper and peeled back one of the slices of bread. 'Corned beef,' he murmured and nudged the corpse on the floor with the toe of his shoe. 'Now how on earth did you know they were my favourite?'

CHAPTER 7

Kate arrived home late in the afternoon, to find a plain van and Lewis's distinctive red Jaguar parked in the drive of the cottage and the place virtually taken over by a team of scenes-of-crime officers. Lewis was waiting for her in the living-room and he looked apprehensive, as if unsure of her likely reaction.

'Sorry, Kate,' he said, 'but Guv'nor wanted a detailed examination carried out, in case our visitor left any traces.'

'Did he?' she commented grimly. 'So he still doesn't believe me then?'

He was quick to reassure her. 'Oh, I don't think it's that,' he replied, 'But he'll have no choice now anyway – SOCO found marks on the little pantry window which suggest that that is how our man got in, shutting it after him and probably leaving by the front door.'

He hesitated and her eyes narrowed. 'There's something else, isn't there, Hayden?' she said. 'Come on, out with it.'

He sighed and nodded towards the stairs. She followed him up to the bedroom, but stopped dead in the doorway.

The wreath lay on the coverlet of the bed, a card attached by a black ribbon to one side of it. Moving closer, she saw that the card was face up, the message, written in a thick black pen, unmistakable: 'In memory of Kate Hamblin. RIP'.

'Don't touch it,' Lewis said quickly. 'SOCO will be taking it with them for forensics to have a look at.'

Kate treated him to an old-fashioned glance. 'What is it they say about teaching granny to suck eggs?' she said tartly.

He flushed. 'He must have put it here when you left for the nick,' he went on. 'And there's worse.'

She faced him. 'How much worse?'

'Spare front door key is missing from the hook,' he replied.

She closed her eyes for a second. 'So he can come and go as he pleases now, eh? Brilliant.'

He shook his head. 'I've got a local security firm coming over tomorrow to fit new locks to the doors and security bolts to the windows,' he said.

'And meanwhile, I have to sleep here?'

'I don't think he'll come back again today. He's made his point.' He frowned. 'I just can't understand why he's going to all this trouble. If he wanted to … er….'

'Kill me?'

He looked embarrassed. 'Well, you know, he could have done it at the beginning before anyone realized he was back. Why all this charade?'

'He likes to play, Hayden,' she said grimly, staring out of the bedroom window. 'I'm only at risk when he tires of the whole thing.'

'I think you should go away for a few days – until we nail the bugger,' he said suddenly. 'Have a little holiday.'

She glared at him. 'Like hell I will. I'm going to see this thing through to the end, whatever happens. I'm not running away like some scared little kitten.' She snorted. 'Anyway, Ansell's insisting I go two-up when I'm on duty as a safety precaution. I ask you, a police sergeant with a chaperone? I'll be an absolute bloody laughing-stock.'

'It's better that than dead,' he reminded her.

She snorted. 'I am quite capable of taking care of myself, thank you.'

He looked worried. 'I'm sure you are, but on that score, I have to go back on duty this evening, so you'll be on your own. Might be better if you bolted the front door on the inside, as our man might now have a key. I've already wedged the French doors to stop any forced entries there.'

'I'll be fine,' she said a little tersely.

He nodded. 'Well, it's only for today. New locks will be fitted from tomorrow. He hesitated. 'I can hang on here for a while after SOCO have left anyway, so you should be able to get your head down for a few hours,' and he grinned, 'unless you have … er … anything else in mind…?'

'Don't even think of going there, Hayden,' she said. 'Not for just a second.'

Twister had found his victim's body a lot heavier than he had expected, but he managed to carry it over one shoulder to the edge of the lake. Then, stripping it completely, he waded into the water and pulled the cadaver under the hide, wedging it in a small cavity below the ramp and securing it to a wooden pile with some rope he had brought with him. 'That should hold you for a while,' he murmured, confident that he would be long gone before decomposition of the body brought it to notice.

Returning to the car park, he dumped his victim's clothes in the back of his Land Rover and transferred a black briefcase from the front seat of the Volvo to the other vehicle's front seat. Then, checking to make sure the car park was still empty, he slid behind the wheel of the Land Rover, started the engine and drove to the entrance, where he left the vehicle for a few moments with its engine running. Finally returning to the Volvo, he unlocked the fuel cap flap, removed the cap itself and inserted a length of petrol-soaked rag into the filler pipe before lighting the rag and taking to his heels.

The car exploded in a ball of flame seconds after he rumbled out of the reserve in the Land Rover and, glancing in his rear view mirror, he saw the angry red and yellow tongues leaping above the trees that separated the car park from the main road. It was done and the police would be cursing the joy-riders responsible when they were called to the smouldering wreck. Now all he had to do was dump the clothes in the appropriate recycling bin at the local supermarket and move on to the next stage of the game.

Just half an hour later, he swung the Land Rover into a narrow lane off the back road from Wedmore to Glastonbury and, a few hundred yards further on, turned right into a wide gravel drive flanked by brick pillars and seven-foot-high hedges. Climbing out of the car briefly to open the heavy wrought-iron gates that blocked his way, he drove through, without closing them after him, and pulled up beside an imposing detached house, with squared bay windows and a large double garage. Getting out of the vehicle, he looked around him. The property was well shielded from the road, as he'd seen from earlier reconnoitres, which suited him fine, and he'd been careful to ensure no one had seen him turn in.

Approaching the garage, he unlocked the double doors and pushed them back. Then, returning to the Land Rover, he drove it inside, switching off the engine and smiling at the sleek black Mercedes saloon, which he knew he would be parking alongside. 'Just the job,' he murmured. 'Am I looking forward to driving you.'

The front door of the house opened easily with his stolen keys and he stood for a moment in the hallway, listening. Not a sound; the place was as dead, as he had expected. Taking his time, he carefully checked each room in turn, looking for photographs. There were none. So his research had not played him false then. His victim lived alone and had no family ties – he was the solitary bird-watching freak his inquiries had indicated. Brilliant. A place to doss – provided he kept out of sight, of course – a full larder, and a nice new Mercedes motor to use; what more could a man want?

Making his way back to the study off the hallway, which he had already cursorily checked, he now interrogated the answer phone. Nothing. He nodded his satisfaction. It was all going according to plan, which was excellent – and there looked like being something of a bonus to it all too. Picking up a bottle from the desk with one gloved hand, he read the label, 'Talisker Single Malt 12 years old,' he murmured. He beamed as he reached for a glass. Mr Twitcher was a whisky drinker too. Well now, wasn't that just perfect?

Opening his briefcase on an adjacent coffee table, he carefully checked that the electronic equipment inside was working satisfactorily for later use, then closed it again and settled into the high-backed swivel chair with his generously filled glass, thinking carefully about his next move.

CHAPTER 8

Bad dreams. Old memories coming back. Twister bending over the bed, huge hands outstretched, his dead eyes wide and staring. Kate jumped violently and uttered an involuntary cry. A beamed ceiling jerked into focus as she opened her eyes, her body steaming with perspiration, yet icy cold inside the tangle of cotton sheets that seemed to be sticking to her, as if backed with adhesive.

She rolled over in the bed and tore herself free of their clammy embrace, gasping for air, lying there for several minutes, willing her hammering heart to slow down as she acclimatized herself to her surroundings. The dream had been so vivid that she still couldn't believe it had only been a dream.

She glanced at the clock on the bedside cabinet, then shot up in a different sort of panic. It was already 8.30 in the evening and she had to be on night duty by ten.

'Hayden?' she yelled, but there was no response. Crossing groggily to the window, she peered down at the driveway. His Jag was not there, which meant he had to be still at work. Damn it!

Dragging herself to the bathroom, she slipped into the shower and stood there for twenty minutes, as if trying to purge herself of the dream in the hot clean water. Then she dried herself with a big fluffy towel and padded down to the kitchen in her bare feet, pulling on her dressing-gown as she went.

A quick snack of cheese on toast and coffee, then it was back to the bedroom to put on her face and slip into her uniform. It was nearly half-past nine when she finally left the house – clean, refreshed and more or less back in control. But her horrific dream was still as vivid in her mind as it had been an hour earlier and, climbing into her blue Mazda MX5 and pulling out on to the main Burtle to Mark road, she prayed for a busy night shift, in the hope that it would provide the healing distraction she needed. She was soon to learn, however, that it is always wise to be careful about what you pray for, because you can easily end up with a lot more than you envisaged.

The duty inspector, Doug Harrison, was scowling when he hauled Kate into his office 'for a chat' after the shift briefing at ten. Like her, he had had to run the gauntlet of an army of journalists and photographers, who had shown their dissatisfaction with the terse statement on the murder issued by the headquarters press office by besieging the police station. He was plainly unnerved by it all.

'Gather you are to have your own bodyguard,' he growled.

'Not my idea, sir,' she said. 'DCI insisted.'

He grunted. 'Don't know how we're going to do this with the numbers *we* turn out on the streets on a night shift,' he said, ignoring her explanation. 'Bloody ridiculous. I mean, are you a police officer or not?'

She flared immediately. 'With respect, *sir*, don't blame me for it,' she retorted. 'I don't like it any more than you do.'

But it was obvious that he wasn't listening. 'Bloody press camped outside the nick, clamouring for information,' he grumbled, 'two of the shift off sick and now I've got to find you a flaming chaperone.' Striding to the door of his office, he shouted down the corridor. 'Taylor.'

The young, spotty-faced constable appeared almost at a trot – a first year probationer. Inwardly, Kate groaned. Talk about rubbing it in.

Harrison's eyes gleamed. 'There you are, Sergeant,' he sneered. 'Your very own personal Rottweiler. I hope you two will be very happy together.' Then he stalked off towards the custody office.

'Sorry, Sergeant,' the young bobby said, his face reddening.

Kate studied him for a moment, noting the close cropped fair hair, bright blue eyes and the fine golden line on his upper lip, marking his attempt at a moustache. 'What's your first name?' she queried.

He looked even more uncomfortable. 'Eugene,' he replied.

Kate winced. 'Great,' she breathed. 'The final ignominy.'

'Pardon, Sergeant,' he said, frowning.

She clapped him on the shoulder. 'Never mind, Eugene, let's get out there and see what's about.'

The streets were rain washed, lamp standards throwing distorted yellow moons into the puddles and vehicle headlights producing 3D reflections in the black ribbon of the A38. Kate drove slowly, scanning the pavements for anything untoward and giving every vehicle that passed them a brief once-over before returning her gaze to the road ahead.

Eugene Taylor sat in the front seat beside her in silence and Kate could sense his acute embarrassment, as if it were a tangible thing. Several times she tried to make conversation, but on each occasion his answers were hesitant and awkward. In the end, she gave up trying and called Control for a rendezvous with one of the other units.

They drew alongside each other in the car park of a local public house, facing in opposite directions, and Kate wound down the window. 'Anything?' she called across to the driver.

Jimmy Noble was an old sweat and she could sense, even with his arm half covering his rugged face as he leaned an elbow on the sill and held on to the top of the door, that he was laughing at her.

'Not a thing, Skipper,' he said, but then couldn't resist adding: 'Quiet as a mortuary fridge.'

She scowled. 'Don't give up your day job, Jimmy,' she retorted and, slipping the car into gear, headed back out on to the road, conscious of his chuckles chasing after her.

The call from Control came in just minutes later with a 'Burglary in progress' at an address on the Bridgwater Road and the hairs on the back of Kate's neck quivered. 'Bloody hell, that's Pauline Cross's old house,' she exclaimed and spun the car round in the road with a screech of tyres to head back the other way.

'Pauline Cross?' Taylor queried, animated for the first time. 'Wasn't that the wife of the copper who did her husband for the insurance money?'

She threw him a swift glance in the intermittent flashes of light that washed through the interior of the car from passing vehicles. Not being part of the current murder investigation, he would not have known much about the background and he was too new to have been around during Operation Firetrap.

'You're very switched on,' she said, swinging out to race past a slow-moving petrol tanker.

'I read a lot,' he replied, for the first time showing his even white teeth in a broad grin.

'Eugene,' she said, swinging into the kerb in front of a terrace of houses. 'I reckon you're OK.'

Jimmy Noble swung in behind their car as Kate leaped out and slammed through the rusty garden gate of one of the houses. The light from an adjacent street lamp revealed that the tiny handkerchief of a front garden was overgrown and choked with rubbish and the downstairs windows were boarded up with plywood panels nailed to the frames. Pauline's home had been derelict as long as Wadman's Funeral Directors and for the same reason – no one wanted to live there.

Someone seemed to have shown some interest now, however, for the front door was half open, the padlock which had replaced the broken Yale lock lying in pieces on the step.

Kate paused, experience warning her to exercise caution.

'What is it?' Taylor whispered hoarsely at her elbow, almost pushing her forward in his eagerness to get inside.

Very carefully she pushed the door open and shone her torch down the rubbish strewn hallway, noting the electric cables hanging in festoons from the broken asbestos ceiling and the radiator leaning out from the wall, its copper pipework missing.

A heavy goods lorry thundered past towards Bristol and she waited until the noise had faded before stepping over the threshold into the hall.

Taylor was behind her, but Jimmy Noble had disappeared. She guessed he had driven off to go round the back.

'I'll check the bedrooms,' Taylor whispered and before she could say anything to stop him, he was gone, his feet producing loud cracking noises on the stairs.

The front-room was empty, bits of furniture littering the room and the usual graffiti plastering the walls. The dining-room was the same, except for one important difference – candles. Kate noticed the faint glow as she approached the doorway and she stiffened when she peered through and saw the little display on the overturned tea chest. There were six candles in all, arranged in a neat circle, in the same way as on a birthday cake. But this particular display had nothing to do with birthdays and her eyes widened as her gaze fastened on the bulbous, wooden vase-like object in the middle of the circle, its brass inscription plate winking at her in the flickering light.

She was still staring at it, as if transfixed, when she heard footsteps crunching through broken glass in the kitchen and sensed someone behind her. 'What the hell—?' Jimmy Noble breathed. 'It's a bloody cremation urn.'

'I know what it is,' Kate said tightly. 'Read the inscription for me, will you.'

Noble stepped past her to peer at the urn more closely, then whistled. 'You won't like it,' he said.

She nodded. 'I guessed I wouldn't. What does it say?'

He hesitated, then straightened up. 'Kate Hamblin. 1984–2012,' he said.

'The bastard,' she grated. 'So that's what this shout was all about – another bloody threat.'

He grunted. 'Likes his candles, though, doesn't he – your man? Must have a private store.' Then he added: 'Anyway, where's young Eugene? He's very quiet.'

Something jolted in her stomach and she threw a quick alarmed glance in his direction. The glance was unnecessary, for the same thought had occurred to them both simultaneously. In a second Noble was following her back along the hallway at a run. Then they were taking the stairs two at a time, regardless of the loose uneven treads and the structure shivering beneath their pounding feet.

The young policeman was in the small bedroom on the right of the stairs, but Kate didn't see him until the door had started to close behind her and she turned to go out again. PC Eugene Taylor had served just four months in the force and had been keen to follow in the footsteps of his policeman father, who had risen to the rank of chief superintendent before retiring, but on this wet dismal night in an unremarkable Somerset town, his career had come to an abrupt end. Someone had broken his neck and left him hanging from a hook on the back of the bedroom door.

CHAPTER 9

Dawn had long broken by the time a distraught Kate got back to the police station from the murder scene and her hands were shaking as she sat on the edge of the chair in the incident-room with a cup of coffee clutched perilously between her knees.

'Why?' she jerked out in a cracked voice that sounded nothing like her own. 'He was no threat – he was just a kid.'

Detective Chief Inspector Ansell nodded, his pale face even more ashen as he dropped into a chair opposite. 'We'll come to that later, Kate,' he said gently. 'But I need some questions answered first. I'd already arranged a press conference on the Jennifer Malone murder for ten this morning and the jackals will be all over me when they hear about this new incident.'

She nodded, staring at the floor. DI Roscoe stepped forward and grabbed her mug as it began to tip over towards her lap and placed it on a nearby table.

'First the obvious question, did you see anyone at all?'

She shook her head. 'When we got there, there was no sign of the intruder, just a broken front door lock. Jimmy Noble checked the back garden while I did the ground floor and Eugene upstairs, but there was nothing. Then we went upstairs and … and….'

'Found Eugene suspended from a coat-hook behind the door?'

She took a deep trembling breath. 'Bloody hook snapped with the weight as I stood there and he hit the floor, but he was already dead.'

Roscoe cut in suddenly. 'So where did the murdering bastard go? You and Noble used the stairs, so how the hell did he get out?'

Kate swallowed hard. 'Jimmy rushed over from another room when he heard me yell. While we were checking Eugene out, we heard someone race across the landing and down the stairs. The killer must have been hiding in one of the other rooms.'

'And you didn't go after him?' Roscoe demanded.

Kate's mouth tightened, reading the accusation in his eyes. 'Eugene's body was partially blocking the doorway,' she snapped back. 'By the time we got out on to the landing, whoever it was had gone.'

'And who do you think this "whoever" was?' Ansell said.

She clenched her hands tightly for a second. 'It's obviously got to be Twister,' she replied.

He frowned. 'But what possible motive could this Twister have for murdering young Eugene Taylor if his gripe is with you?'

'I don't know, sir. Maybe he was lying in wait for me and Eugene happened to walk in on him.'

'Hardly likely, though, is it? He could have got to you at any time – he didn't have to set up this elaborate hoax call – and he must have known that you would turn up mob-handed to this kind of shout. There seems no purpose in luring you to the house.'

Kate shook her head in resignation. 'Unless it was to remind me about Pauline Cross,' she went on. 'As I've said before, Twister likes to play games, hence the cremation urn and the candles again.'

He grunted. 'Some game this is. Anyway, we'll see what Doctor Norton thinks.'

'Doctor Norton?'

Ansell climbed to his feet. 'Forensic psychologist and criminal profiler. He'll be joining us in' – and he consulted his wristwatch – 'about half an hour.'

'But – but if we *know* who the killer is, what's the point in getting a shrink involved?'

Ansell studied her coldly. 'We *know* nothing of the sort, Sergeant,' he replied. 'As a former detective, you must appreciate that we should never prejudge an investigation. Furthermore, apparently Doctor Norton is a very well thought of criminal psychologist – used by several other forces. As he lives on our ground, Mr Willoughby thought we might as well make use of him.'

'We didn't use a criminal psychologist on the previous Operation Firetrap case,' Kate persisted stubbornly, fearing that Ansell was still not convinced Larry Wadman was their man and was seeking to look for other suspects.

'That was two years ago,' Ansell countered. 'Things have changed a lot since then – and anyway, had the senior investigating officer at that time used a criminal psychologist, you might have identified your killer earlier in the investigation.'

'That's not fair, sir.'

'Nor is murder, Sergeant Hamblin, and the Chief Constable will not be amused if we foul up this time.'

He turned towards the door, snapped his fingers and wheeled to face her again. 'Oh yes, and he'll want to interview you – and Noble, of course – and no doubt visit both crime scenes. You're on quick changeover from nights to late turn duty today aren't you?'

'On again at 1400 hours, sir,' Kate confirmed.

'Right, come on at 1300 hours and see Doctor Norton before the 1400 hours incident-room briefing.'

'But my inspector—' she began.

'I've already cleared it with the territorial superintendent, so your inspector will do as he is told,' he said. 'Just *be* there – and come in civvies.'

'Civvies, sir?'

'That's what I said. You're no good to me prancing about the streets in uniform. I need you where I can find you.'

Despite the night's awful event, Kate felt a surge of excitement. 'I'm joining the team, sir?' she exclaimed.

He grunted. 'Just an attachment, Sergeant, nothing more,' he said, 'but you'd better be worth it.'

And DI Roscoe winked at her as Ansell strode from the room to prepare for his press conference.

Doctor Clement Norton was nothing like Kate had imagined. Tall and angular with collar-length blond hair and a slight stoop, he wore tinted steel-framed glasses that turned a deep mauve colour in the light, plus a stud earring in his left ear that boasted a silver crucifix. The tan coloured leather jacket, green needle corduroys and blue suede shoes completed the image of someone more arty than clinical and she could not help but smile when Ansell introduced him to her in the incident-room commander's office. Norton responded with a courteous, 'Delighted to meet you,' in a soft almost weary tone that carried a slight lisp and she blinked as she stepped forward to shake his limp hand and was enveloped in a cloud of strong, sweet perfume.

It was apparent from the start that the psychologist had been fully briefed about the two murders, but he insisted that Kate went over the same ground again and listened intently as she recounted the gruesome details, nodding and occasionally interjecting in a gentle probing manner when he sought clarification.

When she had finished, he sat back and stared at the ceiling for a few moments without saying anything, as if digesting the information. Then, leaning forward, he studied her intently.

'The suspect, Twister, I believe you called him, what do we know about this man, apart from the fact that he kills his victims by breaking their necks?'

Kate frowned, then abruptly reeled off the information as if paraphrasing the CRO file she knew so well. 'Real name

Larry Wadman. Ex-SAS, but dishonourably discharged. Then worked for crime syndicates in the North as an enforcer and a night-club bouncer. Got eighteen months imprisonment for benefit fraud. Came down to Highbridge on release, ostensibly to help his sick father manage his undertaker's business in the town, but inherited the business on the old man's death, which he ran into the ground.'

She took a deep breath before continuing, even the mention of Twister giving her palpitations.

'He must be in his late forties now. Last time I saw him he was a big muscular man with a full black beard,' she wrinkled her nose in disgust, 'plus a really unpleasant body odour, and, according to his descriptive file, he has numerous body scars and what have been described as cold dead eyes – like a fish.'

Norton made a face and shook his head almost irritably.

'Yes, yes, yes, all very interesting, but what do we know of the man himself? What is he like? How does he think? What rings his bell?'

Kate stared at the psychologist levelly. 'He's a cold-blooded killer, sir; a man who kills effectively and dispassionately. He is incredibly strong and cunning, and he likes to play games with his prospective victims – a bit like the game he is playing with me now.'

Norton raised an eyebrow. 'Indeed. An interesting subject then?'

She grunted. 'Not how I would describe him, sir.'

He grinned. 'Touché, Sergeant Hamblin. And you think he is behind these murders and has come back to torment and ultimately kill you?'

'I know it, sir.'

He sat back in his chair again and threw a quizzical glance at Ansell. 'Then we'd better catch him first, hadn't we, Chief Inspector?' he said.

The incident-room briefing was short and sweet and Kate was not surprised to see the effect Norton had on the team of cynical hard-bitten coppers. If spot assessments were the order of the day, this lot had already made up their minds about the flamboyant psychologist the moment he was introduced and it was smirks and side-glances all round. However, with Ansell beside him and Willoughby sitting in the wings, still looking uncomfortable and out of his depth – as he had at the disastrous dismembering press conference earlier – no one dared to come out with the usual homophobic cracks that might otherwise have been expected.

And the humour died altogether when reference was made to young Eugene Taylor; a dark sombre atmosphere descending on the room as Kate related the incident, speaking in a husky halting tone and holding back her tears with an effort.

'So why did this bastard kill a kid like Eugene?' a thickset detective snarled from the back. 'It don't make no sense.'

Norton crinkled his brow in thought. 'I can't be certain at this early stage,' he said, 'but from the information I have gleaned about the main suspect, it is possible it was an act of bravado.'

'Bravado?' the detective snorted. 'What does that mean?'

Norton nodded. 'It would not have mattered who had drawn the short straw to check the upstairs part of the house,' he explained. 'Any policeman would have done. Your killer, I believe, was making a statement – he was letting Sergeant Hamblin know that he could still get to her whether she had a chaperone or not.'

Roscoe turned on him. 'You're saying he set up the burglary at Pauline Cross's place just to kill a copper?'

'Not entirely – he was making you a promise as well by leaving the burial urn – but killing young Taylor was a part of it, yes.'

'So how could he have known that Kate wouldn't be the one to check the upstairs?'

'He couldn't, but I am quite sure he would have had a Plan B in that event. He needed to demonstrate his power, that was all there was to it, and if not young Taylor, he would have selected someone else – perhaps PC Noble.'

'Me?' The contempt in Jimmy Noble's voice was obvious. 'I wish he *had* chosen me; I'd have fixed him good and proper.'

There was a faint patronizing smile on Norton's face as he turned his head to look at the policeman. 'I think it is important to understand what we are dealing with here,' he said quietly. 'Plainly, this man is not just a psychopath, but a trained killing machine who needs to be treated with the utmost respect. He has a total lack of empathy or any genuine sense of emotion. Cold and calculating, he will not feel guilt or remorse for any act he carries out, but will be driven solely by expediency and the desire to kill.'

'But surely, if he lacks emotion,' Willoughby cut in, 'how could he be capable of revenge? That involves emotions like passion and hate, does it not?'

Another patronizing smile. 'Agreed, Superintendent, but you see, for him, this isn't revenge in the normal sense of the word. Miss Hamblin here represents unfinished business – a challenge that needs to be overcome. He will almost certainly admire and respect her for managing to elude him for so long, and stretching things out now – what Miss Hamblin referred to as playing a game – will actually serve to enhance his satisfaction when he finally completes his task. It's a bit like sexual bondage – someone delaying the inevitable orgasm as long as possible to reach maximum fulfilment.'

'Sounds like a load of crap to me,' Noble commented again with barely suppressed fury. 'All this boils down to is the fact that we're dealing with a bleedin' nutter and the sooner we stick him in a loony bin the better.'

Norton nodded slowly. 'Excellent sentiments, Constable,' he agreed. 'But remember this, psychopaths are not lunatics with staring eyes, who are prone to screaming and foaming at the mouth. They are, to all intents and purposes, normal people just like you and me; you could be sitting next to one on a bus or in the cinema without knowing it. Herein lies the danger and catching this particular individual may be a lot more difficult than you appreciate.'

'So what do you recommend?' Ansell asked quietly, his dark eyes fixed on Norton with an unwavering – almost hungry – intensity.

The psychologist met his gaze with equal candour, pushing his tinted glasses up on his nose before returning to his audience. 'We try to understand our adversary,' he replied. 'Try to get inside his head to see what makes him tick.'

'And where will that get us?' Roscoe growled.

Norton's patronizing smile was back. 'Knowing your enemy will help you catch him, Inspector,' he said. 'So let's summarize the information we have acquired so far.'

He picked up a black marker pen and turned to the white board behind him, making notes on the squeaky surface as he continued. 'We have already perceived that our chief suspect is an efficient assassin and that he is clever, ruthless and focused. It is also apparent that he is a meticulous planner – the murders of Jennifer Malone and PC Taylor tell us that – which means he will have worked out, down to the finest detail, what and when the endgame will be.

'But, more importantly from an investigative point of view, he is an obvious risk-taker; someone who enjoys the challenge of operating on the very edge, as part of an obsession with power and a belief in his own infallibility. This could be his Achilles heel and may cause him to make a mistake. What we have to do is to wait for that mistake to be made.'

Roscoe was plainly unimpressed. 'And what do we do while we are waiting?' he said drily.

Norton studied him, his face grim. 'We watch our backs,' he replied. 'We watch our backs very carefully indeed.'

CHAPTER 10

Uniformed police officers were still on guard at the front and back of Wadman's Funeral Directors when Kate drove Doctor Norton to the derelict property and a couple of reporters materialized as soon as they got out of the police car, one, a willowy blonde woman of about 25, with dark rimmed glasses, clutching a mic in her hand. Norton had the good sense to keep walking, head down and plainly keen to keep a low profile as he headed for the rear gate, but it seemed the girl with the mic was more interested in Kate.

'Naomi Betjeman, Bridgwater Clarion,' she said as a couple of cameras flashed nearby. 'Kate Hamblin, isn't it – Sergeant Kate Hamblin?'

Kate frowned. Damned press. Well informed, as usual, she thought, ignoring her and quickening her step, but finding the woman easily keeping pace with her.

'Is it true the dead prostitute found in the chapel of rest was dumped in a coffin and kitted out in a police uniform?'

Kate felt a spurt of acid in her stomach. Someone had been opening their mouth too wide. As far as she knew, that information had not been released. 'No comment,' she replied and tried to keep walking, but the other stepped in front of her, thrusting the mic towards her face.

'Is there a link between this murder and the murder of the police officer in Highbridge last night?' she said.

Kate physically pushed her aside. 'I said, no comment.'

But this was one reporter who was not about to give up that easily, especially after the reluctance of the police hierarchy to answer questions at the press conference earlier. 'Is it true the police have called in a criminal psychologist to help solve the murders?' she persisted, walking alongside her.

Kate was tempted to snatch her mic and stick it somewhere personal, but resisted the urge. 'No comment,' she repeated.

The girl tried to get in front of her again. 'I understand it's a Doctor Clement Norton. Is that true?'

Kate brushed her aside for a second time, but made an inadvertent slip as the uniformed constable on the gate stepped forward to bar the psychologist's passage. 'Let Doctor Norton through,' she called out.

'So you're Doctor Norton then?' the press girl shouted when the constable on the gate complied. 'Do you think we're dealing with a serial killer here, Doctor?'

But neither Kate or Norton bothered to reply and the constable guarding the back entrance then shut the gate behind them.

The rear yard was full of late afternoon shadows and it was completely deserted, as was the building itself – the SOCO team having been pulled off, after finishing their initial crime-scene examination, to cover Pauline Cross's house. Kate sensed a heavy menacing presence when they stepped inside and, as a police officer, she felt angry with herself for finding reassurance in Norton's presence.

Norton himself seemed unaffected by the atmosphere, which pressed down on Kate like some tangible force. Switching on his torch, he emitted a tuneless whistle as he peered through the taped-off doorway of the chapel of rest.

'Where do you think he got his coffin from?' he queried, directing the beam very slowly around the room.

Kate shivered, examining the hallway behind them with her own torch as if she sensed something lurking there. 'The place *was* an undertakers,' she replied tightly.

'Liked his candles, though, didn't he?' he went on, unwittingly echoing PC Noble's words. 'I gather he put on quite a display?'

'You could say that.'

Norton faced her in the gloom. 'I hear that in the Operation Firetrap case he swopped bodies.'

She nodded. 'Pauline Cross had hired him to carry out the murder of her husband, Alf, but there was an argument when things started to go pear-shaped, during which she apparently stabbed him in the gut. So he killed her, then removed the corpse of a lady due to be cremated the following day from her coffin, putting her back in the fridge and substituting Pauline's body instead.'

'And this Pauline was eventually cremated?'

'Yes, but we didn't know until after the funeral what had happened – not until one of the staff here found the other woman in the fridge, still with the label on her toe.'

To her astonishment, he chuckled. 'You must admit, there's a certain black humour there.'

She scowled. 'I don't find any of it in the least bit funny,' she retorted tartly.

He cleared his throat, suddenly humbled. 'No, of course not. Not in the least bit.'

For some reason, perhaps just curiosity, Norton insisted on the full tour of the premises, despite Kate's obvious reluctance, and they ended up in the big garage at the back. The vehicles she remembered from before were still in situ and clearly visible in the light penetrating the garage through the skylights – two black Daimlers, a green van and the sinister Land Rover that had featured so much in the case two years ago.

'Strange that the local authority haven't done something about this place before now,' he commented. 'Bit of an eyesore – and those vehicles must be worth a fair bit.'

Kate shrugged again. 'Larry Wadman is still the legal owner,' she replied. 'I suppose they can't do much in his absence.'

He chuckled. 'Bit of a problem all round, our Twister, isn't he?'

She treated him to a cold stare. 'I'd describe him as much more than a bit of a problem, Doctor Norton,' she retorted.

He clapped her on the shoulder. 'Sorry, Kate, I didn't mean to be insensitive, just thinking aloud. Let's take a look in the cellar, shall we?'

Kate's stomach churned. The cellar was the last place she wanted to visit. She remembered how she had found Hayden trussed to a chair down there – his face covered in blood after a beating from Twister – and then how she had had to confront the killer in the blacked out hallway as she'd tried to get the injured detective out of the house.

The chair hadn't been removed either, the sticky tape used to tie up the detective still attached to it in places.

'This where your fiancé was held then?' Norton queried, peering at the chair.

Kate didn't answer and he grunted, flicking one of the lengths of tape with his fingers. 'Strong stuff by the look of it. How did you free him?'

'I cut it with a scalpel from the mortuary,' she replied.

An army of shadows encircled them in the light of their torches and Kate edged back towards the rickety staircase leading up to the hallway. 'I – I can't stay down here, Doctor Norton,' she said. 'I must get some air.'

He wasn't far behind her either and, out in the lengthening shadows of the street, he studied her over the bonnet of the CID car. 'Made a lasting impression on you, that place, hasn't it?' he said, quickly climbing into the front passenger seat when he saw Naomi Betjeman and an army of colleagues heading their way at a trot.

She slid behind the wheel and started the engine, pulling away just in time. 'A recurring nightmare actually,' she said. 'I'll be glad to see it pulled down.'

SOCO were still working at Pauline Cross's house when they pulled up in front of the place, to be greeted by another army of press reporters and photographers. Norton pushed through them without preamble, again shielding his face from the flash-cameras – not a man who enjoyed publicity, Kate thought with a grin – but he had to wait for her to show her warrant card to the constable on the front door before they were allowed inside. Even then, it was made very plain by the crime-scene manager that their presence was resented and they were specifically denied access to the room where Eugene Taylor had died.

'We found a built-in cupboard in the rear bedroom,' the crime scene manager grudgingly revealed. 'Must have been where your man hid after killing young Taylor. Found some fibres on the door catch where he could have caught part of his clothing. Not much good on their own, though.'

Kate felt her senses swim again as she visualized the killer creeping up behind the young policeman – maybe on the landing itself – then, like a big black spider carting its prey off to its lair, dragging the body into the small bedroom while she wandered about downstairs, unaware of what was happening above her head. She knew she would never forgive herself for what had happened to him – never!

'Fancy a bite?' Norton said suddenly, breaking in on her unpleasant reverie.

She stared at him for a moment. 'Sorry?'

'Something to eat. My treat after your excellent tour this afternoon.'

She hesitated. 'Well, I should really be getting back....'

'So police forces don't allow their staff meal breaks then?'

She flushed and smiled. 'We do have a canteen.'

'Canteen? You must be joking. Come on, I know a little place that will do just fine.'

The little restaurant was in a side-street in Burnham-on-Sea and it was practically empty. Norton ordered a lasagne for each of them, together with a glass of white wine, then sat back in his chair, eyeing her curiously. 'So, Miss Kate Hamblin,' he said. 'What exactly makes you tick?'

'I beg your pardon?'

He gave a short laugh. 'Sorry. As a psychologist, I have a natural interest in people and what motivates them.'

'I thought you were here to help us catch a serial killer.'

He made a grimace. 'Ouch! You're right, of course, but it helps me to know a bit about the witness/victim too. I can then see where the killer is coming from.'

She took a sip of her wine and also sat back in her chair, meeting his gaze frankly. 'So what do you want to know? My bra or knicker size? Whether I had sex last night?'

He laughed again, unfazed by her directness. 'OK, so I asked for that. Let me start by asking you why you joined the police?'

She pursed her lips reflectively. 'I suppose I wanted to make a difference.'

'Have you?'

'Have I what?'

'Made a difference.'

'That's not for me to say.'

'And do you enjoy what you do?'

'Yes, I suppose I do – except this business.'

He nodded. 'It really bugs you, doesn't it – the fact that Twister got away?'

'I just want to finish it.'

'How do you feel about this psycho?'

'Revulsion mainly.'

'Are you frightened of him?'

'Only a fool wouldn't be.'

He sighed. 'Catching him won't be easy. Psychopaths tend to be very clever people and he is bound to have the measure of the likely police response – may even be ahead of it.'

'So what do you suggest?'

He frowned. 'As I said at the briefing, we can only wait to see what moves he makes next.'

‘So you’re saying the ball is in his court?’

‘I’m afraid so. Still, you have got me,’ and he chuckled at his tongue in cheek vanity. ‘Anyway, I see the lasagne is on its way, so I suggest we forget Master Twister and enjoy our meal.’

Kate smiled and leaned back slightly as the waitress deposited the plates of lasagne and garlic bread in front of her, but she was so engrossed in an appraisal of the enormous meal, that she failed to notice that she was being watched from the street outside. Hayden Lewis had gone into Burnham to buy Kate some flowers and, seeing her enjoying a meal with Clement Norton, he was not at all amused.

CHAPTER 11

'There's been a development.' Hayden Lewis greeted Kate coldly as she got out of the CID car in the floodlit rear yard of the police station, nodding perfunctorily to Norton as he headed for the back door, then adding when he was out of earshot, 'Boss has been trying to get hold of you and he's not best pleased.'

Kate's jaw dropped and she dived into her pocket. 'Bloody hell!' she said, staring at the digital radio she had tugged free of the lining. 'I turned the damned thing off and forgot to turn it on again.'

Lewis's face was wooden, his eyes bleak. 'Was that when you were having your little tête-a-tête with Norton?' he sniped.

She jumped as if she had been stung, surprised by the unfamiliar hardness of his tone, which was totally out of character for the slightly eccentric and good-natured Hayden she knew and loved.

'And what do you mean by that?' she snapped.

He snorted. '*I* was trying to get hold of you, too,' he said. 'I thought we might go out somewhere for a quick drink to cheer you up, but then I discovered you were already spoken for.'

She raised her eyes to heaven as the penny dropped. 'So you saw us in the restaurant?' she breathed. 'Hayden, he invited me for a meal as a thank you for showing him the crime scenes, that's all.'

'Well, I hope you enjoyed it,' he replied haughtily, '*and* his company.'

She stared at him, a smile hovering over her lips. 'You're jealous,' she exclaimed. 'Hayden Lewis, you're jealous. How really sweet.'

He snorted, his face reddening. 'I'm nothing of the sort,' he retorted. 'Just disappointed in you.'

Before he could react she had leaned forward and kissed him quickly on the mouth, grinning at the cat-calls from a couple of uniformed policemen making their way to a parked traffic car. 'You stupid duffer,' she said. 'Why would I go after a man who wears mauve-tinted glasses and blue-suede shoes? Come on, Hayden, get real, will you?'

But he was already stalking away from her towards the rear door of the police station in an apparent huff and she soon had a lot more to think about than his hurt feelings anyway.

'Hamblin, get up here now!' DI Roscoe had never been a man of tact and diplomacy and he could not have demonstrated this more effectively than he did at that moment, yelling down at her through the open window of the incident commander's office on the top floor.

Kate blanched. This was all she needed – Roscoe on the warpath – and she headed for the rear door at a rate of knots that would have put an Olympic sprinter to shame.

Norton was already there, a half-smile on his face as he leaned against the radiator, but Roscoe was certainly not smiling and he went for her the moment she pushed through the door. 'Where the hell have you been, Kate?' he blazed. 'I've been calling you for an hour.'

'Slight exaggeration, I think, Inspector,' Norton drawled, coming off the radiator. 'And it's my fault anyway. I took her to dinner.'

Roscoe's eyes seemed to start from their sockets. 'Took her to—?' he choked, unable to finish the sentence. 'Don't you both realize that this is a bloody murder inquiry. We *don't do dinner*!'

He turned away, shaking his head, his chest heaving as he tried to regain his breath.

'Sorry, Guv,' Kate said quietly, automatically dropping the usual 'Sir' in favour of the more colloquial CID form of address now she was on the team. 'It won't happen again.'

Roscoe swung round and glared at her again. 'It had better not either, young lady,' he growled, slightly mollified by her apology. 'Now get yourself down to the interview room. We pulled in Jennifer Malone's pimp for questioning two hours ago—'

'Malone's pimp?' Kate echoed, unable to contain herself. 'But I thought we had decided who we were looking for?'

Roscoe looked like flaring up again at the interruption, but controlled himself with an effort. 'Guv'nor's orders,' he said. 'It's all political. We have to go through the motions to keep the press happy – show we are doing something. Mr Ansell also felt the arrest might lull whoever is responsible into a false sense of security. Get anything you can out of him.'

Kate looked nonplussed. 'But why is it so important for me to do the interview? I'm very happy to do it, of course, but—'

'How very gracious of you,' Roscoe said sarcastically. 'Just get on with it, will you? For some reason, he'll only talk to you.'

Mystified, Kate headed for the basement, where the station's two brand new American-style interview-rooms had been constructed the year before. She peered through the one-way observation window of Room Number 2 and studied the thin mousey-haired man sitting behind the interview table, smoking a cigarette. He was older now, but she recognized Del Shaylor straight away. The shifty little eyes and beak-like nose were characteristics that would never change, whatever age he was, and she guessed he would still smell as bad as he always had. But then the little villain's assets had never had anything to do with looks or personal hygiene. He had been one of Kate's first snouts when she'd originally joined CID and very little that was going on in the area escaped this one's sharp eyes and ears. So he was pimping now, was he? Well, well, well....

'Hello, Del,' she greeted him as she entered the room, sitting down opposite him.

He grinned, flashing rotten teeth. 'Hi, Kate. Skipper now, I hear. You done well.'

'And you're into pimping now, I understand,' she retorted. 'Real bottom of the heap stuff.'

He grinned again. 'Have to earn a crust like everyone else, Kate,' he said. 'Mind you, all me girls is top notch – clean, obligin' an'—'

'Expensive,' she finished for him drily. 'Now, what have you got for me?'

He threw a quick glance at the tape machine, crouched malevolently in the corner, as if eager to be activated again. 'That on?' he queried. 'I given your lot the nothin' doin' already, but what I got to say to you ain't for tapin', see?'

She shook her head. 'Not yet – unless you've done something you shouldn't have,' she replied. 'Then it goes back on.'

He nodded and drew more smoke into his lungs before stubbing out the cigarette on the table and leaning forward in his usual dramatic conspiratorial way. 'I seen the guy what done for Jenny,' he said suddenly.

Kate felt her senses start to tingle, but she tried to conceal her excitement to keep Shaylor's price down. There would be a price too, she knew that only too well; she could see it in his eager shitty little face.

'Go on,' she encouraged.

'It's like this,' he said. 'I'm a bit short of funds at the moment an'—'

'Forget it, Del,' she snapped. 'You've been nicked on suspicion. I'm your only ticket out of here.'

He scowled. 'They know I ain't done it, an' a ton is what this one's worth.'

'I'll talk to my guv'nor and you might, only might, get fifty.'

He scowled. 'No deal, girl.'

Kate stood up. 'Then you stay in here, Del, and we start a vice inquiry and have a chat with the brew about your benefits claims.'

His grin returned, wavered uncertainly, then stayed. 'OK, OK, seein' as I'm a good citizen an' all that – but you will speak to your guv'nor, won't you?'

Kate sat down. 'So what have you got to tell me.'

He bent forward again, glancing around him as if the whole world were listening in on their conversation. 'I was out checkin' me girls about midnight the night Jenny copped it when I sees this motor drive slowly by an' pick her up from her patch. A red Volvo, it were – one of them big old 'uns – an' missin' a back bumper bar too. Anyway, I writ the number down on a ciggy packet.'

'What made you do that?'

He fidgeted for a moment and Kate nodded in understanding. 'Some of your girls been cutting you out of the action, have they, Del?' she suggested. 'Doing a bit of business on their own account?'

He forced another smile. 'Nah, they're all good girls, Kate. I'm like a bleedin' father to each an' every one of 'em.'

Kate sighed her impatience. 'OK, so you took the number? What was it?'

He made a deprecating gesture with his hands. 'Dunno. Can't remember – E4 something. Left the ciggy packet at my stash,' his grin returned, 'but I can get it once I got me fifty.'

Kate didn't bother pursuing the issue; she could easily turn his place over after the interview anyway. 'And Jenny drove off with this feller?' she said.

He nodded. 'Never saw her again. Then Ol' Bill come round an' told me she was brown bread. I felt real sick, I can tell you.'

'I bet you did,' she replied. 'It's always a shock to lose an earner.'

He didn't seem to hear her. 'Thing is,' he added, 'this geezer had been with Jenny night before. I seen his car outside her flat and he were there most of the night, so it must have cost him a bundle.'

Kate's eagerness was showing now and she found herself leaning towards him across the table. 'Did you get a look at the punter?'

To her disappointment, he shook his head with a sour grimace. 'Nah. Only time I saw him was the night of the murder an' then it were just a – a what you call it, shape thing in the drivin' seat—'

'Silhouette?'

'Yeah, that's it – so what about my fifty?'

Kate gave a thin smile. 'Ciggy packet, then we'll see.'

'That ain't fair.'

Kate stood up again. 'Life isn't fair, Del,' she replied. 'But if you're a very good boy, I'll drive you to your place myself. Then you can hand me the car number personally.'

It was well past eight when Kate finally drove out of the police station in a marked patrol car, with Jimmy Noble, still grumbling after drawing the short straw, sitting in the back with what Noble called 'Bridgwater's own health hazard' in the shape of Del Shaylor. 'RHP,' Kate had explained to the disgruntled bobby when she had broken the news. 'Rank has privileges.' And that had gone down like a lead balloon.

Roscoe had been reluctant to release Shaylor so early – even more reluctant to consider making an application on his behalf to the informant's fund – but Kate's persuasion had won the day and he had capitulated in the end, although his warning had been clear. 'Come back with the goods or else.'

It was only a short drive to Bridgwater and within minutes of crossing the town's boundary, they were pulling up in a seedy district not far from the canal. There were no lights on in Shaylor's dingy flat and it was only as he fumbled with his keys to the communal front door that it suddenly dawned on the three of them that it was already ajar. Closer inspection with Kate's torch revealed that the Yale lock had been forced so violently that part of the door frame had splintered.

Noble and Kate exchanged narrowed glances. 'You've got a visitor,' Noble breathed to the little pimp. 'Keep close to us.'

Shaylor's hesitation was understandable. 'You go in and see first,' he whined. 'I ain't in no hurry.'

Kate smiled grimly. 'Would you rather wait in the car on your own?' she queried and abruptly Shaylor changed his mind.

The hallway smelled of stale cabbage and something scurried away from them in the gloom. 'Nice place you've got here,' Kate said close to his ear and paused by an internal door bearing the number 1.

'Ain't no one living in there,' Shaylor said. 'It's empty.'

Noble grunted. 'Why doesn't that surprise me?' he said.

Shaylor didn't bite. 'My place is next one up,' he said, clutching at Kate's arm.

She pushed his hand away, but grabbed Noble's arm. 'We stay together, Jimmy,' she directed. 'No lone-wolf stuff.'

The stairs made surprisingly little sound, despite the apparent dereliction of the place, and they reached the landing with hardly a creak. Flat Two and Flat Three opened off on either side and Kate smelled rather than saw the bathroom in front of them. 'Which one?' she asked Shaylor and he pointed to Flat Three.

A check revealed that the door had also been forced and for a moment all three stood there listening. Nothing, save the blare of a television from the flat opposite.

Shaylor was on the point of pushing the front door open, when Kate smelled the petrol. 'Out!' she screamed and slammed into Noble, sending him staggering back down the stairs as Shaylor thudded after them in a panic.

They had only just made the hall when the explosion lifted them off their feet and a massive orange fireball rolled down the stairs in pursuit, literally blowing them out through the front door into the street.

Behind them the whole building was engulfed in flames as windows blew out with a sound like snapping limbs, and the screams of those trapped inside were shortly drowned by the crash of collapsing timbers.

Once again, Twister had proved himself to be ahead of the game and once again carnage had followed in his wake.

CHAPTER 12

'No one dead, but three badly burned – Shaylor and two other guys in the next flat,' Hayden Lewis said, the shock still written into his expression as he brought Kate her breakfast in bed on a tray. 'Forensics say they think the swine disconnected a gas-pipe, then attached some sort of explosive device to a couple of petrol cans.'

Kate nodded. 'Quicker than searching for the cigarette packet Shaylor left there,' she observed with a grimace, 'though how the hell our man knew that Shaylor had the car number in the first place is a total mystery to me. How's Jimmy Noble?'

Lewis gave a faint smile. 'A bit scorched, that's all. Still swearing his head off in hospital apparently, but he should be released shortly.'

He stared at Kate intently. 'You don't look so hot yourself, you know.'

'I think hot is the wrong word under the circumstances,' she replied. 'And I'm sorry about poor old Shaylor and the two residents, but at least we all survived. This creature is like a one-man war.'

He settled on the corner of the bed. 'Listen,' he began. 'Sorry about my touch of pique yesterday. I was just rather upset and—'

She laid a hand on his wrist and smiled wearily. 'The flowers downstairs are lovely,' she said. 'And you don't have to say anything else. In fact, I was rather chuffed.'

He frowned. 'Chuffed?'

'Yes, no one has been jealous of me before.'

His frown deepened. 'Well, it won't happen again, I promise.'

She feigned indignation. 'And why not?'

He gaped and then shook his head several times. 'No, no, I didn't mean that I won't be jealous again.... Well, I did, but what I actually meant was—'

In spite of everything, Kate was laughing now. 'Hayden, you are such a lovable nitwit. If you're in a hole, as they say, just stop digging, OK?'

He gave her a sheepish smile and patted her arm, before getting up to go. 'Well, I have to be off. DI says you're to stay in bed until you feel fit enough to get up.'

'He said that?'

He grinned. 'Not exactly. What he actually said was "I suppose the lazy bitch won't be in today at all now?"'

He got to the door, then half-turned. 'Oh, by the way, they've found what they think is Shaylor's mysterious Volvo.'

She sat up quickly. 'You what? Where?'

'Car park of a nature reserve out on the Levels. Burned out apparently. Early turn uniform responded to a fire service call day before yesterday, but put it down to joy-riders until all this got out.'

'And it's definitely the car?'

'Seems so. One index plate was found some yards away. Someone's been to see Shaylor in hospital and he says that the number sounds about right. DVLC have confirmed it was a red Volvo and the rear bumper bar is certainly missing. Motor was stolen from the forecourt of a Taunton used-car dealer about a week ago apparently. Some idiot of a salesman left the keys in the ignition.'

Kate's legs were already pushing out from under the duvet and Lewis frowned. 'And where the devil do you think you are going,' he snapped.

She grinned. 'Well, a shower first,' she replied. 'But then the nick. After all, we mustn't add to poor old Roscoe's blood pressure, must we?'

The haunting boom of a bittern erupted from the depths of the wetland reserve, like the low resonant sound of a ship's foghorn, as Kate stepped out of her car into the car park. She was just in time to see the burned out Volvo more or less in situ – a low-loader was already in the process of lifting it on to the back of the truck and the driver cast her the usual appreciative once-over with the sort of grin she knew so well.

He wasn't the only one there either. Phil Sharp was just about to get into his CID car as she arrived and he turned towards her, a quizzical look on his face. 'Thought you were sick?' he said, walking over to her.

'I don't know where you got that idea from,' she retorted. 'I'm just on my way in.'

'So what are you doing here?'

'Thought I'd drop by on the way.'

'How did you know where to come?'

She shrugged. 'I do have the control-room's number, you know.'

He grimaced. 'Guv'nor won't like it. He don't like free-range operators – and you're supposed to have a chaperone with you everywhere you go anyway.'

'He won't know, unless you tell him.'

His cocky grin surfaced suddenly and he jerked a thumb towards the lorry, now trundling away towards the exit with its load of scorched metal. 'Not much left of that anyway. Why do you suppose your psycho mate dumped it here – it's miles from anywhere.'

She shrugged. 'Your guess is as good as mine. I'm more interested in how he got away afterwards.'

'What do you mean?'

She sighed, as if trying to explain something to a backward child. 'Well, either he likes long distance walking or he drove away again after torching the Volvo and, since even he couldn't drive two cars at once, he must have been in another motor.'

Sharp frowned and stared about him, as if trying to draw inspiration from the encircling trees. 'So you're saying he must have nicked another car – maybe from here?'

She shook her head in disbelief. 'Bravo, Phil, you're there.'

The sarcasm was lost on him, however, and he frowned again. 'Nothing in our bulletins about a car being nicked from around here.'

A sudden chill possessed her. 'Given Twister's track record, maybe the driver wasn't in any fit state to report his car stolen.'

Sharp's eyes widened and he glanced around him again, a little nervously this time. 'I'll suggest that to the Guv'nor when I get back,' he said, turning away from her towards his car. 'Get a team out here.'

'You do that,' she called after him. 'I'm just going to have a bit of a mooch around first.'

'Better watch out for the bogeyman then,' he chortled through the open window and promptly drove off.

The big brown rat had returned. Ever since finding the corpse under the hide she had been helping herself to the most succulent bits, instinct leading her to the softer parts of the abdomen first. With a large family to feed, she knew that she could not afford to pass up the opportunity.

But another denizen had also sniffed out the partially gutted remains and the only thing that until now had kept the mangy fox away was the glint of the water in which the body lay partially submerged. Finally, however, Reynard's empty belly had won the day and, plucking up the courage, he scrambled down the shallow bank into the reeds and sent the rat racing to safety as he began to take his share of the feast. The ropes holding the corpse in place were already frayed from the rat's attentions and the weight of the fox severed the remaining strands on one side. As the body began to drift outwards with the water, Reynard bolted even faster than the rat, leaving the corpse projecting slightly from under the hide, held by just one rope; its empty eye-sockets – pecked clean by feathered marauders – staring sightlessly up through the narrow gaps in the planking above.

Kate heard the fox's panic-stricken flight through the boggy reeds as she approached the hide and she turned quickly at the sound, her heart thumping. Then she caught a brief glimpse of the scavenger as he disappeared into the woods and released her breath in a heavy relieved sigh. 'Bloody Reynard,' she mouthed silently, one hand held against her chest; he'd given her the fright of her life.

She heard the boom of the bittern again as she went up the ramp to the door of the hide and jerked it open, her knee-length black boots clumping hollowly on the wooden planks. As she'd expected, the long timbered building was empty and the viewing hatches were all shut. Reaching across the bench seat, she opened one of them and secured it with its wooden latch. The lake seemed somehow dark and threatening and very little bird life was in evidence on the water. Once she heard something make a loud 'plopping' noise below the hatch and glimpsed the tell-tale air bubbles of a large fish, but otherwise everywhere was deathly still.

What the hell was she looking for? A body perhaps? But why here? If Twister *had* topped the driver of the car he was now using, he would hardly have stuck him in the hide for some visiting twitcher to find; he would have buried him somewhere deep in the undergrowth outside or dumped him in the lake.

She frowned and turned for the door, only to stop abruptly. The aluminium flask glinted at her from the shelf which ran the length of the hide under the hatches. Curious, she picked it up and unscrewed the top, making a face when she sniffed the stale coffee inside. The beverage was cold, so it had been here awhile. She screwed up the flask again and slipped it into the pocket of her woollen coat. It could have been left there by anyone, of course. The hide was probably used a lot by twitchers and nature lovers - any one of them could have left it behind, but she felt strangely uneasy about it and her gut instinct was to hang on to it for the time being anyway.

Closing the hatch she had just opened, she went outside again, blinking in a sudden burst of sunshine. More booming from the invisible bittern accompanied by the splashing and squabbling of a few ducks somewhere on the lake. A heron rose from the reeds to one side of the hide and she watched it soar gracefully over the trees, its huge wings making hardly a sound. Had it not been for the circumstances which had brought her here, she could quite easily have stayed awhile and listened to the vibrant sounds around her. Maybe there was something to all this bird-watching after all and perhaps twitchers were a lot brighter than she had once believed.

Yes, but if that was the case, why had one of them left his precious flask behind and where was he now? She had a really bad feeling about it and, as she made her way back to her car along the boardwalk, the musty smell of rotting vegetation rising from among the trees bordering the track assailed her nostrils like the stench of a newly opened grave.

CHAPTER 13

'You left her there?' Hayden Lewis's normally good-natured face had become an ashen mask and his fists were clenched into tight balls by his sides. Phil Sharp stepped back hurriedly, as if fearing a physical attack.

'But – but she said she'd be OK,' the DS bleated. 'And there was no sign of anyone else there anyway.'

'You waste of a skin,' Lewis grated, even in the midst of his anger refraining from using the sort of obscene expletives his other colleagues might have produced in such circumstances.

The incident-room was hushed, the faces of the other members of the team fixed on the pair in gleeful anticipation. Phil Sharp had never been a popular member of the department because of his arrogant toadying nature and the confrontation was a welcome development as far as his colleagues were concerned.

'You can't talk to me like that,' Sharp exclaimed. 'I'm a detective sergeant.'

'You're still a waste of a skin,' Lewis retorted, turning towards the board holding the ignition keys for the team's car pool. 'It could have been given to someone else.'

But even as he reached for a black key tab, Kate pushed through the double doors of the incident-room, with a grim expression on her face.

'See? What did I tell you?' Sharp snarled. 'She's fine. Just wants to make a bloody entrance, like the proper little drama queen she is!'

'At least she doesn't cut and run when a leaf rustles,' Lewis threw back and followed Kate into the SIO's office, where the DI was waiting with a quizzical expression on his battered face.

As Sharp made to join them, Roscoe kicked the door shut in his face.

'Right, Kate,' Roscoe growled, turning to face her, with his back against the door, 'Mr Ansell's at the morgue for the PM on Malone, but you've obviously got something you're bursting to unload. So, you'd better let me have it before he gets back?'

She frowned, throwing a quick glance in Lewis's direction as he perched on the DI's usual window sill seat. 'There was another car in the reserve car park when the Volvo was dumped there and torched,' she said abruptly.

'What sort of car?'

'I don't know, but there had to be one to enable the killer to quit the scene – unless he was picked up afterwards by an accomplice, which I doubt. Assuming it *was* Twister, he always works alone.'

'He could have belled for a taxi?'

'Hardly likely under the circumstances, though, is it, Guv?' Lewis joined in, then shut up quickly under the DI's glare.

'Tyre tracks?' Roscoe went on.

'Lots – the place is used regularly by twitchers, dog walkers and, of course, the reserve's wardens, so there's nothing for us in that respect. But I did find something else rather interesting.'

She reached into her pocket and produced the slim aluminium flask. 'It was on a shelf inside the hide.'

The DI looked unimpressed. 'So it's a coffee or tea flask. I should think any number of twitchers carry them and this one was obviously forgotten by the owner.'

'Maybe it was, but it looks quite expensive to me and, if you look closely at the base, you will see it is engraved with the initials RCJN. Someone obviously valued it enough to have that done, so I would have thought they'd have been back for it before now – unless something nasty happened to them.'

He snorted. 'Now you *are* jumping the gun.'

'Am I, Guv'nor? Think about it. Someone visited that hide pretty damned recently – was probably the last one there before me – otherwise something like this would either have ended up in the lucky finder's pocket or been handed in. And anyway, as I've said already, whoever dumped and torched that Volvo must have had wheels to enable them to get away afterwards. Whether both things are linked or not, the whole thing stinks to me.'

'So you're saying we've got a stiff out there?'

'I don't know, but my gut tells me it's possible, yes.'

'Possible?' He gave her an old-fashioned look. 'And you expect me to authorize a plod team to carry out a search of a two hundred hectare reserve on the basis of your gut?'

She shrugged. 'Your call, not mine.'

'Thanks.' He turned for the door. 'Any other bright ideas?'

She saw Hayden wink and she flushed for a second. 'Not as yet, Guv, no.'

The big brown rat had been put to flight once again by the arrival of the heavy boots and from a safe distance among the reeds her little gimlet eyes had watched the uniformed police officers in their gumboots spread out along the bank of the lake on either side of the hide, probing the undergrowth with their long wooden poles, as their digital radios crackled incessantly. It was already 3.30 in the afternoon and she knew instinctively that she wouldn't have long to wait before she was able to resume her feast. The watery sun had already disappeared and the shadows were rapidly lengthening. Soon it would be too dark to see anything – unless you were a rat, of course.

Under the hide, the remains of the corpse bobbed up and down in the shallows, just the single length of frayed rope lashed to one of the supporting piles now preventing it from floating out into the middle of the lake. In the building above, Kate tapped the toe of one boot impatiently on the rough plank floor as she scanned the hide in the dim light which filtered into the place through the wide open hatches for anything she might have missed on her earlier visit.

She was still trying to puzzle things out when the door creaked open behind her. At first she thought it was Lewis, but started when the lisping voice spoke. 'Doing a spot of bird-watching then?' Clement Norton said with a short laugh.

She swung round in surprise. 'What are you doing here?' she exclaimed, unwittingly wrinkling her nose at the strong perfume smell he brought with him.

He shrugged, thrusting his hands into his pockets and giving the hide a cursory glance in the gathering gloom. 'Heard where you all were, so I thought I'd pop over to see if you'd turned up anything,' he said, letting the door close behind him. 'Visiting crime scenes is part and parcel of a criminal psychologist's job nowadays. Helps him to get a flavour of things first-hand and to form judgments based on his own perceptions, rather than what he is told by others.'

She flicked her eyebrows in acknowledgment. 'So what do you make of all this then?' she said.

He adjusted the tinted glasses on his nose and stared round the hide more intently. 'I gather from Mr Roscoe that you believe our psychotic friend murdered someone else in here?'

She nodded. 'I'm positive that's what happened.'

'No sign of a body, though?'

'Not yet, but it could have been dumped anywhere in a place like this; there are acres of marsh and woodland out there, then there's the lake, of course.'

'So why would our man kill again in an isolated wildlife reserve?'

'My hunch is he dumped his stolen Volvo here, torched it and nicked his victim's car after killing him.'

He shook his head. 'Unlikely. As I pointed out at the briefing, this particular individual is a meticulous planner. He would hardly have dumped a car here on the off-chance of being able to pick up a replacement. What if he'd ended up with the car park to himself? It would all have been rather hit and miss – not his style at all.'

'You could be wrong.'

'I'm never wrong.'

She laughed. 'Mr Perfect than?'

'More or less, yes.' He grinned and moved closer. 'You and I are each perfect in our own way anyway.'

His distinctive perfume seemed to reach out towards her and she drew back quickly, her heart thumping. 'Are you flirting with me, Doctor Norton?' she said, clearing her throat to hide her embarrassment.

'Possibly.'

'Well, please don't. I'm already spoken for.'

He leaned against the wall, partially blocking her exit. 'Spoken for – now there's an old-fashioned term.'

She bit her lip. 'That's because I'm old-fashioned. Now will you let me past?'

He smiled again and for a moment she thought he was going to prevent her leaving. Then abruptly he relaxed with a soft chuckle and stepped to one side, indicating the door with the open palm of his hand. 'Be my guest, Miss Hamblin.'

She couldn't help brushing against him as he held the door open for her and she felt acutely conscious of his eyes following her all the way down the ramp to the boardwalk, mentally undressing her with every step that she took – and she wasn't the only one to be aware of the focus of his interest either.

Hayden Lewis's scowl was almost as dark as the shadows that were beginning to devour the remains of the day and Kate flinched as she saw him look past her at the still grinning psychologist standing in the open doorway of the hide. Not again, she thought as her stomach sank into her jeans.

Before she could say anything, however, Roscoe emerged from some scrub to her left, puffing heavily. 'I'm calling this farce off altogether,' he rapped. 'We're wasting our bloody time here.'

Kate tore her gaze away from her fiancé's glowering face and shook her head in protest. 'Guv, I still think —' she began.

But the DI was in no mood to listen. 'You think too much, young lady,' he cut in. 'And I need a brew like yesterday.'

The atmosphere in the incident-room could not have been more tense. Still weighed down by the cruel murder of Eugene Taylor and frustrated by the lack of progress with the investigation so far, the morale of the thirty-strong investigative team was plainly in need of a substantial boost, but that was unlikely to materialize with the present ineffectual SIO at the helm and his personal Rottweiler actually running the show.

DS Sharp was in a particularly low mood – but for rather more selfish, personal reasons. Having the door slammed in his face by his own DI was bad enough, but then to be relegated to incident-room admin duties afterwards as a kind of punishment for rubbishing Kate Hamblin, instead of joining the rest of the team for the search of the wildlife reserve, was a humiliation too far. His thin face carried a venomous scowl as he sat there, throwing dagger glances around the room at anyone and everyone – especially in the direction of Kate Hamblin. There would be a reckoning, he promised himself, staring down at the polished table top; sometime soon there would be a reckoning and when it happened, that conceited bitch would laugh on the other side of her pretty little face! He just had to wait and watch. Then he stiffened, sensing he was being watched himself. Glancing up quickly, he caught a glimpse of Ansell's cold gaze fixed on him and felt his stomach juices stir uneasily, wondering why he was being singled out for scrutiny.

The DCI's dark saturnine face was almost expressionless, the hard analytical eyes carefully studying him, as if reading the inner secrets of his mind and copying that information to some cerebral database buried deep in his own subconscious.

Then, to his relief, the cold gaze left him and swept around the table. 'So,' Ansell said softly, 'where is this investigation going? Two murders – one of a police officer – a major arson and the forced entry of another police officer's own home. And what have we come up with so far? Absolute zilch!'

He shook his head and leaned forward across the table. 'I had a rush job done on the prints found at the two murder scenes and they match those we have on record for Larry Wadman, which means we now know for certain who our killer is. So why is it that we haven't been able to get so much as a sniff of him? Ideas, people, that's what I'm looking for – ideas and *results*!'

There was silence for a few moments and one or two of the detectives shuffled their feet self-consciously, unable to come up with any feasible suggestions and unwilling to make themselves look stupid in the eyes of their boss by resorting to guesswork.

Roscoe wasn't so inhibited and cleared his throat noisily. 'Kate reckons our man nicked a car from the wildlife reserve when he dumped the Volvo in the car park, stiffed the driver, then buried him somewhere in the woods. I've had a team out there, but we found nothing.'

Ansell pursed his lips for a second. 'So why kill the driver? Why not simply steal the car when it was left there?'

Roscoe shrugged. 'Dunno. Maybe the guy tried to stop him taking it or he thought he would be able to identify him?'

'Oh for goodness sake, why would he bother?' Doctor Norton cut in almost irritably from the far end of the table. 'One of the features of this case is that our psychopath has not tried to hide his identity at any stage. His *raison d'être* thus far has been to make sure we *know* he is the culprit – that's what turns him on. You will undoubtedly find his DNA as well as his fingerprints all over the scenes of his crimes simply because he is not trying to conceal who he is. Why then would he be worried about someone identifying him?'

'Accepting your argument, Doctor,' Willoughby put in suddenly, no doubt keen to raise his profile with the team, 'if our man is not worried about being identified, why would he first fire-bomb Del Shaylor's flat – presumably with the intention of preventing us finding out the registration number of the stolen Volvo he was using – and also torch the car itself when he abandoned it?'

For a moment Norton looked as though he was lost for an answer and Willoughby directed a smug grin around the room, but then the psychologist simply kicked the question to touch with more than a hint of arrogance. 'I would think it was all part of his game to muddy the waters and frustrate the police inquiry,' he said smoothly and gave his most patronizing smile. 'All very much in accord with his profile, Superintendent.'

Ansell also smirked, obviously delighted with the obvious put-down. 'More importantly,' the DCI went on, as if the point Willoughby had raised was irrelevant, 'and forgetting the whys and wherefores, how come the killer knows so much about the progress of our inquiry?'

He raised a hand to silence Roscoe as the DI started to interrupt. 'In particular, how did he find out that Shaylor had been brought in, that he held details of the car at his flat and would be going back there to pick it up? OK, so it would have been easy enough for our man to find out, by means of a simple phone call, when Sergeant Hamblin was on duty, so that he could stage his next sick event at precisely the right moment, but not the Shaylor connection which was known to just a handful of officers. We have a leak, ladies and gentlemen, it's as simple as that.'

'Not a leak, Guv,' Kate exclaimed, 'a bug'.

Ansell's gaze fastened on her curiously. 'I beg your pardon?'

Kate now also leaned forward across the table. 'The incident-room commander's office – probably the incident-room itself – must be bugged. Twister's ex-SAS. He knows all about surveillance kit and, as I said to you before, he actually put an electronic tracker on my car during the Operation Firetrap inquiry.'

Ansell pursed his lips, nodding slowly. 'Then we shall have to get our technical support unit to carry out a sweep, shan't we?' he said, then fixed her with a cold smile and added, 'But if what you say is true, Sergeant Hamblin, our man will certainly know that we're on to him *now*, won't he?'

And as Kate caught his meaning and realized the amateurish blunder she had made, she suddenly felt sick.

CHAPTER 14

Kate spotted the box of chocolates on the desk she had been allocated as soon as she arrived back in the incident-room the following morning.

She had had a bad night again, with very little sleep, and it showed. Hayden had refused to share her bed, still believing that something had been going on between her and Clement Norton in the wildlife reserve hide, and they had had a flaming row. Lewis seemed to have forgotten his earlier apology and was displaying all the tendencies of paranoid jealousy. Kate had been unable to get through to him and he had left for work well before she had dragged herself out of bed, without so much as a 'goodbye'. But her problems on the domestic front turned out to be far from over.

'Got an admirer then, Kate?' one of her colleagues called, looking up from the pile of files she was studying on the adjacent desk.

Kate threw the woman detective an old-fashioned look, noting the broad grin on her face and that of a couple more detectives seated opposite as she bent down to detach the card from the box. She smiled at first, thinking that, like her flowers before, it was good old soft-hearted Hayden again.

But she couldn't have been more wrong and her smile quickly faded when she read the words on the card.

'Hi Kate, Sorry if I was a bit pushy at the reserve yesterday. These are for you. Enjoy.' It was signed 'Affectionately, Clement Norton'.

Kate's mouth clamped shut, her eyes glittering. The man was becoming a bloody liability. Why didn't he leave her alone? She was marrying Hayden at the end of the year and she wasn't at all interested in this prat with his blue suede shoes. Why didn't he get that through his thick head?

'Do you call him Clem on the quiet?' another voice spoke at her elbow and she turned quickly to find Sharp leering over her shoulder.

'Just shut it,' she snarled, tearing the card in half and dropping it into the wastepaper bin before dumping the box after it.

Sharp reached down and retrieved the chocolates. 'Well, if you're not going to eat them, allow me,' he said and waltzed off, studying the box as he went. 'Cadbury's,' she heard him comment. 'Hayden would have liked them.'

'Hayden would have liked what?'

Kate closed her eyes tightly for a second as Lewis pushed through the incident-room doors. She forced a smile and turned towards him, anxious to divert his attention. 'Fancy a coffee, Hayden,' she said.

'I said, "Hayden would have liked what?"' Lewis persisted, the heavy frown on his face warning her that he was still not over his chagrin.

Sharp turned with a grin. 'Nice box of chocs, mate,' he said. 'Courtesy of Kate's secret admirer, Clement Norton.'

Lewis moved a lot faster than Sharp had anticipated and the ex-Rugby Blue's fist planted itself on his jaw before he realized what was happening, sending him crashing into a coffee machine perched on a side table and bringing the whole lot down on top of him.

'Leave it!' Roscoe's voice shouted from the doorway, as Lewis stood over the sprawling DS.

Kate stared wide-eyed at her fiancé's red face and the clenched fist raised for a second blow. This wasn't the quiet gentle man she knew and she was totally shocked.

'I said *leave it*!' Roscoe snarled, stepping between the two policemen.

'Bastard hit me,' Sharp choked as he hauled himself to his feet, using the overturned coffee table as a prop. 'Look at the mark on my face. That's an assault, that is.'

'And if you don't shut your mouth, *I'll* bloody hit you,' Roscoe threatened, then turned to stare around the room at the other half-dozen astonished faces. 'Anyone here see what happened?'

He was treated to shrugs and shaking heads as they all returned to the work on their desks.

'There you are, Sharp,' the DI said grimly. 'No one saw a thing. Your word against his.'

'I – I don't believe this,' Sharp exclaimed. 'He *hit* me. I want to press charges.'

Roscoe thrust his face so close to Sharp's that it looked as though he was about to take a bite out of him. 'Listen, you little turd,' he said, 'So far I've got two bloody murders and a serious arson to investigate, plus a wanted psychopath on the loose. I can do without this sort of aggro on top of everything else, OK? So take the rest of the day off and go home. I don't want to see your ugly face in here again until tomorrow. Got that?'

Sharp swallowed hard, nodding like a scolded Labrador, and Roscoe turned away from him to glare at Lewis. 'As for you, I've got a very nice little job that's right up your street. You can call and see Albert Price, Wadman's ex-manager, to see if he or his missus have any useful information for us on their former employer.' His eyes gleamed. 'And when you've done that, you can pop in to see ex-DCI Roz Callow to see if she has anything to add—'

'What, the Wicked Witch of the North?' Lewis cut in hotly. 'What could she possibly know?'

Roscoe's face darkened. 'OK, so I'm scraping the barrel,' he snarled. 'But we've got nothing else – no witnesses, no leads, no forensic results, nothing – so we can't afford to leave any stone unturned. She was the DCI on Operation Firetrap and could know something, so get on with it!'

'Even if we find something nasty under the stone?' Lewis muttered, chancing his arm.

For a moment it looked as though the DI would explode, but he controlled himself with an effort. 'Just do it!' he rasped. 'Or, so help me, I'll get you transferred to traffic. And you can take Hamblin with you; she's become a real pain in the arse.'

Sharp would have put it a lot stronger if he had he been present and given the opportunity. As he checked his swollen cheekbone in the mirror of the gents toilet along the corridor a few minutes later, he vowed that 'fixing the little Hamblin bitch' would now become his overriding priority.

Naomi Betjeman needed a break – anything that would get her the best angle on potentially the biggest story of her career and enable her to escape from the humdrum existence of a reporter on a regional tabloid to what she imagined to be a high-octane job on one of the big nationals, but so far she had zilch.

In fact, as far as she was concerned, she had less than zilch. Still smarting from Kate Hamblin's rebuff at the scene of Jennifer Malone's murder and frustrated by the police hierarchy's refusal, either via the force's press office or at the subsequent press conference, to elaborate on the separate press statements they had already put out regarding this and the killing of the young police officer, she felt as if she were up against a stone wall. The bloody fuzz wouldn't even *talk* about the dodgy fire at the Bridgwater flat or why they had been carrying out a search of a local wildlife reserve. She knew full well that Kate Hamblin was somehow connected with all the incidents, which suggested there was a link between them, but beyond that, she had nothing. If cover-ups were capable of winning awards, the Highbridge murder team would have been top of the heap for her nomination.

The pub and a very large brandy beckoned and she found both on the outskirts of the town. More importantly, she also found Detective Sergeant Philip Sharp.

Already on his fourth double whisky and swaying unsteadily as he tried to remain upright by clinging to the edge of the bar, he was a chicken ready for the plucking and Naomi Betjeman's face lit up the moment she clapped eyes on him.

Sharp was well known to her. A useful leak in the past on other much lower profile cases, she had greased his palm on numerous occasions and, although the DS would never have got rich on a regional newspaper's meagre bungs, he had not done too badly out of it overall – especially as he was also known to be taking backhanders from journalists on other papers, including a couple of the nationals.

'Hi Phil,' she said after ordering a brandy and soda and sliding the drink along the counter beside her as she went over to him. 'You look a bit peed off.'

He turned his head to fasten his bleary gaze on her prominent cleavage. 'Well, well,' he sneered in a thick slurred voice, ''Tis the lady of the press.'

She tapped his glass with one neatly manicured red fingernail. 'Want another of those?'

'Rather have a jump with you,' he said lewdly, looking her up and down.

She snorted. 'You couldn't manage a hop and a skip at the moment,' she retorted, 'let alone a jump. Anyway, you should be working, shouldn't you, not in here getting pissed.'

Sharp seemed not to have heard her, but stared morosely into his half-empty glass. 'Sent home,' he muttered, 'just like a soddin' kid.'

Naomi caught on quickly. 'Sent home? Whatever for?'

He took another gulp of his whisky. 'Bastard hit *me*,' he snarled, pointing at his swollen cheekbone. 'Yet *I* get sent home. Can you believe it?'

She raised an eyebrow. 'Who hit you?'

'Hamblin's bloody boyfriend, DC Scumbag Lewis.'

'But you're a sergeant, aren't you?'

He belched. 'Yeah, but don't make no difference when the boss has it in for you.' He belched. 'Just 'cause this bleedin' psycho is running rings round 'em and the inquiry is falling apart.'

Naomi's journalist's nose twitched. 'Why don't we sit over there in the corner?' she suggested, trying hard not to appear too curious.

'If you're buying,' he said and lurched in the direction she indicated.

She watched him slump into a wooden bench seat with his back to the window and smiled encouragingly from the bar as she ordered him another double.

'So, why is the inquiry falling apart?' she said, setting the drink in front of him and staring almost too casually around the room.

'Lost the plot, haven't they?' he said, belching again. 'Whole thing's a total cock-up.'

The glint of the wolf surfaced in Naomi's blue eyes and they fastened almost hungrily on his thin sweating face.

'Why do you say that?' she breathed, fearful that her continuing questions might make him clam up, but Sharp was too far gone to care.

He gulped some more whisky. 'Obvious, isn't it?' he said. 'SIO is a prat – Ethelred the Unready they call him – and the DCI is like a bloody android.'

'That's a bit unkind.'

He shrugged. 'Only speaking the truth.' He leaned towards her and tapped her arm with one finger, almost toppling over in the process. 'Bleedin' psycho's running rings around 'em. Like he did two years ago – Op … Operation Firetrap thing.'

Thinking of the connection between the two cases that her editor had already suggested, Naomi couldn't contain her excitement any more. 'So it *is* the same killer then?'

Sharp's face twisted into a cunning leer and he leaned towards her. 'Not so fast, love – what's it worth first?'

She made an irritable grimace. Pissed, but not so far gone as to miss an opportunity for a nice little earner. 'Depends what you've got,' she retorted, the irritation in her tone as sharp as a wasp sting.

He set his glass down unsteadily on the table once more and sat back in his seat, tilting over slightly on one side like a sinking ship. 'Let's not play around, sweetness,' he said. 'This thing's bloody big and if you want the whole SP, it'll cost you a grand.'

She emitted an incredulous laugh, her eyes widening in disbelief. 'A grand? You've got to be joking. The Clarion couldn't come up with that sort of money – even for an exclusive.'

He shrugged again. 'Your loss. I can always try somewhere else.'

She snorted. 'Like where, for instance? Anyway, you've already told me enough. I can soon find out the rest from your guv'nor.'

Sharp grunted. 'Think he'll talk to *you*? I doubt it.'

Her eyes glittered. So the little shit wanted to play hardball, did he? 'He might if I agreed to tell him where I got my info,' she said.

The cocky expression on his face died instantly. 'You wouldn't dare.'

'Try me.'

The DS studied her for a moment, his face twitching uneasily. 'There's a lot more to this than you realize,' he said, leaning forward again and lowering his voice after quickly glancing around him. 'There's why Jennifer Malone and Eugene Taylor were topped, for instance, the reason the Bridgwater flat was fire-bombed and why we were searching the wildlife reserve. It's worth a grand, easy.'

She didn't answer and he hesitated before her hard uncompromising stare. 'OK, five hundred,' he said sullenly, then grinned again, 'plus an extra.'

Naomi looked puzzled. 'What sort of extra?'

His grin widened. 'You – in the sack.'

She glared at him. 'In your dreams.'

He sat back again, finishing his drink and wiping the back of one hand across his thin lips. 'That's the deal. Final offer.'

She stared at him with absolute incredulity. She could hardly believe what he had just come out with. No virgin, but a hard cynical woman with a bisexual appetite and few moral scruples if she wanted something badly enough, she nevertheless found the idea of sleeping with Sharp utterly abhorrent, even for an exclusive that could set her on the road to stardom.

'No way, José,' she said tightly.

He levered himself upright. 'Suit yourself,' he said, 'but if you *do* go to my guv'nor, remember one thing, bribing a police officer is a criminal offence. So, do you worst.'

For a moment she hesitated, gnawing at her lip as she watched him clumsily negotiate his way round the table on his way to the door. Then, abruptly draining her glass, she reached out to grab his arm. 'I think I'd better drive, don't you?' she said drily.

CHAPTER 15

'So what the hell is eating you?'

Kate tackled Lewis the moment they were clear of the police station and climbing into the CID car in the rear yard.

He threw her a sour glance as he closed the driver's door after him. 'Leave it,' he retorted morosely, starting the engine. 'We've got inquiries to make.'

'Bollocks to the inquiries,' she exclaimed, turning sideways in the front passenger seat to face him. 'Just answer the question, will you? What is wrong with you?'

He scowled. 'You know very well what. We're supposed to be getting married in a few months, but that seems to have slipped your mind.'

'Don't talk crap!' she grated. 'Just because some loser sends me chocolates, doesn't mean I'm over the side with him. Use your head, man – he's doing it deliberately.'

He looked unconvinced. 'So why would he do that?'

She sighed heavily. 'To drive a wedge between us, you idiot. He fancies me and thinks if he can turn you against me, he might be in with a chance. Simple as that.'

'And what about the business in the hide?' he countered.

She swore under her breath, her frustration breaking through. 'There *was* no business in the hide. It was all in your bloody imagination. I'm not interested in this pillock and never will be, so will you get that into your thick public-school brain?'

Roscoe appeared in the yard, walking briskly to his car, and they saw him stop and stare intently their way. Lewis started the engine and slipped the car into gear. 'Better get mobile,' he muttered, releasing the handbrake and lurching forward. 'We're in enough trouble already.'

'You're the one in trouble,' she blazed as they drove out of the yard. 'What you did in there was bloody stupid.'

'Sharp's an idiot,' he threw back at her. 'Deserved all he got.'

She snorted. 'Fat lot of good that would have done you at a court hearing for ABH,' she retaliated. 'Out of a job and maybe looking at three months inside or a heavy fine at the very least.'

To her surprise, he grinned, his truculent mood suddenly evaporating.

'Mind you, I did enjoy it,' he chuckled. 'Always wanted to thump the little tyke.'

And as their eyes met across the car, they couldn't help laughing uproariously, but they would not have been laughing if they had known who was tailing them.

Twister had turned round quickly in the mouth of a small development, abandoning his original plan and giving a van driver a two-fingered salute when he pulled back across the road in front of him. He had seen Kate and her boyfriend swing out of the police station yard on his approach and his curiosity had been instantly aroused.

'Now where are you two off to?' he murmured and headed after them, keeping his speed down and staying well back to avoid being spotted in their rear-view mirrors.

His whole body tingled with excitement as he thought about the auburn-haired cop sitting in the front passenger seat now a couple of hundred yards in front of him and the very special end he had planned for her in the not too distant future.

Ironically, the feeling of excitement in itself surprised him, suggesting a subtle change in his personality he had not experienced before. He had always enjoyed taking life, of course. First it had been cats and dogs, but by puberty the growing compulsion to kill *people* had become impossible to resist. The fat boy at his school had been his first and he still remembered, with a sense of nostalgia, the day he had plunged the chisel into Jerome Cassidy's throat in the local park, then sat and watched him die. The scantily clad jogger and the middle-aged nurse had followed. Both had been pretty enough women to stir any normal man's juices, but he had simply strangled them, without any attempt at sexual interference.

The thing was, sex had never been what it was about. It was the act of killing itself that had always interested him. But even this had never really excited him or given him the merest semblance of a hard-on. He had simply killed out of a sense of compulsion and had gained his satisfaction from watching the light go out in his victims' eyes.

Joining the army and then the SAS had enabled him to extend his murderous activities and develop a much more varied skills portfolio. He mastered a variety of weapons and methods to kill silently and efficiently in operations all around the world – and in the end, earned himself the nickname, Twister, for his favoured method of executing targets by snapping their spinal cords with a sharp, powerful twist of the neck.

Although a keen, dedicated assassin, he had shown little emotion in carrying out these tasks. Like an alcoholic or drug addict, he had been driven solely by need, deriving satisfaction from extinguishing life in a cold clinical way that had both surprised and disturbed his comrades and had ultimately led to a court martial and dishonourable discharge when his well-known maverick approach and disobedience to orders was blamed for the death of a fellow soldier on a training exercise.

The smothering of his own father some years later, in order to inherit his funeral business, had also been carried out with the same cold, unemotional efficiency and he'd felt no guilt or remorse for what he had done – or any sense of enjoyment either – merely satisfaction that once again he had got away with his crime.

Now, though, after all these years, the prospect of wasting some nondescript woman cop had affected him in a way no previous target had ever managed to do, destroying his characteristic ambivalence and arousing in him a latent passion that was almost sexual and heightened his senses to fever pitch.

He still couldn't quite fathom why he had risked everything by coming back to the Levels to kill Kate Hamblin; why he had constructed this long drawn-out game as a lead-up to the final event, when he could so easily have snapped her neck at the start and been done with it. Ironically, he didn't hate the woman, didn't really feel vengeful towards her. In fact, in a way, as Doctor Norton had surmised at one of the police incident-room briefings, he actually liked and respected her. He just wanted – no, felt compelled – to destroy her. And now, on top of that, there was this emerging carnal desire to cloud the issue.

It was an interesting novel feeling, but he had to regain control, and fast, or he would end up making mistakes and that would certainly not do at all.

Patience, that was the watchword. His moment would come, but only when the game he was playing reached its planned finale and, although that day was not far off, they weren't quite there yet. Still, he mused, the wait could only serve to sweeten what he now knew would be a truly orgasmic experience.

Naomi Betjeman climbed out of bed naked and crossed to the chair opposite where she had left her clothes. She dressed quickly but quietly, throwing repeated glances at the rumpled bed and the naked, prostrate figure of Phil Sharp lying there on his back with his eyes closed and his mouth wide open.

She treated him to a look of contempt. The skinny arms and legs, the faint smudge of blond hair on his narrow chest and his pathetic manhood poking above the pushed-down sheets, Sharp had about as much sexual appeal as a stick insect. She'd been dreading going to bed with him, but she need not have worried. He was so drunk by the time he had given up what he knew on the police operation, that he had promptly fallen asleep in an alcoholic stupor. It couldn't have worked out better and she smiled faintly as she bent over the adjacent chest of drawers to scoop up Sharp's five hundred notes she had just drawn out of her savings – well, the paper wouldn't have paid that much for the information, would they?

Peeling off a hundred, she tossed it on to the bed and slipped the rest into her handbag. 'Don't spend it all at once,' she breathed at the insensible detective and turned for the door. 'Now let's see if I can stir up a hornet's nest.'

Albert Price was of little help to the police inquiry. Twister's former administrator was in the first stages of dementia and was only a shadow of the man who had once been running things at the funeral parlour. His other half had died of a heart attack only weeks after the Operation Firetrap investigation had been mothballed and he could barely remember the case, let alone provide any useful information about Larry Wadman. After more than half an hour of gentle questioning in the living room of his one-bed bungalow, during which the old man constantly asked where his wife had gone for the afternoon, Kate and Hayden abandoned the interview leaving him to his confused ramblings and the imminent arrival of one of his regular carers.

The experience had a sobering effect on Kate and she couldn't help feeling a heel leaving him to his miserable surreal world with its whispering phantoms and half-assembled memories. But that was the nature of the job – ask the necessary questions, then move on – and above all, don't get personally involved. And that's exactly what she did. Yeah, she mused cynically, just like the good efficient police officer she had sworn to be.

Their second visit could not have been more different and Kate had no difficulty in engaging her sympathy bypass. Roz Callow lived in a detached house bordered by large trees on the fringes of the picturesque village of Wedmore. She took a few moments to answer the door and when she did, Kate and Lewis saw why. She was leaning heavily on a steel walking stick.

The lean figure and sour hatchet-face hadn't changed a lot, although the former DCI looked much older than her forty-odd years. The pain lines were deeply etched into her pallid complexion, and her red woollen top and black trousers were stained and creased as though they had been slept in. There was an odour about her too – a stale morning-after smell that suggested she had been drinking heavily.

She seemed unsurprised by the visit and treated Kate to a thin humourless smile, completely ignoring Lewis. 'Well, well, well,' she murmured, 'if it isn't Kate Hamblin, the new sergeant on the block. Congratulations.'

Kate felt the muscles in her stomach knot as she faced the twisted lesbian woman who had made her life so much of a hell and had mounted a campaign of harassment against her during the Operation Firetrap inquiry, simply because she had rejected her sexual advances. For a moment she had difficulty finding her voice.

In the end, after an awkward, pregnant pause, Lewis spoke for her. 'Can we have a word, Roz?' he said.

Callow continued to ignore him, studying Kate keenly instead. 'He's back, isn't he?' she grated. 'Twister's come back?'

Kate's lips tightened. 'Better if we talked in the house,' she replied.

Callow stepped to one side to allow them through and for the first time Kate saw the smoke trailing from a cigarette in her hand. All the vices now, it seemed. One day's time it had been extra-strong peppermints, now it was booze and nicotine. Her old boss had certainly let herself go and she wondered whether she still lived alone or had shacked up with another lesbian lover.

'So, to what do I owe this delightful visit?' Callow said sarcastically, waving Kate and Hayden to adjoining armchairs in the shabby sitting-room. 'Run out of experienced detectives, have they?'

'Roz,' Kate said quietly, 'We need to know all you can remember about Larry Wadman.'

Callow drew on her cigarette and smiled coldly through the smoke. 'Everything I know?' she murmured. 'Well, isn't that something? Inquiry at a standstill, is it?'

Lewis emitted an impatient grunt. 'We haven't got time to play games, Roz,' he snapped. 'There's a dangerous psycho out there and people's lives are at risk.'

Callow seemed unperturbed. 'Like Kate Hamblin's, you mean? Now, that is something to worry about, isn't it? Especially as, according to the papers, he seems to be running rings around you.'

'You should take no comfort from that,' Kate pointed out. 'You could be next on his list.'

Callow emitted a hollow laugh. 'I doubt it. I'm of no interest to him.'

'Nor was PC Taylor, but Twister still snapped his neck,' Lewis put in. 'Depends what message he wants to send.'

Callow's humour faded and, despite her apparent self-confidence, Kate saw the quick glance she directed at the window.

'So what can I possibly know about Wadman?' she said, taking another pull on her cigarette, then lifting a half-filled glass to her lips from the adjacent coffee table. 'I saw him for the first time on the night I was injured. Before that, I didn't even know he existed.'

'But you were pretty close to him at one stage. You must have formed some sort of impression of him.'

Callow made a face. 'Only that he had a very nasty B.O. problem.'

'Pauline never mentioned him when you were – er – together then?' Kate said as tactfully as she could manage.

Callow's thin lips curled in contempt. 'You mean when we were having it off?' she replied. 'Why don't you just say what you mean? And, as I told the police inquiry two years ago, the answer is "no"; we were too busy with each other.'

'So you can't tell us anything about him?' Lewis cut in hastily, sensing the increasing hostility building between the two women.

Callow shrugged and blew more smoke across the room. 'Only what's in his file.'

Kate nodded and abruptly stood up. 'Well, since you can't help us with anything else, we'll be on our way.'

Callow stubbed out her cigarette and stood up. 'There's one thing you might like to know that I didn't tell the inquiry,' she said, studying her fixedly as she prepared her parting shot.

'Oh? And what's that?'

'Pauline wasn't dead when Twister sealed her up in Mary May's coffin.'

'What?'

Callow treated her to a smile that was pure relish. 'He snapped her spine all right, but he didn't make a proper job of it,' she gloated. 'She was paralysed, but still alive – I heard him mocking her while she was lying on top of me at the foot of the stairs where I'd fallen.'

Both Kate and Lewis froze in the doorway. 'Gordon Bennett,' Lewis breathed. 'What are you saying?'

Callow's eyes were hard and glinting. 'I'm *saying*,' she said, 'that the bitch was still alive when she was cremated!' She leaned forward like a cobra about to strike. 'Burned alive, Sergeant Hamblin,' she added. 'Now, I wonder what he's got lined up for you?'

And crouched below the open window, listening intently to the conversation, Twister smiled a knowing smile before quietly slipping away.

CHAPTER 16

The technical support unit had turned up at Highbridge police station at just after eleven and Ansell gave instructions that the incident room be completely vacated while they carried out their electronic sweep for the bugs Kate suspected had been planted there. Roscoe was sceptical about the whole thing. 'Bloody waste of time,' he declared to Ansell before his boss left for a case conference with the ACC at police headquarters. 'Hamblin's off with the Wizard of Oz.'

But his opinion abruptly changed when the Tech Unit manager poked her head round the door of the DI's own office in the CID wing downstairs a couple of hours later.

Laura Talbot's face wore a triumphant grin as she carefully set the tray on the desk in front of him. Roscoe stared curiously at the two black, rectangular boxes, about 3 ½" x 1 ½" x ½" in size, that had been placed in it.

'Two in all, sir,' she said. 'And we're confident that's the lot. Nice little beauties, aren't they? They're called lithium transmitters and operate on a UHF frequency band. They will pick up conversations within about thirty feet and will transmit even through walls. One was fitted in the SIO's office, under his desk, and another under a table in the incident-room. They have a range of about 600 metres, so your man would probably have had his receiver quite close by – if not in the nick itself, maybe in a car or building.'

Roscoe gaped. 'The cheeky bastard,' he breathed. 'But what I want to know is how he got in here to fit them in the first place?'

Talbot nodded. 'One of my team's just had a chat with the nick's civvy admin officer and he remembers a BT engineer turning up to check the telephone system about a week ago. The only problem is he wasn't a BT engineer – despite his very realistic ID card and the kit he brought with him.'

'How do you know all this?'

'Your admin man gave BT a bell and they have no knowledge of any visit by one of their engineers.'

'Well, I'll be buggered!'

'Hopefully not, sir,' she said with a chuckle. 'But if it's OK with you, I'll bag these up for SOCO. I've already had pics taken of them in situ, but you will obviously want them checked for prints.'

Roscoe nodded. 'Go ahead,' he growled. 'I'll tell Mr Ansell when he gets back from his meeting with the ACC,' and he added sarcastically: 'He'll be highly delighted.'

As Talbot left the office with her prize, he stood up and, crossing to the window, peered out into the police station yards, chewing furiously and frowning as he thought about the cunning assassin who had blatantly walked into the police station to bug the place and had been eavesdropping on their briefings ever since. 'So, you piece of shit,' he said heavily, 'where the hell have you been hiding? And where the bloody hell are you now?'

Kate still looked shaken when she climbed into the CID car beside Lewis. 'I wish Callow hadn't just told me that about Pauline Cross,' she breathed, slamming her door shut and fumbling with her seat belt. 'It's the stuff of nightmares.'

Lewis nodded and started the engine. 'If it's true, of course,' he said, glancing over his shoulder before pulling away. 'After all, why didn't she tell the inquiry team about it at the time and why bring it up now?'

Kate's shrug turned into a long shudder. 'I really don't know, Hayden,' she replied. 'But I reckon it's true enough – I mean, why would she go to the extent of inventing something so perversely awful? Callow is certainly vindictive, and she'll cut herself on her tongue one day if she's not careful, but I can't see her concocting a story like that.'

He chuckled and she was pleased to hear the warmth in the sound, suggesting he had put his bad mood behind him. 'The Wicked Witch of the North certainly doesn't like *you* anyway,' he said, then frowned. 'Thing is, she must also be pretty stupid to come out with that sort of admission anyway. It means she would have been aware that Pauline Cross was alive hours before the cremation, but did nothing about it. Could be a criminal offence there.'

Kate shook her head. 'She knows we can't do anything on just her admission. She could easily retract it later and we have no means of proving or disproving it after all this time. Ashes to ashes, dust to dust really does mean that and there won't be any ashes or dust left now either.'

Lewis flicked up his sleeve to glance at his watch. 'Well, anyway, enough about death and disaster,' he said. 'It's well past my lunchtime and I know a certain pub out on the Levels where we can get a nice little snack before we head back to the nick.'

Kate raised an eyebrow. 'Mr Roscoe told me we don't do dinner on a murder inquiry,' she replied, thinking of the meal with Norton and the grief it had caused her.

Another chuckle and Lewis winked at her as he slammed the car into gear and, hitting the accelerator, pulled away with a screech of tyres. 'Ah, but I bet he didn't say anything about snacks,' he said. 'Pie and chips OK with you?'

Twister watched Kate and Lewis drive away with a grim smile. So the inquiry was going so badly they were into fishing expeditions now, were they? Well, maybe it was time to liven things up a bit for them. First, though, he had a more pressing job to do and, with this in mind, he made no attempt to continue tailing them, but pulled out of the gateway in which he had parked and headed back to Highbridge.

The derelict, boarded-up shop was part of a terrace of shabby premises and stood right next door to the police station. There was a small plot of overgrown waste-ground at the rear, bordered by the wall of the police station yard on one side and the garden wall of the next terraced property on the other. A broken-down fence marked the rear boundary, which separated it from the narrow lane running along the backs of the terrace, and an assortment of faded signs leaned over the fence from inside, declaring that the place was for sale.

Twister pulled in as close to the fence as he could – no sense attracting unwelcome attention by causing an obstruction – then sat for a few moments smoking a cigarette and studying the lane both in front of him and in his rear-view mirror. Nothing moved.

The old shop had served his purpose well, he mused, but the time had now come to abandon it for good. He was quite sure the police would find the two bugs he had planted in the incident-room and he guessed it would not be long before they carried out a search of the immediate area in an effort to locate the UHF receiver. He didn't much care that they had rumbled him, but he couldn't afford to lose an expensive automatic receiver/recorder that he might need again in the future. He knew he was cutting it fine and he should have retrieved the equipment over an hour ago – as he had originally intended before deciding to follow Kate Hamblin and her boyfriend instead – but he felt sure he still had enough time before the plods appeared.

Stubbing out his cigarette in the ashtray, he eased himself out of the car and, locking the doors with the infra-red remote, he ducked through a gap in the fence, confident that he could be in and out of the place in minutes without anyone being the wiser.

Unbeknown to him, however, his arrival had not escaped notice, for someone was actually there before him – someone who was very surprised indeed to see him making his way through the tramped down grass to the back door and was determined to see what he was up to.

Naomi Betjeman had already written her story and submitted it to her editor, but an eleventh hour hold had been placed on it to give her an opportunity to try to elicit some comment from the police SIO or his deputy for what was going to be a major front-page splash. Getting into the police station to buttonhole someone, however, was not going to be easy. The internal door beside the front inquiry desk could only be accessed by means of an official security card slotted into a card reader, so that was an absolute no-no, while the entrance to the rear yard was now guarded by uniformed police officers who were checking everyone going in and out.

She had to look for an alternative entry point and, although the rear gateway currently presented a problem, the yard itself provided her with her best means of accessing the building. Once there, she could try and slip in the back door behind someone else – look confident and official so no one would challenge her – or hide behind one of the many parked vehicles until someone important came out. It was all very hit and miss, but it was the only strategy she could come up with, so she had to stick with it.

The problem was how to get into the yard in the first place. The wall was around seven feet high. Attempting to climb over in broad daylight was only likely to get her arrested – if she didn't break her neck in the first place – and she couldn't see one of the bobbies on the entrance letting her through the gateway even after a substantial bung.

It was then that she spotted the lane running along the back of the yard and the adjoining terrace and decided to take a look. Almost immediately she found the broken-down fence at the rear of the shop adjoining the police station and felt a surge of excitement. Maybe there was a way in from this side? It was worth a check anyway.

Someone had been there before her too. She spotted the ribbon of trampled grass leading to the back of the shop as she ducked through a hole in the fence, but didn't give it much thought: kids probably or a tramp looking for somewhere to doss.

Striking off the improvised path deeper into the undergrowth, she found the wall of the police station yard and followed it carefully along as far as the shop itself. Damn! Not a gap anywhere. She was snookered. Ah well, it had been worth a try.

She turned around and was on the point of heading back to the path when she heard a vehicle bump slowly along the lane, then come to an abrupt stop just yards away. Crouching down behind a hawthorn bush, feeling vulnerable and guilty after her trespass – like a small child caught scrumping for apples in a neighbour's garden – she froze as she heard the creak of the fence, followed by the swish of undergrowth brushed by advancing feet.

Intensely curious in spite of her predicament, she peered around the bush and caught a glimpse of what looked like a man in a long, hooded coat striding purposefully along the strip of trampled grass to the back door of the derelict.

He turned once to stare back down the garden when he reached the half-open door, then pushed against it and disappeared inside.

Naomi forgot the reason she was there and followed him. It was daylight after all; what was there to fear?

CHAPTER 17

Twister found the briefcase containing his receiver/recorder exactly where he had left it – set up behind some boxes in an upstairs room. He smiled to himself as he closed it down and snapped the briefcase shut. Be interesting to update himself on what the cop murder team had been talking about since he had last interrogated the machine. Yes, a nice glass of whisky or three, sitting in the twitcher's armchair while he sat back and listened to the recordings – what could make a nicer evening?

Then he stiffened and cocked his head on one side. The footfall had only been faint, but it had been enough of a giveaway for his sharp hearing. Someone was moving about downstairs and, by the sound of it, in their bare feet or just socks.

Frowning, he crept to the door and peered out on to the landing. The grey afternoon light filtering in through the broken window was enough for him to see the mark of his own rubber-soled shoes in the dust of the bare floorboards: a trail someone could easily follow.

Stepping backwards across the hall, placing his feet exactly in the imprints he had left on his arrival, he slipped into what had obviously once been a bathroom and waited silently behind the door. Whoever had followed him into the house was sure to see his footprints in the hallway downstairs and, with a bit of luck, would follow them to the bedroom he had just vacated. Setting his briefcase carefully on the floor, he flexed his large hands with a smile of anticipation.

Naomi was scared – not terrified, but scared nevertheless. Her heart was thumping and her mouth was dry as she mounted the single step and peered through the back door of the shop. A large square room made up the space downstairs, running the full length of the premises from the back door to the boarded up front windows. A splintered screen to her right provided what had once no doubt been an office of some sort and the remains of a long counter stood in front of it. Rubbish littered the floor and someone had scrawled 'Psycho' on one of the walls in big black letters. She grimaced. Very appropriate.

To her left she glimpsed a narrow flight of stairs dropping away through a low doorway – apparently to a basement – while another wider staircase, just past the doorway, climbed to the upper floor. At first she was undecided, then she noticed the imprint of what looked like crepe-soled shoes in the dust in front of her, a neat trail that led across the floor diagonally and stopped before the lower step of the ascending staircase. Ah, so that was where he had gone.

Removing her shoes, she forced them into the pockets of her coat and, stepping into the shop in her bare feet, approached the stairs cautiously. More footprints on the treads, but she hesitated.

This was stupid. She had no business being here in the first place. She was trespassing. What if the man she had seen was the owner of the place or an estate agent checking on something? What possible excuse could she give for her presence there if she ran into him? And, worse still, what if he was a dosser with an eye for the ladies? She could be in big trouble then.

A warning voice in her head told her to get out while she could. Stick to the story she was investigating already and leave well alone in this creepy derelict. But her journalist's nose was twitching. Something was going on here, she could feel it in her water, something out of the ordinary, and she knew she would never forgive herself if she walked away from it now.

The stairs were surprisingly firm and didn't raise a single creak as she made her way to the upper floor, pausing at the top to listen. The sound of traffic on the main road and someone blasting their horn, but nothing stirred inside the house. Maybe she was wrong; maybe her man had gone into the basement instead. But then why were the footprints going up and across the landing?

She moved off again, heading on tip-toe towards the doorway through which the footprints seemed to disappear, then frowning her puzzlement when she peered through into a seemingly empty room. Where on earth had he gone?

The single scraping sound answered her question, but before she could turn, Twister was on to her, one arm round her neck, cutting off her air supply as his other hand jerked her head to one side in a vice-like grip. 'Nosy, nosy,' he breathed in her ear as he tensed his muscles for that fatal sideways wrench.

Roscoe went to the front door of the derelict shop first and peered through a split in one boarded-up window, but he could see nothing in the gloom beyond and, testing the door handle, he found it was securely locked.

If the range for these particular electronic bugs was only 600 metres, this empty premises would be ideal for the killer's purposes and he was determined to take a look inside. 'Stay here,' he directed the uniformed officer with him. 'I'm going round the back.'

'Do you want me to call someone off one of the other search teams to meet you there, sir,' the constable queried. 'Shouldn't be doing it on your own.'

Even Roscoe was touched by his concern and grinned with genuine amusement. As a tough ex-marine, who had earned a formidable reputation among his colleagues where physical confrontations were concerned, the DI was quite confident he could take on any man and he squeezed the policeman's arm with a grip that made the latter wince before heading off along the main road.

'I think I can manage,' he threw back over his shoulder and, marching briskly past the front of the police station, barged through a group of reporters hanging around outside and turned into the street which ran down the side of the building.

He saw the brake lights of the big Mercedes come on at the far end of the back lane as he turned into it, but he took no real notice of the car, apart from thinking that it was going a bit fast for the conditions. Even if he had been interested, the departing vehicle would have been much too far away for him to have picked out any detail and he was too preoccupied with other things anyway.

He found the gap in the fence easily enough – muttering an oath as a ragged timber plucked his pork pie hat from his head when he ducked through – and his eyes narrowed the moment he saw the ribbon of trampled grass leading to the back door. So someone had been here earlier, had they? By the look of things, not too long ago either. Maybe they were still inside? And his heartbeat quickened as he thought about that.

He saw the footprints in the dust as soon as he stepped through the back door and immediately bent down to examine them, feeling a bit like an Indian tracker out of a 1950s Western. One, a set of what looked like crepe or heavy rubber soles and the other, what were plainly bare feet – he could see the mark of the small toes of either a woman or a child – and both heading for a flight of stairs which connected with the upper floor. Most peculiar.

Frowning, he approached the stairs cautiously and stared into the gloom above. And it was then that he heard the faint moaning, coming from directly above his head. Throwing caution to the winds, he mounted the stairs two at a time, his gruff voice shouting, 'Police! Stay where you are!'

Naomi was just seconds away from oblivion, she realized that with a sense of anger and indignation, silly thoughts crowding her head. She still hadn't submitted her story, so she couldn't die now – not here in this obscure derelict, in the gloom and the dust. She hadn't made her mark yet, which meant she would become just another faceless crime statistic, a nondescript reporter on a regional rag, whose rape and murder would be mourned briefly, but soon forgotten. No one would know what she had achieved, that she had been on the verge of the biggest story ever to hit the south-west. No, it wasn't right; she had to have the fifteen minutes of fame Andy Warhol had once promised everyone; she had to *live*!

The self-defence classes she had attended just six months before had been a waste of time and money; the cynic inside her had told her that. Confronted by a powerful man, a woman had no chance whatsoever and she had been convinced that all the moves and clever steps the hairy, balding instructor had recommended were nothing but bullshit. Yet for some reason she remembered them now.

Twister knew nothing about the classes and, had he known, he would probably have laughed derisively. That he didn't laugh was due to the fact that he was caught completely unawares. He had expected Naomi to struggle, to throw herself forward in a panic or reach up to grab his arm in an effort to break his grip; he hadn't expected her to suddenly throw herself backwards towards him.

Caught off balance in spite of his size, he sensed the stairs immediately behind him and instinctively relaxed his grip to steady himself and avoid pitching head over heels to the ground floor. Before he could recover, Naomi had torn herself free and was stumbling away from him.

She had reached the bathroom and was slamming the door shut before he could recover and he heard the snap of the lock being engaged even as he went after her.

The door would not have held against him for long, but time was not on his side. The blast of the police radio sent him racing to the window at the end of the corridor and, glimpsing the blue helmet in the street below, he snarled his frustration and headed for the stairs. It had all gone wrong. For the first time since he had returned to the Levels, he had lost an intended target and, to make matters worse, he had had to abandon the audio-surveillance equipment he had left in the bathroom as well. Maybe it was time to finish the game and get out before his luck deserted him completely. But no, not just yet. He was enjoying his stay in the twitcher's house too much and there were still several varieties of malt whisky to savour, plus some nice smoked salmon in the fridge.

He glimpsed Roscoe approaching along the lane as he climbed into the car and drove off at speed. There was no mistaking the DI's squat muscular build and his distinctive pork pie hat, and he grinned wolfishly. Out in the nick of time, it seemed, and he was too far away even for the index number of his car to be clocked. Maybe his luck was holding after all.

CHAPTER 18

The car park of the wildlife reserve was empty. Tracy Long was nervous as she got out of the car and followed her three friends along the track into the woods, the towel in the haversack on her back seeming to weigh a ton. She had never done this sort of thing before, but a dare was a dare and, despite the coldness of the afternoon, she knew she had to go through with it.

Her Irish boyfriend, Josh, had suggested they bunked off college and went skinny-dipping. 'No one'll be there in the afternoon this time of year,' he'd promised. 'It'll be a great craic.'

Her two friends, Lisa and John, were of the same opinion. 'Real cool,' Lisa said with a grin. Tracy frowned. It would be that all right – more like bloody freezing.

They got to the hide without seeing a soul and Josh checked inside to make sure no one was there. Then, stepping on to the wooden landing stage that jutted out a few feet into the lake from one side of the wooden building, he began stripping off. Tracy watched him, biting her lip and pulling her anorak more closely about her. 'I don't think …' she began, but Josh was already naked and lowering himself into the water lapping the reeds. Turning to look at her other two friends, she saw that Lisa and John were already pulling off their clothes to follow him.

'Come on Tracy,' Lisa chuckled. 'It's only a bit of fun.'

Tracy stared at her, embarrassed by her blatant nudity, and trying hard not to look at John in his own virgin state. 'What if someone comes?' she exclaimed.

For reply, Lisa ran on to the landing stage and jumped straight into a patch of clear water to one side of the reeds, and screamed at the cold. John smiled at Tracy and ran after her, hitting the water like a bomb.

Still Tracy hesitated, plucking at her anorak, but doing nothing else. 'Tracy, you agreed,' John called from the reeds. 'Don't be a chicken. Get your kit off.'

Tracy undressed slowly, dropping her clothes where she stood and removing her underwear only after further jibes from Josh and Lisa.

The water was icy cold and took her breath away as she lowered herself carefully into it, feeling the reeds clutching at her thighs and the slime out of which they sprouted forcing itself up between her toes.

Hands grabbed her round the waist, pulling her away from the safety of the shallows. She went under, then surfaced in a panic, coughing up filthy water and kicking out at Josh as he tried to grab her again, laughing hysterically.

'Not funny,' she gasped. 'I'm getting out.'

She managed to swim back to the reeds and pull herself upright, using a corner of the overhanging hide for support, but a second later felt something brush her calf. 'Josh, will you stop it,' she yelled, reaching down to pull his hand away.

There was certainly a hand there, but it did not belong to Josh, nor did the ruined, half-eaten face and empty eye-sockets that stared up at her from just under the surface. And, as she shrank backwards in the water with a piercing scream, the rope that had held the twitcher's body in place for so many days snagged on her leg, jerking the corpse up among the reeds as if it were in the act of rising out of the slimy water to greet her.

Detective Chief Inspector Ansell was poring over the post mortem report on Jennifer Malone when Doctor Norton stepped into the incident-room commander's office and carefully closed the door behind him.

Ansell looked tired and drawn. Only days into what was now a double murder inquiry, he was beginning to wish he'd never been given the job in the first place. Everything seemed to be going pear-shaped. The ACC had made a point of emphasizing that fact at the meeting earlier and he nursed the growing apprehension that, if he and his boss weren't careful, they would fare as badly as their predecessors on the original Operation Firetrap inquiry, both of whom had ended up on the career scrapheap. OK, so Willoughby was the SIO and, therefore, in theory carried the can, but the man was already known to be an absolute tosser which was why Ansell had been given the job of wet-nursing him in the first place. Whatever his illustrious leader did, he couldn't really end up as any more of a tosser than he already was; the trouble was, if the ship went down with him on board, his DCI would go down with it and Ansell just couldn't let that happen.

'Nothing surprising here,' he said wearily, pushing the reports away. 'Malone died from a broken neck, as we all thought. We'll have to wait and see what Taylor's PM turns up when I pop over to the morgue,' and he glanced at his watch, 'in half an hour.'

Norton gave a cynical smile. 'At least that's something to look forward to anyway,' he commented drily. 'Will you be back for the afternoon briefing?'

The DCI nodded. 'Shouldn't take that long, and I don't expect any real surprises with this one either. Just a formality really.'

Norton grunted. 'Any luck with the bugs?'

Ansell frowned. 'The technical support unit carried out quite a thorough sweep this morning,' he said. 'Found two of the little bastards concealed under desks. All Roscoe and his merry men have got to do now is find out where our eavesdropper is holed up. They're on to that as we speak.' He lifted his jacket from the back of the chair. 'Still, I'd best be off. Don't want to be late for the dismembering.'

'Mr Willoughby not going?'

Ansell's face twisted into a cynical knowing smile. 'Mr Willoughby has gone to headquarters to see the Assistant Chief Constable,' he said, resisting the temptation to add, 'to sniff his shirt-tails and safeguard his career', and saying instead, 'Why do you ask?'

Norton hesitated, then asked, 'Don't suppose I could come instead?'

Ansell threw him a surprised glance. 'It's not very pleasant.'

Norton shrugged. 'It won't bother me. I've been to too many of these things before to be squeamish about them and seeing the PM usually enables me to improve my understanding of the killer by seeing his handiwork close up.'

Ansell held out an open hand towards the door, inviting Norton to precede him. 'Be my guest then, Doctor,' he said with a look of grim amusement and, jerking a packet of extra-strong mints from his pocket, he pressed it into the other's hand. 'Always carry a couple of packets with me,' he explained. 'Helps to take away the smell.'

Kate had picked up the call on her police radio as she and Lewis climbed back into the CID car after their guilt-laden lunch of steak pie and chips and the uniformed patrol officer was waiting for them at the entrance to the wildlife reserve car park.

'Got a stiff in the lake, skipper,' the policeman explained grimly. 'Some kids found it by the hide half an hour ago. Sergeant Casey's there with them.'

The four youngsters in question were sitting quietly on the ramp leading up to the hide, another uniformed constable standing with them, and, although they were all now fully clothed, Kate saw that the hair of the two girls particularly was soaking wet and they were shivering. She cast them a brief reassuring smile.

Sergeant Len Casey was a former DC on the drug squad and he had seen many a sight in his fifteen years' service, but his face was ashen now.

'Last time they'll go skinny-dipping,' he said, leading Kate and Lewis over to the landing stage at the side of the hide. 'Got a nasty shock, I think.'

The corpse was naked, not even a remnant of clothing attached to it, and the lower abdomen, part of one thigh and the face had been largely stripped of flesh. Kate noted the length of frayed rope tied tightly round the other thigh and a second shorter length around the corresponding upper arm.

'Who got him out of the water?' Lewis demanded.

Casey hesitated. 'One of the officers who first attended,' he said, but was not forthcoming with a name.

Kate sighed her irritation. 'Should have left him in situ until SOCO got here,' she commented. 'He's plainly very dead.'

'My officer didn't know that until he pulled him out,' Casey retorted defensively, then nodded towards the four youngsters. 'One of them called us on their mobile. Pretty plucky thing to do, considering they shouldn't have been swimming in the lake in the first place.'

'Any idea who he is?' Lewis queried.

Casey shook his head. 'And it'll be a bit difficult trying to find out, the state he's in,' he pointed out unnecessarily.

Kate nodded grimly. 'Oh I think we might be part way there,' she said.

The sergeant stared at her. 'You do?'

Kate grunted, thinking of the abandoned flask she had seized earlier in the week. 'I think he was a twitcher, that his initials are RCJN and his car was stolen from the car park back there before he was stiffed.'

'And how the devil do you know all this?'

Kate threw Lewis a sideways glance and faced the sergeant again. 'Elementary, my dear Casey,' she said with heavy sarcasm. 'That's why we are detectives.'

CHAPTER 19

Ansell found Roscoe waiting for him in the cramped SIO's office when he and Norton returned to the police station from the mortuary and Eugene Taylor's post-mortem.

The DI had a satisfied gleam in his eyes and he pointed to a briefcase standing open on the desk. 'Got a present for you, Guv,' he said.

Ansell glanced into the briefcase and gave a low whistle when he saw the electronic equipment it contained, although, as an experienced investigator, he refrained from touching it. 'So you found the receiver,' he said softly.

Roscoe nodded, 'SOCO will be collecting it shortly for fingerprinting and photographing.'

Ansell grunted. 'Where did you find it?'

'Derelict next *door* – upstairs bathroom.'

'Next door? The cheeky sod.'

Roscoe grunted. 'Yeah, and it seems I only just missed him.'

Ansell raised an eyebrow. 'How do you know that?'

The gleam in the DI's eyes intensified. 'Lady of the press told me.'

'Who?'

'One Naomi Betjeman. She's a reporter on the regional rag.'

'Good name for a journalist,' Norton cut in and was treated to blank looks. 'You know – John Betjeman, the poet? Wonder if she's a relative?'

The witticism was lost on Roscoe, while Ansell merely threw the psychologist an old-fashioned glance and turned back to his deputy. 'So how did *she* know you'd just missed him?' he went on heavily, his impatience with the DI's bit-by-bit story beginning to show.

Roscoe's face hardened. 'She followed our man into the place apparently and nearly ended up as his next victim – lucky I arrived when I did.'

'And where is she now?'

'Downstairs. Interview-room one. Thought you would want a word with her.'

'Damned right I do,' Ansell retorted, 'and right away.'

Roscoe cleared his throat. 'Bit of a hard nut this one, Guv,' he ventured. 'No friend of the police and she's got previous for rubbishing our investigations.'

Ansell gave one of his watery smiles. 'Thanks, Ted,' he acknowledged, heading for the door, 'I'll bear that in mind.'

'Mind if I accompany you again?' Norton said suddenly.

Ansell shrugged. 'As you wish, Doctor,' he said, 'though I hardly think it will be a particularly riveting experience.'

But he was wrong about that.

Naomi was still pretty shaken up and the cigarette trembled slightly in her hand as she held it to her lips. Her glasses had fallen off in her struggle with the intruder and, although she had managed to recover them, they had been stepped on and the left-hand frame was broken and only held together by some Sellotape provided by the civvy manning the front desk at Highbridge police station.

Ansell gave her the once-over as he walked into the room, closely followed by Norton. Even from where she was sitting, Naomi caught the whiff of the psychologist's strong perfume and she made a face, eyeing him with distaste. He returned her stare with a faint smile, his tinted glasses in one hand, while he polished the lenses with the other. His gaze fixed on her analytically, making her feel more than a little uncomfortable. The contrast between the ramrod straight Ansell, in his dark suit, college tie and shiny black shoes, and the slightly stooped, arty psychologist, with his collar length blond hair, green cords and blue suede shoes, could not have been more marked: at any other time Naomi would have found the duo a hilarious sight.

'You've broken your glasses,' Ansell commented, sitting down on the other side of the desk.'

'I can see why you're a detective,' she replied sarcastically, watching Norton cross the room and deposit himself on the edge of a table holding what she knew to be interview recording equipment. 'Is that thing on?' she queried.

Ansell shook his head. 'You're not under arrest,' he replied, 'just—'

'Helping you with your inquiries,' she cut in before he could finish.

'Quite so,' and Ansell smiled. 'Tea, coffee?'

She indicated a mug on the table beside her. 'Already provided, thank you. Now, shall we get on, Superintendent?'

His eyes glittered for a second. 'Detective *Chief Inspector*,' he corrected.

She grimaced. 'Big boss not about then?'

'He's busy,' he retorted. 'You'll have to make do with me. Now, I would very much like to know what happened to you this afternoon.'

She shrugged. 'All I can tell you is that I was in the lane behind your nick' – she wasn't about to admit to being in the garden of the derelict – 'and saw this character drive up to the place and climb through a hole in the fence. I was curious, so I followed him inside and then upstairs, but he was evidently lying in wait for me and he attacked me when I got to the landing. I managed to break loose and lock myself in an old bathroom and he ran off when one of your plods arrived.'

'So, to the most important question, what did he look like?'

'I haven't the faintest. I never saw his face and he was wearing some kind of hooded coat with the hood up. Tall, powerful guy, though. He grabbed me round the neck from behind and I reckon if I hadn't broken his grip, he would have twisted my head off.'

'So that's all you can tell us about him? Tall and powerful?'

She frowned, apparently thinking. 'Well, there *was* something else, something that stuck in my mind, but I just can't put my finger on it.'

'OK, what sort of car was he driving?'

She thought again for a second. 'A black Mercedes saloon – a big one – and, before you ask, no, I didn't get the number.'

'And what were you doing in the lane in the first place?'

'Taking a stroll – any law against that, is there?'

Ansell sat back in his chair and studied her for a moment, perturbed by her blatant hostility. 'Not as yet, no.'

She stubbed out her cigarette on the table and immediately lit another one. 'Good. Now I've answered your questions, maybe you'll answer mine?'

The DCI treated her to a wary frown, but then, after a slight hesitation, gave another smile and held out his hands in an inviting gesture. 'If I can, yes.'

There was a gleam of anticipation in the sharp, blue eyes studying him from behind the dark rimmed glasses.

'Do you suspect that the murder of Jennifer Malone and PC Taylor, plus the arson at the flats in Bridgwater are the work of the same man?'

He shook his head. 'I cannot comment on what lines of inquiry we are following at present.'

'Do you think there is a link between these crimes and the Operation Firetrap murders two years ago?'

'I cannot answer that either.'

She made a face. 'I'll take that as a "yes" then,' she said. 'But it is a fact, is it not, that you are looking for Larry Wadman, the former owner of Wadman's Undertakers, in connection with these crimes?'

'We are currently following up various lines of inquiry.'

But Naomi had no intention of giving up. 'A ruthless killer who has managed to evade the police for at least two years?'

'I can confirm we have no knowledge of Mr Wadman's present whereabouts, yes.'

'But he *is* still wanted?'

'It is possible he could help us with our inquiries, yes.'

'And if he had been caught originally, these murders could have been prevented, could they not?'

'No comment.'

'And is it not the case that your Detective Sergeant Kate Hamblin is this killer's main target and that the other murders were actually committed as part of a sick revenge game he is playing?'

Ansell's eyes narrowed, but he didn't answer the question, and, pushing his chair back, snapped to his feet, indicating that the interview was at an end. 'I suggest we stop there,' he said.

Naomi drew on her cigarette, savouring the moment before hitting him with the question she had saved until last. 'OK, but just one more thing,' she said, meeting his hard stare with one of her own. 'Can you explain how a wanted killer you haven't been able to find for two years was able to walk unchecked into Highbridge police station and actually bug your own incident-room?'

The effect of the question on Ansell was almost electrical and she had the satisfaction of seeing his thin frame tense and his Adam's apple jerk in a sudden tell-tale spasm as he swallowed his shock.

'Where did you get that information?' he rasped, recovering almost immediately.

Naomi snorted. 'Do me a favour. You know I will never tell you that.'

The DCI's face was so pale now that his dark eyes seemed to stand out in contrast like black marbles. 'Maybe not,' he said, resting the knuckles of both hands on the table and leaning across towards her, 'but print any of it and you could find yourself facing charges of impeding a criminal investigation as well as breaching the Contempt of Court Act.'

She laughed out loud. 'Oh p-lease,' she mocked, 'that's balls and you know it. I'm impeding nothing by printing the facts and the Contempt Act doesn't apply because you haven't arrested anyone yet.'

'Is that so?' he breathed. 'Well, *Miss*, let me tell you something. Identifying a possible suspect in advance of his arrest and charge could certainly impede our investigations and also prejudice a subsequent trial, so think on it – I'm sure your editor will.'

'All that I've said is right then, is it?' Naomi sneered. 'I'm sure my readers will be very interested to learn how a wanted man has not only been able to evade arrest for two years, but also to return to the scene of his crime for a repeat performance.'

She had the satisfaction of seeing just a hint of alarm in Ansell's dark eyes. 'Believe me, Miss Betjeman,' he warned, 'I shall find out who gave you all this information and, if I discover money changed hands, you will be on the sheet for bribing a police officer, so think about that as well.'

'That sounds like a threat.'

Ansell turned for the door, closely followed by Norton. 'No, Miss Betjeman,' he corrected, 'it's a promise. Now, I have a briefing to attend to – I'll get someone to show you out.'

Naomi glared at him. 'You do that, Chief Inspector, but,' and she dropped a couple of business cards on to the table, 'in case you decide to come clean before we go to press, I'll leave you my home address and telephone number. Feel free to contact me any time.'

Ansell ignored the offer, turning his back on her and stalking from the room, without a backward glance, and it was left to Norton to pick up the cards with a mocking smile as he followed him out.

'Arsehole!' Naomi snarled after them, savagely stubbing out her cigarette on the table top again. 'You don't know what's about to hit you.'

That was true, but then neither did Naomi.

CHAPTER 20

Naomi Betjeman stalked out of Highbridge police station tight-faced and angry. She didn't take kindly to being threatened – it made her all the more determined to hit the police where it hurt – and that lizard, Ansell, had got right under her skin. Who the hell did he think he was, treating her like some common villain?

Nevertheless, his threats had made her very uneasy. She knew his type only too well. Cold, calculating and utterly ruthless, he would have no hesitation in making good his threat to stick a bribery charge on her if he could prove she had paid for her inside information.

OK, so as yet he had nothing to go on, save his own suspicions, which were valueless without some hard facts to back them up. But she knew he would leave no stone unturned to uncover the leak on his team and, if he succeeded and managed to get a cough from Sharp, it could not only mean the end of her journalistic career, but, in the present political climate where media phone hacking had given rise to a vicious witch-hunt, a possible prison sentence too. It was vital that Sharp kept his mouth shut or they were both in the cart, but could the insipid little DS be relied upon to hold his nerve if Ansell got his hooks into him? She had her doubts about that. He needed to be warned – and PDQ.

Pulling over into a lay-by, she snatched her mobile from the front passenger seat. But, even as she started to dial the number of his flat, she was interrupted by an incoming call.

'You frigging bitch,' Sharp snarled. 'Where's my other four hundred?'

'Just woken up, have you?' Naomi commented tartly. 'I was just about to ring you.'

'We had a deal,' he retorted. 'I want the rest of the money you nicked.'

She emitted a hard laugh. 'You've got a lot more to worry about than that, Sharp,' she cut in. 'Ansell's on the warpath and he's out for blood over his leaking ship.'

There was silence for a moment and when the DS spoke again, it was in a much more mollified tone. 'You didn't have a go at him over what I told you?' he breathed.

Naomi was tempted to tell him about the attack on her in the derelict to explain how she had ended up talking to Ansell, but couldn't be bothered to go through it all again. Instead, she said, 'What's the point in paying for information if you don't use it?'

His voice erupted down the phone in a choking wail. 'You stupid cow, he'll crucify me.'

'Only if he finds out you are the leak. So stay calm and keep shtum.'

'Easy for you to say that; you don't know what a nasty bastard he can be.'

She made a grimace. 'Oh, I think I have some idea.'

The malice was back in his tone now. 'If I go down, you go down with me, remember that.'

She bit back the angry retort that flew to her tongue. She couldn't afford to wind him up any more than he was wound up already and, after her run in with Ansell, she was in no mood for the hassle anyway.

'No need for that,' she said with exaggerated patience. 'But we should meet to discuss things, so we're singing from the same hymn sheet.'

'OK, when?'

'Not for a couple of hours anyway. I'm going home for a bath and a bite to eat first, then I've got some work to do at the Clarion's offices in Bridgwater. I'll be in the basement archives below the main offices at eight-ish.'

'The Clarion Building?' he exclaimed. 'Are you mad? Ansell is already on your case and you're proposing I simply walk into your newspaper's offices for a chat, in full view of everyone? Why don't I just publish my confession on the Clarion's front page and have done with it?'

'Don't be so stupid – you're overreacting,' she snapped. 'No one will see you. All the editorial staff will have gone home by six and, as we outsource the printing of the paper, no one will be working overnight on the premises – that is, except me, and I have my own key to archives.'

'I don't care. There's no way I'm risking it.'

She tried another tack, appealing directly to his avaricious nature, 'Suit yourself, but then you can say goodbye to the rest of your money.'

Her tactic worked. There was a moment's hesitation before he capitulated with another snarl. 'You'd better bring the full four hundred,' he warned.

She gave a smile that, if he had been present, would have told him she had no intention of bringing anything. 'See you at around eight then,' she replied. 'I'll leave the back door ajar for you.'

Willoughby stared at the pale dismembered corpse lying on the jetty under the spot-lit SOCO tent and swallowed hard. 'Dreadful,' he whispered, 'just dreadful.'

Ansell threw him a contemptuous glance. 'I'd put it a lot stronger than that,' he grated and fixed his gaze on the pathologist who was still bending over the dead man. 'Been in the water long, Doctor?' he queried.

Doctor Lydia Summers stood up and pursed her lips in thought. 'Difficult to say accurately. After death, in the first stages of decomposition, a body will start to lose its heat until it reaches the ambient temperature of its environment. The rate at which that happens can be influenced by a variety of factors. In this case, the temperature of the water, lack of clothing, and the body mass and condition of the deceased will have had a significant impact on that rate and therefore on any estimate re time of death—'

'With respect, I'm not looking for a lecture on pathology, Doctor,' Ansell interjected sharply. 'I just want an estimate of time of death, if that's at all possible.'

His censure was greeted with an indulgent smile. 'I would say about seventy-two hours, maybe less,' she said, 'but that's very approximate. Looks like the local carnivores have had a feast too. Face is virtually gone and most of his abdomen.' She ran a hand through her hair. 'Oh yes, and his neck has been broken – just like Jennifer Malone and your young policeman.'

'Same killer then?' Willoughby put in.

Summers shrugged. 'Looks like it. And this time you're going to find identification pretty difficult.'

Ansell nodded. 'It's going to be down to fingerprints and dental records by the look of it.'

'You could try facial reconstruction techniques, if necessary.'

'Whatever we do, it's going to take time to get anywhere, Doctor,' Willoughby pointed out, 'and, with this madman roaming about, time is not on our side.'

She shrugged. 'Not my problem, Mr Willoughby.'

Ansell nodded. 'Thanks, Doctor. See you at the PM.'

Turning on his heel, he pushed the tent flap aside and stepped out into the early evening moonlight, Willoughby following at his heels like an overweight sheepdog.

He spied Kate Hamblin and DI Roscoe standing by the ramp to the hide as he was pulling off the blue plastic booties he had been wearing to protect the crime scene. 'Seems you were right, Kate,' he said, leaving Willoughby struggling to remove his own booties and walking over to her. 'Pity no one believed you.' And he directed a keen critical glance at Roscoe.

Kate flushed with embarrassment in the gloom. 'I must admit it did sound a bit far-fetched at the time, Guv,' she said, tactfully empathizing with the DI. 'Question is, why was he killed?'

Ansell shrugged. 'As you said before, probably for his car.'

Kate shook her head quickly. 'I'm still quite sure the killer took the car after torching the Volvo, but I can't see that he came all the way out here just for that purpose. It doesn't make sense. I think there's more to it than just the car.'

'Such as?'

'Maybe he knew the dead man and had to get rid of him – an accomplice who knew too much perhaps – or he was sleeping rough somewhere on the reserve and accidentally came face to face with him.'

Ansell was plainly sceptical. 'I don't buy either of those two theories,' he commented.

Willoughby materialized beside Ansell. 'What was it Sherlock Holmes used to say?' he put in. 'Something about "when you have eliminated the impossible, whatever remains, however improbable, must be the truth".'

For a second none of them spoke, all plainly stunned by his off the wall comment. Sensing their reaction, Willoughby grunted and promptly wandered over to where Doctor Norton was standing on his own by some trees, apparently trying to come to terms with the horror of what he had just seen, the butt of his cigarette glowing fiercely in the shadows as he sucked the poisonous smoke into his lungs.

'Well, Sherlock Holmes aside,' Ansell resumed drily, 'a more thorough search of the reserve would certainly not be a bad idea. We should also check missing person reports – see if someone hasn't come home when they should've done. But the real key to our man's ID has to be his car. Once we have the make and number, we may be able to short-circuit the ID process through an RO check.'

'The flask Hamblin found could be another way of achieving the same end if the prints match?' Roscoe put in. 'Maybe the man *was* a twitcher, as Hamblin first thought.

The flask is not only distinctive, but carries some initials. Someone in the bird-watching community might recognize it or know whose initials they could be.'

'Pity we didn't follow up on the flask originally,' Ansell said, his tone dripping acid. 'But I'll leave you to do that now, shall I, Ted? You can also get someone on to missing persons while we're waiting for fingerprint matching and dental records to be checked. Oh, and get hold of some plods to give this place a more thorough going-over too, will you?' He gave a humourless smile. 'Think you can manage all that?'

Roscoe didn't answer, which was probably just as well under the circumstances, for, had it not been dark, his unspoken thoughts would have been clearly reflected in the baleful look he directed towards his boss. At least the gloom concealed the full sourness of his expression, however, and that was not all it concealed either.

In the shadows of the wood bordering the boardwalk, Twister watched the proceedings through narrowed eyes. Time for another rethink, he mused. Things were beginning to unravel around him. He hadn't expected the corpse to be discovered so early and once police forensics got their hands on it, identification was inevitable in the end. That wouldn't be immediate, but time was certainly running out for him.

Yeah, then there was that reporter cow. He wasn't bothered about Old Bill knowing he was behind the killings – that was an inevitable consequence of his little game, but he couldn't risk her coming up with something that would give the inquiry team even the slightest edge in tracking him down – at least not before he had concluded his business with Kate Hamblin anyway. A little more tidying up was required and his fingers were already itching.

CHAPTER 21

The air was cold, but fresh when Naomi left her flat in Bridgwater and drove the short distance to the offices of the Bridgwater Clarion, unaware that she had been followed home and that the same vehicle was on her tail again. A hot bath and an Indian take-away, delivered to her door, had set her up for the night's work and she felt a tingle of excitement as she headed through the lamp-lit streets.

After finally agreeing on the release of her story over the phone with her editor, she could hardly wait for the morning edition of the newspaper to hit the shops and news-stands, although she knew it would not make her any friends in the police. Filing her additional copy with Tom Caxton, the paper's editor, detailing the assault on her and her subsequent interview with Ansell, she hadn't been surprised to learn that the DCI had already been on to him with carefully veiled threats. It hadn't done her any harm, however; just the opposite – Tom was now even more anxious for her to provide a follow-up for the next edition.

To research the background for this, she could have accessed the digital records in the newspaper's archives through her own laptop at home, but had decided to do her research at work where there were no distractions and there was also access to other non-digital information that could prove useful. Besides which, it was an ideal place for her to meet Sharp, away from prying eyes.

The place was in darkness, just as she had expected. Flicking a switch inside the door, she put the lock on the snib and waited until the strip-lights sprang into life. She was standing on a platform separating two halves of an iron staircase, the longest section ascending to a fire door on a landing directly above her head and also giving access to the editorial offices where she worked. The other half plunged into a vaulted basement which held the newspaper's archives.

Half a dozen individual workstations stood in a line at the foot of the staircase, each with its own computer and printer, like some corporate library, and a row of at least twenty steel tambour filing units, containing horizontally accommodated paper records behind lockable steel shutters and separated by deep shadowy aisles, marched along the far wall from one end of the room to the other.

Two of the three rows of high-level strip-lights were still flickering annoyingly when she got to the bottom of the staircase and she tutted her irritation as she dumped her handbag on the floor beside the nearest workstation and sat down. Outside, a two-stroke motor cycle roared past with a sound like an enraged hornet, but otherwise the night was ominously still and for no real reason she shivered and glanced around her, half-expecting to find someone standing there.

Finally, pouring a black coffee from the flask she had brought with her, she set the plastic cup on the edge of the desk, switched on the computer and waited. The screen flashed into life, within a couple of seconds, accompanied by a faint 'fizz' and, tapping in her password to access the company's intranet, she waited for the list of options to appear on the light blue screen. When they finally jerked into place, she selected the appropriate icon, then typed in the necessary subject information request in the browser and clicked on.

The system seemed to hold its breath, then abruptly the front page of a two-year old edition of the Clarion appeared on the screen, bearing the headline 'Murder Mayhem' and a photograph embedded in the text of an apparently burned-out Transit van on a rutted marshland track. She scrolled down and stiffened as a man's bearded face stared back at her from a centre page. Even without reading the caption underneath, she knew instinctively that the picture was that of Larry Wadman and for several moments she simply froze in her chair.

She had not joined the Clarion from university until well after the Operation Firetrap inquiry had finished, so this was the first time she had seen a close-up of the psychopath Sharp had referred to as Twister. But her heart began making strange sucking noises as her gaze became riveted on that cold, hard face and the empty soulless eyes – eyes that lacked even the slightest hint of emotion or humanity and bore a macabre resemblance to those of a corpse.

And as she stared into them, something clicked in her brain, an incredible realization that made her skin crawl and sent her thoughts careering off into cyberspace. Her intention had been to access the newspaper's archives for background information on the old Firetrap investigation, but instead, by pure accident, she had stumbled upon something far more significant, something so mind-blowing that she could hardly believe it. And on top of that, she could now also remember with startling clarity what it was about her assailant that she had been trying to recall after he had attacked her in the derelict house – in itself a very small detail, but one which, together with the revelations provided by the computer's archived newspaper report, had assumed major significance.

Returning to terra firma, she took a gulp of her coffee and sat back in the chair to think things out. She would have to inform the police inquiry team immediately; it was her moral duty – and, of course, she mused with a grim tightening of her mouth, it would also earn her the recognition she craved. This time, however, she was going to call the shots; this time Ansell and his crew would have to play by her rules, whether they liked it or not.

She heard the door open at the top of the stairs as she reached for the telephone and cursed under her breath. The last thing she wanted to do was to share her information with Sharp and she wished now she hadn't arranged the meet in the first place.

'Be with you in a minute, Phil,' she called as she quickly exited the digital archives. 'Take a seat somewhere.'

But the figure now standing behind her, his face reflected in the dying screen, was definitely not who she was expecting.

Phil Sharp had the mother of a hangover and the last thing he wanted to do was go out. But the prospect of retrieving the four hundred he was owed overcame his natural inclination to go back to bed and continue to sleep it off.

Just before eight in the evening, without bothering to shower or shave and pulling on an old tracksuit and trainers, he dosed up on a couple of mugs of black coffee and a handful of painkillers before ringing for a taxi to take him to the pub where he had left his car.

His flashy unaffordable Subaru was exactly where he had left it – surprising with all the villains there were about in the area – and it started with the usual satisfying roar that gave the poser in him so much satisfaction.

He knew he should never have been driving in his condition. With the number of double whiskies he had poured down his throat that morning, he had to be well over the limit, even after several hours sleep, but he didn't see that he had a choice if he wanted his money and, hopefully, his uniformed colleagues would be too busy hunting a serial killer to bother too much about drinking and driving offences.

To avoid drawing attention to himself, he drove with particular care, but if there was one thing Detective Sergeant Sharp should have learned after several years' police experience was that, however careful one driver is, there are always others who are not.

The supermarket van driver was in a hurry; he was late with a delivery and it was the third time in as many days.

Sacked from his previous job because of poor performance and already on a verbal warning with his present employers, he couldn't afford another slip up. Nevertheless, he made one – and in the most public way possible.

He didn't see the silver Subaru when he pulled out of the turning on to the main Bridgwater Road and by the time the headlights blazed in his side window, it was already too late.

Had Sharp not been suffering from the effects of alcohol, he might have avoided a collision, but on this occasion he was a fraction slower than usual and that was all that was necessary. Although he hit the brake pedal hard and swerved to his nearside, he ploughed into the driver's door of the van at a little over 40 mph, sending it careering across the road into the path of an articulated lorry, which braked hard, and jackknifed across both lanes.

The thud of more collisions followed in quick succession, but Sharp hardly heard them and he was still sitting in the driving seat of his wrecked Subaru, shocked, bruised but otherwise uninjured, when the police traffic officer finally approached him.

'You OK sir?' she queried and he nodded vaguely as she helped him out of the car.

'Your car is it? You driving at the time? Good, then I must require you to take a breath test. I realize the accident probably wasn't your fault, but each driver will have to be tested.'

He stared at her, uncomprehending, and she added, 'Nothing to worry about. It's just routine.'

CHAPTER 22

Twister knew from bitter experience that Naomi Betjeman was a handful. What he didn't anticipate was that she would see his reflection in the computer screen before he got to her and react with the speed that she did.

The coffee hit him full in the face as she whirled round, sending him staggering back with a cry of pain, and before he could recover, she was racing for the iron staircase leading to the street. But Twister could react with equal speed when he needed to and he got to her just as she reached the door at the top, grabbing her arm and pitching her into the opposite wall before swinging round to block her exit.

The only way Naomi could go was up, but she didn't hesitate, stumbling away from him with blood dripping from a re-opened split eyebrow caused by the broken frame of her taped-up glasses. She just prayed that the door on the ground-floor landing above, giving access to editorial offices, was not locked – and she was in luck.

The heavy fire door took all her strength to pull open, and she was only just through when Twister got to the landing and made a grab for the handle as the door swung to behind her.

The moon was out and its brilliance flooded into the room through the large windows, providing enough light for Naomi to see by as she stumbled along a narrow aisle between two rows of work-stations, but the light also enabled her pursuer to follow her more easily and she sensed him just a couple of yards behind her, panting heavily.

Approaching the door to the front foyer at the other end of the room, she suddenly swung sideways, away from the reach of the moonlight, and, as the darkness folded around her, she dropped to her knees between two workstations and scrambled into a deep kneehole. She heard Twister jerk to a stop, still panting, and sensed his eyes – those frightening dead eyes – staring about him in the gloom, trying to pinpoint her position. She waited for him to switch on the main lights, but nothing happened and she breathed a sigh of relief when it dawned on her that he probably didn't want to attract attention from outside the building by such a move.

But her relief was short-lived and the next moment she froze as she heard him squeeze between two of the workstations just feet from where she crouched, groping for her in the gloom.

'You might as well give it up, Naomi,' he said suddenly. 'I shall find you in the end, you know that, don't you?'

The voice was low and confident, if slightly wheezy, but there was no trace of malice in the tone. In a weird kind of way, it was almost soothing, but his statement carried absolute conviction and she shuddered. The creature was a virtual automaton.

'Naomi, where are you?' she heard him call, this time in a sing-song voice, like a child playing a game, adding with a heavy sigh, 'OK, coming, ready or not.'

It was all like some kind of nightmare and she screwed up her eyes and clenched her fists in an effort to hold back the panic that was threatening to engulf her in an irrational burst of hysteria.

'Naomi? Naomi?' he called again in the same sing-song voice. 'Come out, come out wherever you are?'

Now he was standing directly in front of her hideaway, just his lower legs and feet visible in a shard of moonlight probing the gap.

Silence. She could feel her heart racing, like an engine with the clutch out, and felt sure its frantic beat could be heard all over the room. He gave no indication of this, however, and moved on. Still she remained where she was, suspecting that he was standing among the other workstations, just waiting for her to give herself away.

'Naomi, sweetheart, give us a clue?'

The voice was now much further away, to her right. Dare she take the chance and make a run for it? Just as she was about to risk it, however, there was another development and she stiffened as heavy footsteps crunched in the gravel outside the row of windows through which the moonlight blazed. The beam of a powerful torch grazed the top of the desk beneath which she crouched and she heard the muffled rattle of heavy glass entrance doors being shaken in the front foyer towards which she had been fleeing.

Security! The paper's bloody security patrol was checking the premises – due to a broken alarm system, it was the Clarion's only defence against break-ins – and, stuck under a desk in the virtually blacked out office, she had no way of attracting the man's attention before Twister got to her. Her only hope was that the security officer would now go down the steps to the lower car park at the back of the building, find the basement door unlocked and investigate.

But even if he did, would he be a match for a creature like Twister? Pretty unlikely. Most of the security officers she had seen were either elderly retired coppers or spotty-faced university students trying to earn a crust while they decided on their future careers – a pushover for the psychopath – so she would still be dead at the end of any confrontation anyway. All she could do was to treat this distraction as an opportunity to effect her escape.

Creeping out of her hiding place on all fours, she carefully crawled between the rows of workstations. Heading back towards the door leading to the basement, she hoped that Twister would assume she would try to make for the front foyer instead – especially after hearing the security man checking the main entrance doors.

Peering round the last desk in the row, she could see the door clearly outlined in the moonlight, the aisle between it and the door to the foyer completely empty. Where the hell had the psychopath gone? She glanced over her shoulder between the workstations. Slivers of moonlight traced faint lines along the floor, but otherwise everything was in deep shadow.

Gritting her teeth, she raised herself on her haunches, gripped the edge of the desk for a second and then ran full tilt for the door. She expected firm resistance as she grabbed the handle, but to her surprise, the door opened easily, throwing her off-balance and pitching her forwards on to the landing. She caught a brief glimpse of Twister holding the door back on the other side, but before she could recover, he had released it and was reaching for her. In a desperate attempt to evade those deadly hands, she threw herself sideways, but lost her balance and pitched headfirst over the guard-rail, hitting the concrete floor thirty feet below with a sickening crunch of shattered bone.

Fred Jarvis had only worked as a security officer for eight months and, if he was honest with himself, after thirty-eight years in the police force, eight as a civilian office manager on CID, he saw it as a bit of a come-down. Shaking the door-handles of factories and offices as a pseudo policeman left him cold, but he needed the job, both for the money and to make up his National Insurance contributions until he qualified for his state pension, which would then top up the small police pension he now received as a former detective constable.

As a fifty-nine year old, heavily built man suffering from gout, Jarvis moved only slowly and he often wondered how he would ever manage to detain a villain at his age and in his condition if he was to catch a fit, young toe-rag breaking into one of the properties on his rounds. He would have a go obviously – old habits died hard – but he didn't rate his chances very high.

He moved slowly now as he approached the rear of the Clarion's offices, after satisfying himself that the doors at the front of the building were secure, but jumped, his senses tingling, when he saw the basement door standing partially open and the lights on inside. Hearing a faint sound a few yards away, he flicked on his powerful torch and caught a glimpse of what he thought was a shadow moving swiftly away from him along the wall of the place towards a service road, but when he focused the torch on the spot, the beam met only bare brickwork and he relaxed with a sense of relief, putting his intruder down to nothing more than a trick of the moonlight.

Approaching the open door, still with some trepidation, he peered inside and immediately stiffened, hardly able to believe his eyes. The prostrate figure was lying motionless on the floor of the basement directly below him, a pool of blood spreading out from underneath her body like the contents of a broken wine bottle.

'Bloody hell!' he muttered and stumbled over to her.

He recognized the woman at once; she was the nice young reporter who had given him a cup of coffee a couple of times when he was on his evening rounds and it seemed she had been working late again. He glanced up at the staircase as he bent over her. Even from where he knelt, he could see that the handrail on the topmost landing was badly twisted. Poor little begger, he mused, thinking she must have tripped in some way and pitched over.

He felt her throat and, to his relief, detected a faint pulse. Then, to his surprise, her eyes flickered open and she muttered something he couldn't quite make out. He shook his head sadly. 'Now you just lie still, love,' he said in an attempt at reassurance and depressed the transmit button of his radio to call for an ambulance.

On a piece of waste-ground on the other side of the service road, Twister started the engine of his stolen Mercedes and pulled away quietly without lights.

He knew he should have made sure that that reporter bitch was actually dead before he'd quit the building and he'd broken his own golden rule by not doing so – even though it was pretty unlikely that she would have survived a fall from around thirty feet on to solid concrete. OK, so the security patrol had been on his way, but he could easily have disposed of a Wally like that if the man had been foolish enough to turn up before he'd got clear. Trouble was, he'd had no means of knowing if the old duffer had called his control centre immediately he'd spotted the back door open, which meant the police could already be on their way, or whether he had had a partner with him and it wasn't worth hanging around to find out.

In fact, it was probably best to leave the whole thing looking like an accident anyway, just in case Old Bill was persuaded to delve a little too deeply into what Betjeman had been doing in the building so late in the evening. Twister found it difficult to believe that she could have sussed out anything of any significance in their earlier confrontation at the derelict, but he couldn't afford to take the risk – which is why he had decided to go after her again, just in case – and, although he didn't think she had left any incriminating notes anywhere, he could do without Ansell and his crew sniffing around on the outside chance that they might find something.

Turning from the service road on to the main drag, he switched on his lights and accelerated smoothly away, leaving the night to the ambulance and police patrol cars that flashed past him in quick succession as he headed for home.

Kate Hamblin pushed wearily through the doors of the deserted incident-room at just after ten and hung the ignition keys of her CID car on one of the hooks screwed into the edge of the big white board on its school-like easel leaning against one wall.

For a moment she stared at the gruesome SOCO photographs of Jennifer Malone and Eugene Taylor fixed to the board – each with black chinograph pencil scrawls underneath – and took a deep trembling breath. Both dead and all because of her. Now there was another one – still to be identified – that would soon be joining them. How many more were there yet to come? And how long before Twister tired of his sick game and came for her?

She stared at the enlarged photograph of the psychopath in the middle of the board. He was just as she remembered him – the hard wide face, bushy black beard and those awful corpse-like eyes. But would he be the same now? She doubted it. Ansell had engaged a forensic artist to come up with an image of what he might look like after two years, without the beard, but it was a tall order and, to her mind, likely to be very much hit and miss.

But what else had they to go on? The only people who had seen him recently were dead – with the exception of Del Shaylor, who was still in hospital with second degree burns and had only seen his silhouette in a car at night, and Naomi Betjeman, who claimed she had not seen much of him at all when he had grabbed her from behind in the derelict next door. They were literally fighting in the dark. All she did know was that Twister's fingerprints had been found all over the coffin in which Jennifer Malone's body had been dumped, as well as in Pauline Cross's old house. The killer had obviously made no effort to conceal his identity. Why would he? As Doctor Norton had already pointed out, that was the main purpose of his killing spree – to let everyone know he was back, and with a vengeance.

'Oh, there you are.'

Lewis's voice cut straight through her musings and she turned as he strode towards her across the room.

'Time for bed, old girl,' he said. 'Guv'nor wants us in first thing, so we'd better be heading home.' He raised one hand and snapped his fingers. 'Oh by the way, have you heard about Phil Sharp?'

She frowned. 'What about him?'

He steered her towards the doors. 'Seems he had a head-on in his motor just outside Bridgwater.'

She gaped at him. 'That's awful. Was he badly hurt?'

He ushered her into the corridor, then held open the doors to the landing. 'Apparently not, but his car is written off and he's in the nick – twice over the limit they tell me. That'll be the end of his career for sure.'

He brightened. 'Still, seeing as he's out of the picture now, there might be a vacancy on CID for you.'

'Hayden!' She stopped on the stairs and stared at him in disbelief. 'That's a rotten thing to say.'

He reddened, then gave a little embarrassed cough, continuing on ahead of her. 'Yes, it is, isn't it? There but for the grace of God and all that. Sorry.' He glanced over his shoulder. 'Er … fancy a Chinese on the way home?'

CHAPTER 23

As an ex-DCI, Roz Callow knew that confidence was all important – confidence and authority. They got you into places which would remain barred to the more timid or hesitant and she needed both qualities to gatecrash the inquiry at Highbridge nick.

She had no intention of chatting to juniors, like Kate Hamblin and Hayden Lewis when she got inside either. She was determined to see the boss himself. Not Willoughby, of course; she knew him of old and he had always been a tosser. No, Ansell was the man; she was going to see him and no one was going to stop her.

She chose her moment carefully. There were three members of the public at the front counter when she marched into the police station foyer just after nine in the morning – all clamouring for the attention of the harassed civilian station duty officer.

One was an elderly woman, apparently complaining about noise caused by her neighbour's dog. The other two, standing immediately behind her, were youngsters with punk hair-styles who, from their impatient demeanour, had obviously been waiting to be seen for some time – no doubt to sign on as a condition of their bail – and were trying to hurry things along by shouting over her shoulder.

Callow made the most of the confusion. Rattling the security door beside the counter and waving her wallet, which contained nothing more official than her credit cards, she barked: 'DCI Callow, headquarters. 'Flick the switch, will you?'

The SDO threw her a startled glance, as his customers continued to shout at him.

'Come on, man, I'm in a hurry,' Callow rapped. 'My bloody card doesn't work in your infernal machine.'

For a moment it was touch and go, but, fortunately for Callow, the beleaguered civilian had obviously never heard of her before. He didn't get much chance to query her identity anyway. The indignant dog-hater suddenly screeched as one of the women behind her tried to push in front. Reaching below the counter, he quickly hit the necessary switch before irritably castigating all three of his customers. There was a loud buzzing noise and, yanking on the door handle, Callow was in.

DCI Ansell had only just arrived and was settling in behind the SIO's desk when his visitor burst in.

'You must be Ansell?' Roz Callow snapped rudely, dropping into the chair opposite, without invitation.

The DCI shot forward in his own chair, his dark eyes narrowed and angry. 'Who the devil are you?' he began, 'and how did you—?'

She cut him short with a wave of one talon-like hand. 'Before your time, Mr Ansell,' she replied. 'Ex-DCI Roz Callow actually.' Then, tapping a newspaper protruding from her coat pocket, she added, 'and in answer to the question you were about to ask, I got in as easily as Larry Wadman did to bug your office.'

To her surprise, Ansell refused to bite on the remark or to show any interest in her newspaper. Instead, regaining his composure with a degree of self-control she couldn't help but admire, he simply sat back in his chair, to study her with the cool analytical gaze of a doctor assessing a difficult patient.

'So, you're Roz Callow, are you?' he commented. 'And to what do I owe this doubtful pleasure?'

'As they say in all the best film dramas,' she finished for him with heavy sarcasm, conscious of the fact that she had used similar words as Ansell when Kate Hamblin and Lewis had called to see her.

He acknowledged the barb with a slight nod of his head. 'Tea? Coffee?' he queried, offering her a smile that completely failed to reach the dark watchful eyes.

'I haven't come here to drink tea or coffee,' she retorted.

'So what can I do for you then?' he went on.

Her eyes glittered. 'It's more a case of what I can do for you, Detective Chief Inspector, especially as your murder inquiry seems to have hit the buffers.'

'Like yours did two years ago, you mean?' he reminded her mildly. 'Rescued, I gather, by a novice DC?'

Her thin lips tightened as she thought of Kate Hamblin. 'Now, it seems, *yours* needs rescuing,' she threw back at him. 'That's why I'm here.'

He rested his elbows on the desk and met her stare over steepled fingers. 'I'm not sure what you can do for us, Ms Callow,' he replied, with the emphasis on the 'Ms'. 'I assume you gave all the information you had to Sergeant Hamblin and DC Lewis when they called to see you before?'

'I told them what I wanted to tell them.'

He raised an eyebrow. 'So you withheld information from a police murder inquiry, is that what you're saying?'

She glared at him, annoyed that she had allowed herself to walk straight into that one. 'You know damned well what I'm saying,' she snapped, 'but if you want me to make it any clearer: I only talk to the organ grinder – not to his bloody monkeys!'

He opened his hands, palms uppermost in an inviting gesture. 'Then I'm all ears, Ms Callow. So what is it that you've got to tell me?'

She shook her head. 'It's not as simple as that. I'll trade what I've got for what you have.'

To her annoyance, he chuckled softly. 'My dear Ms Callow, I do believe you are trying your hand at a little bluff. You don't have anything at all, do you? You've come here simply to try and extract information from me, not to give it?'

Clearly outwitted, she lurched to her feet, gripping the edge of the desk to steady herself. 'Don't you patronize me, Mister,' she blazed. 'You need me on this inquiry, whether you realize it or not. I know this bastard better than anyone. He was closer to me than you are now when he snapped Pauline Cross's neck.'

Ansell sighed and gave another cold smile. 'Oh I think we can manage without your help this time, Ms Callow,' he replied.

'Is that so?' she snarled and, wrenching the newspaper from her pocket, she tossed it on to the desk. 'Well, maybe this will wipe the smug look off your face,' and, turning awkwardly, she limped from the office, leaning heavily on her walking stick.

'Thanks for coming in,' he called after her as he reached for the newspaper. 'Always appreciated.'

Phil Sharp knew he was finished. Released from the police station at just on nine after a further test had revealed that he was no longer over the limit, he'd endured an uncomfortable and humiliating night in the cells. Now he stood blinking in the bright morning light, like a termite emerging from its mound, unshaven, unwashed and hardly able to credit what had happened to him.

He'd known the police breath test at the scene of the accident would be positive, but nearly twice over the limit after so many hours sleeping it off? It didn't seem possible. Yet the evidential breath tests at the police station had supported the fact and now he was in possession of a nice charge sheet, bailing him to the local magistrates court. His world was on the verge of collapse and he cursed himself for a fool. Why hadn't he just scarpered before the traffic patrol had arrived?

Gone into a local pub and downed a few scotches? That way they may not have been able to determine whether his high alcohol level was due to drinking before or after the prang. He could have claimed he was concussed and hadn't realized what he was doing when he had left the scene. Alternatively, he could have managed a swift vanishing act, then claimed his car had been stolen. Others had done this sort of thing before, hadn't they – *and* got away with it? But he had been so shaken up after the collision and so shocked about the severity of the damage to his beloved Subaru, that he had just sat there like a potential road kill, waiting for the inevitable.

He lit a cigarette with trembling fingers. Still, it was too late now to think about what he *could* have done. He was in the shit big time and his impending court appearance could only result in a driving ban and – horror of horrors – a criminal record which could put paid to his career for good.

He swore savagely as he thought about his spiralling misfortunes. Already on the verge of being investigated for leaking information to the press, with nothing to show for his 'exclusive' but a measly hundred quid, he could do without this on top. Then there was his car – not paid for yet and with three years still to go. The repayments would have been tough enough on the pay of a DS, but thrown out on his ear, they would be impossible. The joke was, he wouldn't even be able to afford to get the car repaired – if it hadn't been a write-off already – because he had only taken out third party insurance. What a real shitty mess!

Dropping his cigarette into the gutter, he hailed a passing taxi. 'Better get used to this, Phil,' he thought to himself as he climbed aboard. 'It's the only way you'll be travelling from now on.'

The cabby sniffed several times as he got in. 'You been drinking?' he queried.

Sharp scowled, surprised that the odour was still on him. 'What if I have?' he retorted belligerently.

'Then you can bleedin' well walk,' the other said. 'I'm not havin' you throw up in my motor, so get out.'

Sharp watched the disappearing taxi with a sense of angry frustration. Walk? His flat was miles away. Reaching into his pocket, he flicked his last cigarette out of the packet and headed off in the direction of Burnham, peering through the tobacco smoke at the passing cars with his thumb extended and his feet dragging the pavement.

Fortunately for him, he had only gone about a mile before a car travelling towards him swung across the road and pulled up alongside, facing in the wrong direction.

'Need a good lawyer?' someone chortled.

He scowled and turned his head to stare at the grinning face of the policeman as he leaned out of the window of the police patrol car.

'Piss off!' Sharp retorted and started to walk on.

Jimmy Noble sounded his horn. 'Get in, you wanker,' he shouted. 'Unless you *want* to walk to Burnham.'

Reluctantly Sharp went round to the other side of the car to climb into the front passenger seat and Noble swung out on to his correct side of the road, heading towards Highbridge.

'So, what gives, my man?' Noble queried, glancing quickly at his dishevelled state. 'The jungle drums are saying you've been done for Excess Alcohol.'

Sharp grunted. 'What's it to you?' he said, his sour face confirming the news.

'Happens to the best of us,' Noble said, without meaning it. 'But what are you going to do now?'

Sharp snorted. 'What do you think? Wait to be slung out the job, I suppose.'

Noble winced. 'At least you walked away from that TA in one piece. Pity about your nice motor, though.'

Sharp changed the subject. 'So what were you doing in Bridgwater? Bit off your area, aren't you?'

Noble slowed slightly to study a beaten-up old lorry, laden with what looked like fridges and freezers, limping past them on the other side of the road, then lost interest and increased his speed again. 'Oh, had to drop some stuff off for SOCO at the Bridgwater Clarion's offices.'

Sharp frowned. 'The Clarion? Why, what happened there?'

Noble shrugged. 'Don't know too much now – back on normal duties – but I hear some poor cow of a reporter got mugged or something. She's in hospital in a pretty bad way. They reckon it might be linked to this Twister case.'

He chuckled. 'Don't think the DCI is too unhappy about what happened to her, though. He never did like bloody reporters and this one has really got under his skin with the exposé she's just written.'

Sharp felt his skin crawl. 'Exposé? Who was she then?'

Noble shrugged again. 'Can't remember – same name as some poet or other.'

'What – Betjeman?'

'Yeah, that's it, Naomi Betjeman.' Noble threw him a suspicious glance. 'Didn't know you knew anything about poetry?'

Sharp almost bit his tongue. 'Just an educated guess,' he replied.

Noble grunted, apparently accepting his explanation. 'Well, word is she's got an in with someone at the nick who's been leaking information to her. Wouldn't like to be in their shoes when Ansell gets to grip with 'em, I can tell you.'

Entering Highbridge, Noble slowed down and glanced across at him again. 'Where do you want dropped off – don't suppose it's the nick?'

Sharp grimaced. 'Hardly – going to report sick anyway. Couldn't run me out to Burnham, could you? Drop me off at the Tesco roundabout. I can walk to my flat from there.'

Noble grinned again. 'No problem, my son. Just don't tell the guv'nor, eh? He wouldn't want me running a bent copper home.' And he laughed out loud at his cruel joke, but Sharp hardly heard him; he had other more important things on his mind – like Naomi Betjeman, for example.

CHAPTER 24

Roz Callow was just leaving the police station when Kate and Lewis arrived.

'Good lord, it's the Wicked Witch of the North,' Lewis murmured, as he held the front passenger door of his Jaguar open to let Kate out. 'What the devil is she doing here?'

Lewis had chosen to park in the visitors' bays at the front of the building following scratch marks he had found on his driver's door – almost certainly from the carelessly opened door of a police car while it had been parked in the rear yard – and Roz Callow's old Audi was already parked in the next bay.

'Well, well, well,' the ex-DCI sneered, pausing beside them on the steps to the front door. 'If it isn't the dynamic duo.'

'Hello, Roz,' Kate said quietly, 'looking for a job?'

Callow smirked coldly. 'Very funny,' she retorted. 'Been to see your boss actually – DCI to DCI sort of chat. Like to keep abreast of things, you know.'

Lewis shrugged. 'Then you must have been disappointed. Nothing new unfortunately.'

'Really?' she exclaimed and studied each of their faces in turn, leaning heavily on her stick. 'Your own incident-room bugged by the very killer you're hunting; plus, according to stop press, a body recovered from a lake that your lot failed to discover on a previous search and the reporter who has just rubbished your investigation found lying on the floor of her newspaper offices with multiple injuries? I wouldn't call that nothing new, would you?'

Kate started, recalling Roscoe's revelations a couple of hours before about the attack on Naomi Betjeman in the derelict. 'What, the girl from The Clarion?' she blurted out.

Callow flicked her eyes in acknowledgment. 'Fell down the staircase at work, I understand. Now isn't that sad?'

'Surprised you are keeping such close tabs on this case,' Lewis went on. 'Nothing in it for you anymore, is there?'

Callow's eyes shrunk into narrow slits. 'That bastard, Larry Wadman – or Twister, as he likes to call himself – ruined my life,' she rasped. 'If it hadn't been for him, I wouldn't have this,' And she tapped her leg with her stick. 'And, more to the point, I would still be DCI.'

Lewis couldn't help himself. 'Ah well, Roz,' he grinned, 'every cloud has its silver lining, doesn't it?'

Then he turned away from her and, leading Kate by the elbow, headed up the steps towards the front door of the police station, sensing Callow's eyes burning into the back of his neck with pure malevolence as he went.

'Bet she's put a spell on me now,' he chuckled, stepping back courteously to allow Kate to push through the door ahead of him, but she wasn't listening; her mind was obviously on something else.

'Naomi Betjeman,' she said suddenly, while he slipped his card into the metal box by the security door. 'That's a turn up for the books, isn't it? I don't like the sound of it at all.'

Lewis shrugged, once more stepping aside for her as the door buzzed and opened to his touch. 'You shouldn't read too much into the business; probably just an accident.'

Kate stopped at the bottom of the stairs as he started up towards the first-floor landing and he turned and studied her quizzically.

She shook her head. 'You go on up,' she said. 'I'm just going to pop along to the CID office – see if I can find out who's dealing with the job.'

He sighed. 'OK, suit yourself, but don't take too long. Briefing's in an hour and after the Guv'nor had to cancel last night's briefing because of the stiff in the lake, he won't be very happy if you're late.'

But she wasn't listening to him and was already striding off along the corridor.

'Women!' he muttered disparagingly, then winced under the hard critical look of a uniformed policewoman as she overtook him on the stairs.

Ansell sat for several minutes, staring at the front page of the newspaper Callow had left behind, his thin violinist fingers tapping out a noisy tattoo on the scarred teak surface.

The headline of The Clarion seemed to scream at him like an obscenity, 'What A Mess,' and, reading on, one by one the inflammatory phrases in Naomi Betjeman's front page exposé exploded in his face with the force of a landmine: '… killer strolled into the police station unhindered and bugged incident-room … mind-boggling incompetence of a totally dysfunctional inquiry team … investigation plagued by constant in-fighting and inept leadership … SIO nick-named Ethelred for good reason … reporter threatened by inquiry team's "android" DCI … killer laughing all the way to the mortuary….'

Even after reading the piece, the DCI continued to sit there, sipping his coffee and thinking. He had expected a critical story after his run-in with Naomi Betjeman, but this was way over the top and totally out of order. His only comfort was in the short editorial comment on a bold reverse block at the foot of the page, which reported that the reporter had been seriously injured in a fall from a staircase at her place of work. 'Well now,' he said to himself, 'there *is* some justice in the world after all then.'

Detective Superintendent Willoughby didn't seem to share that view when he put in an appearance shortly afterwards, however, and his face paled when Ansell held up the newspaper in front of him, pinching one corner between finger and thumb, as if it were a piece of dirty linen.

'It appears we have been shafted,' he said quietly.

Snatching the tabloid from him, Willoughby studied the article intently for a few minutes before pulling out a handkerchief and mopping his forehead. 'Good grief, the Chief Constable will go mad when he reads this,' he gasped.'

Ansell shrugged. 'At least it will liven up his morning,' he said drily.

Willoughby stared at him in astonishment, then stabbed a fat finger at the page. 'I don't know how you've got the nerve to say that,' he exclaimed. 'She actually refers to you as a bloody android.'

Ansell's eyes gleamed and he chuckled for the first time with something akin to genuine mirth. 'Better than being referred to as Ethelred,' he commented, adding, 'the Unready.'

Willoughby did not appear to have heard his retort, but peered at the article again and shook his head, frowning heavily. 'So how the devil did she get hold of all this information? It's almost as though she was at one of our briefings.'

Ansell gave another shrug. 'I've said before that we have a leak on the team and now I'm pretty sure who it is.'

'Then we should haul them in pronto.'

Ansell grunted. 'Be a bit difficult at the moment. I suspect our man is Philip Sharp, but since he's been arrested on a positive breath test after a multiple TA last night, it's all a bit academic; he'll be getting the push anyway in due course.' He made a face. 'At least he won't be leaking any more information anyway.'

'Bit late for that now,' Willoughby commented heavily. 'Damage is already done, and this Betjeman creature probably has all she needs by now anyway – could be working on another piece as we speak.'

Ansell shook his head. 'Unlikely. She had a fall at work last night apparently and is on the critical list. All we can do is to try and ride out the storm and hope for some kind of break-through in this damned murder case.'

Willoughby slouched to the window and stared gloomily out into another grey morning, his hands thrust deep into his pockets. 'Any bright ideas?' he went on. 'We could be finished if we don't get somewhere soon.'

Ansell grimaced. 'Fresh out of ideas at present,' he replied. 'Maybe we should ask your Doctor Norton when he turns up for this morning's briefing – though, I have to say, he hasn't been of much use to date – despite the esteem in which you said he was held when he joined us.'

Willoughby swallowed, acutely conscious of the fact that Norton had been engaged on his authority. 'You can't blame me for that,' he protested, 'I'd never actually met the man before, but I did quite a lot of ringing around after he telephoned me to kindly offer his services. And yes, it seems he is held in *very* high esteem, having been an asset to a number of other police investigations.'

Ansell grunted. 'Has he indeed? Well, our so-called expert had better start adding some value to our team now,' he said uncharitably, 'before we all end up down the toilet.'

'And we can't have that, can we?' another voice cut in on the conversation.

Neither Willoughby or Ansell had been aware of the fact that the door was only ajar or that the sound of their voices carried well beyond the precincts of the office and they couldn't have been more surprised – or embarrassed – to find Norton now standing smiling in the open doorway.

'Which is why,' the psychologist continued, unabashed, 'I have put together a possible plan to ensnare our wily psychopath before he kills again.'

Kate knew the Bridgwater DC dealing with Naomi Betjeman's accident very well. Charlie Woo had joined the force from his native Hong Kong at the same time as Kate and they had become good friends at training school. Following her rather non-committal phone call, he was waiting for her at the scene of the incident and, although obviously curious, he nevertheless grinned his pleasure when she walked into the basement archives of The Clarion building.

'Hi Kate,' he said with just a trace of an accent. 'So what's all this about then? You didn't give much away on the phone.'

She smiled back. 'Sorry, Charlie, not being mysterious, but I didn't want to delay things by going into chapter and verse.'

He nodded. 'OK, so you can tell me now then, can't you?'

She stepped past him to look at the large semi-circular stain on the concrete floor, enclosed by police blue and white tapes.

'She didn't have a very nice landing, I'm afraid,' he pointed out unnecessarily. 'Hospital have got her in the CCU; just clinging on apparently. Multiple injuries, including a suspected fractured skull – and that's just for starters, I'm told.'

Kate nodded. 'What's the SP on this one then, Charlie?' she queried.

He pointed to the topmost landing of the staircase. 'We think she fell from up there,' he said. 'Security guard – ex-job actually – found her and called an ambulance. Nothing suspicious about it as far as I could see when I got here last night – just a nasty accident. Handrail's bent.'

'So why is the scene taped off?'

He shrugged. 'Just a precaution when we first arrived – possible suspicious death and all that, but my guv'nor's satisfied that it was simply an accident. We left the tapes up as the paper's insurers are sending an investigator down and there's a possibility the HSE might be interested, since this is the third serious accident the paper have had on their premises in twelve months apparently.'

He studied her quizzically. 'So why are you so interested in the job?'

She ignored his question. 'Can I have a look up top?' she asked.

'Be my guest.'

Kate felt a little uneasy as she climbed the iron staircase. She had never liked stairs you could see through and the steps beneath her feet had been constructed in a latticework pattern of diamond-shaped holes and narrow slits. She felt even worse when she got to the top and peered over the distorted handrail, stepping back quickly after a quick glance at the floor beneath.

Charlie chuckled at her elbow. 'Never did like heights, did you, Kate?' he said, remembering a training-school exercise they had both been assigned to on the top floor of a multi-storey car park. 'About a thirty foot drop we reckon, maybe a bit more. Some basement, eh?'

Kate faced him. 'So how come a fit young woman pitches over a handrail like this?' she said. 'It's at least waist height.'

Another shrug. 'Dunno,' he said. 'Maybe she jumped?'

'I wouldn't think so. This is one ambitious reporter, full of confidence – *and* venom.'

Woo frowned. 'So you're saying what exactly?' he said. 'That she was pushed?'

'I don't know, but it's a bit of a coincidence when she's been covering our current murder inquiry.'

He grinned again. 'Yeah, saw her piece in The Clarion this morning,' he acknowledged. 'Bet your guv'nor's not too happy with it. She's obviously got an 'in' with someone on the team to be able to come out with that sort of detail.'

Kate was determined not to go there. 'Any idea what she was doing here so late?'

'Her editor – he came out last night – says she would have been doing research for a follow-up story tomorrow,' he replied, turning back towards the basement. 'He was pretty upset by it all. Going to the hospital this morning, I understand, to see how she is.'

'And what did the security guard have to say?' she asked, joining him on the lower landing.

He thought a second, leaning back against the wall. 'Not a lot actually. He found the basement door open, key in the lock, and clocked her lying on the floor in a pool of blood.

No sign of a break-in or an intruder …' He broke off, looking worried. 'Look, Kate, if you think this has something to do with the murder inquiry you're on, you should at least—'

'So he saw no one?'

Woo rubbed his nose. 'Well, he said he thought he saw a shadow moving off along the wall outside.'

'A shadow?'

'Yeah, but when he looked again, it was gone, so he put it down to imagination or the poor light.'

'And I suppose there's no CCTV coverage – any more than there's a bloody alarm system?'

'You've got it.'

'And she was unconscious when he found her?'

'More or less, yeah. Oh, she did mumble a couple of words to him, but he couldn't make any sense of 'em.'

Kate stiffened. 'Oh? What sort of words?'

'Dunno – just gibberish, I guess.'

'Gibberish?' she echoed, thinking about the shadow he had mentioned. 'Mind if I call and see him myself? I don't want to step on toes, but …'

Woo grimaced. 'Well, you seem to be doing just that at the moment, Kate, and my guv'nor won't be best pleased. He wasn't particularly happy about you muscling in on the arson at that block of flats and I could be in dead shtook for letting you in on this without speaking to him first. So, are you going to tell me what's going on or not?'

She patted his arm. 'Later, Charlie, later – I promise, but before that, I need to see your security man.'

He sighed, clearly still far from happy. 'I don't suppose that would hurt. Deal is, I come with you, though, OK? You can follow me there in your motor.'

'I've no problem with that.' She stared at him and raised an eyebrow, 'but – like now would be good.'

He opened the rear door for her and followed her through. 'What did your last slave die of?' he threw back over his shoulder.

She chuckled. 'Malnutrition,' she replied. 'He didn't have time to eat.'

CHAPTER 25

Fred Jarvis lived in a small bungalow not far from the church in the village of East Huntspill. A widower – his wife had died just weeks after his retirement – he had never thought to move on. Why would he? He had lived in the village for twenty years and there was no point looking for pastures new at his age. Besides, the place was very convenient for the M5 motorway, enabling him to pop into the security firm's head office in Taunton and to get round the various sites allocated to him during his tours of duty with relative ease.

He was in his garden, tending his greenhouse, having finished his shift at midnight, when Kate and Charlie Woo arrived and he was obviously delighted to receive a visit from members of 'the old firm', as he called it.

Kate was in a hurry, conscious of the fact that she was now going to be very late for the incident-room briefing, but Jarvis was keen to make the most of the company and insisted on rustling up coffee and biscuits for his visitors before sitting down with them in his cramped living-room.

'Bad business,' he acknowledged, after Kate had given him the reason for their visit. 'Young woman and all that. Hope she's going to be OK.'

'In the critical care unit at the moment,' Woo advised him. 'Only time will tell.'

Kate smiled briefly, keen to get underway with her questions. 'Mr Jarvis,' she began, 'I understand you thought you saw someone in the vicinity of the building when you were checking it?'

He frowned. 'Well, I thought I saw a figure walking away from the rear door as I approached, but it could have been a trick of the moonlight. You know what it's like on night patrol; sometimes you see things that aren't there. Had just checked the front doors, see, and was going down the steps to the lower car park when I noticed the rear door was ajar and there was a light on inside—'

'Yes, yes,' Kate cut in impatiently, 'so what did the figure look like?'

Jarvis shook his head slowly. 'Couldn't really say. It was just a shadow, but it looked like a heavy sort of bloke in a hooded coat. That's all I saw.'

'Where did he go?'

'Dunno. One minute he was there and the next …' and he shrugged. 'Like I say, I could have been mistaken. Maybe just imagination.'

'Was there a car in the car park?'

'No, place was empty. I'd left my van up top.' He hesitated, then added, 'But I did hear a motor start up after I'd gone inside the building. Probably parked on the waste-ground on the other side of the offices.'

'No idea of the sort of vehicle it was?'

'Not from inside, no, but I formed the impression it was a powerful car of some sort and it didn't drive away fast – just took it's time. Not at all suspicious. You get an idea when something's wrong, don't you? Sort of gut feeling—'

'So you went in,' Kate summarized, trying to keep him on track, 'and saw the woman lying on the floor?'

'Yeah, in a pool of blood. It looked like she'd fallen from the upper landing of the staircase. Knew the young lady too.

Often used to work there late. Nice woman. Gave me a cup of coffee a couple of times when I called by on my rounds—'

Kate took a deep breath. 'Right, so what did you do?'

'Well, bent over her, of course, to check to see if she was still alive. Found a pulse and radioed in for an ambulance and the police. Then I just waited for them to arrive.'

'Was she unconscious?'

'More or less, yes,' and he frowned again, 'but she did mumble something when I bent over her – said it twice actually, before passing out completely.'

Kate leaned forward, unable to conceal her eagerness. 'What did she say?'

'It was sort of gibberish.'

'OK, but did you pick out anything?'

'Didn't make any sense – gibberish, as I just said.'

Kate's mouth tightened as she tried to control her frustration. 'Look, you were a copper for thirty years, Mr Jarvis; you were trained to notice things. Think hard, gibberish or not, *what did she say*?'

He did think then – for several long seconds – his brows wrinkled with the effort, while Kate waited on the edge of her seat, her fists clenched with the suspense.

'Well,' he said at last, 'it was just two words, if I remember right …'

'Go on.'

'"Red, eyes",' he said, then added quickly, 'No, "dead", that was it, she said "dead eyes".'

Remembering the photograph on the incident-room white board, Kate felt suddenly cold. 'And that was all – just "dead eyes"?'

Jarvis shook his head, again furrowing his brows. 'No, tell a lie, there was something else.' He thought again for a few seconds and then snapped his fingers, his eyes shining. 'Got it! "Smell", she said something about a smell.' He grinned. 'Thought she meant me at first – she was obviously off her trolley.'

'Maybe not,' Kate replied grimly, remembering that Twister had a nasty BO problem. 'But she didn't mention a name – Twister or anything like that?'

The security man shook his head. 'No, just them three words: "dead eyes" and "smell".'

Kate stood up, thanking Jarvis for his time, and Woo, who had sat silently through the whole interview, quickly followed her example. His face registered absolute bewilderment when they finally managed to extricate themselves from Jarvis's hospitality and get outside.

'So what exactly have we got here, Kate?' he said, pausing between their two parked cars. 'Obviously you think this woman's fall has got something to do with the murder inquiry you're on, but my DCI will want to know what.'

Kate nodded. 'Naomi Betjeman was attacked yesterday – we think by the very same killer that we are looking for – a psycho who goes by the name of Twister. Obviously she got away from him then, but I'm pretty sure he must have followed her here and tried to finish the job.'

'Bloody hell,' Woo breathed, gaping at her. 'My guv'nor will go ballistic.'

'Then I suggest you ring him PDQ, Charlie,' she advised, 'and also that you go back here to guard the scene until we can get SOCO down to do a full crime-scene search.'

'And where will you be?'

Kate went round to the driver's door of her car. 'At the hospital,' she said. 'Twister would only have targeted Naomi Betjeman a second time if he'd believed she knew something that could put him at risk. I just hope I can get to her before he tries to silence her for a third time.'

Naomi Betjeman was a ghost. Those parts of her face which were not covered by the oxygen mask were parchment white, with a worrying bluish tinge to the skin. She was connected by a confusion of cables and tubes to various humming, flashing pieces of electronic equipment, eyes closed, breasts gently rising and falling beneath the single white sheet which covered her.

Kate had been refused admission to her room in the hospital's critical care unit and forced to look at her key witness through an internal window, supervised by a staff nurse.

'How is she?' Kate asked.

'Not good,' the other replied. 'Multiple injuries, including a suspected fractured skull, and spinal damage – she's heavily sedated at present.'

'Has she said anything?'

A quick, almost dismissive shake of the head. 'Not as far as I know. She was brought in unconscious – as I told the other lady.'

Kate turned her head quickly to look at her. 'Other lady?' she echoed. 'What other lady?'

The staff nurse shrugged. 'Said she was a close friend. Can't remember her name. Too busy.'

'What did she look like?'

The nurse thought for a moment, plainly surprised at the question. 'Thin, forties, black hair, dark eyes, rather severe face.' She frowned. 'She was leaning on a walking stick.'

'Callow,' Kate breathed. 'When was she here?'

Sudden alarm in the young woman's eyes. 'About … about an hour ago. Are you saying she wasn't who … who she said she was?'

Kate grimaced, but didn't answer the question. 'From now on,' she said, 'you must not let anyone in to see this patient, apart from medical staff, OK? And I mean anyone. She is at great risk. I'll get a uniformed police guard here as soon as I can.'

The staff nurse stiffened and her eyes flashed angrily. 'Will you indeed?' she snapped tartly. 'Well, I suggest you get the Hospital Administrator's permission first.'

Kate took a deep breath, inwardly cursing her own lack of tact. 'Listen to me,' she said heavily. 'The lady in that bed has been the target of a psychopathic killer. He has already tried to kill her once and he will almost certainly try again. Do you understand?'

The nurse didn't answer, but continued to glare at her with obvious hostility. In resignation, Kate produced a business card and handed it to her. 'Look, just let me know if there are any developments – particularly if she says anything – OK?'

The other gave a curt nod, reluctantly accepting the card from her to study it for a moment, and Kate saw that she was still far from convinced. Losing patience with her, Kate emitted a hiss of frustration, and jerking a pen from her pocket, wrote something on the back of it.

'That's my home telephone number,' she explained, returning the card to her. 'You can ring me at any time – day or night. Now, will you do that?'

The nurse gave her a tight smile. 'I'll pass your request on to my colleagues,' she said.

Kate returned her smile with a brief humourless one of her own and, throwing one last look at Naomi Betjeman, she marched off along the corridor, knowing full well that the chances of her request being passed on in a busy critical care unit were almost nil.

She stared round the hospital entrance foyer as she headed for the exit doors to the car park, looking for...? She had no idea what. She was getting jittery again, sensing a presence that she knew instinctively was not there. She realized she probably wouldn't be able to pick out Larry Wadman after all this time anyway and the psychopath was hardly likely to report to the reception desk, even if he did pay a visit to the hospital.

Her personal mobile rang as she climbed into her car and, glancing at the phone's illuminated display, she smiled when she saw it was Hayden Lewis's number. She'd wondered how long it would be before someone rang her to query her whereabouts. It was well past the time for the incident-room briefing, which by now must almost certainly have gone on without her. Certain people would not be at all happy about it and no doubt poor old Hayden was trying to warn her of the fact.

She should have answered the call, but she chose not to; the last thing she wanted was a row with Hayden over the phone and she would soon be back at the nick to face the music anyway. So instead, she put her foot down hard on the accelerator and took off with a screech of rubber that was fully in tune with her current mood.

And as she swung out of the car park on to the hospital's service road, the big black saloon which had been concealed behind a bush in another bay, pulled out after her, the powerful car easily catching her up on the main road, but keeping back a satisfactory distance to avoid attracting suspicion. Behind the wheel, dark hate-filled eyes focused on Kate's profile through the rear window of the CID car as Roz Callow slipped another extra-strong mint between bared teeth and tried to ignore the intense pain building in her gammy leg.

CHAPTER 26

There were three of them in the SIO's office when Kate entered the incident-room – Ansell, Roscoe and Norton – and their eyes seemed to laser her through the internal window as she walked towards them. Two of her colleagues sitting at their workstations, gave her weak smiles as soon as she appeared, then quickly turned back to their computer screens, hunching their shoulders as if trying to pretend they weren't there. Bad news certainly travelled fast, she mused with a cynical grimace – as did the smell of a load of whatnot that was about to drop on her head.

'How nice of you to join us,' Ansell said with an icy smile as she stepped into the room, his eyes resembling the black muzzles of twin pistols.

Roscoe, parked as usual half on and half off the window sill, directed a characteristic scowl in her direction, while Norton, leaning against the wall in the corner of the room simply smiled at her – although she couldn't tell whether it was a smile of sympathy or one of mockery.

'Sorry about the briefing, Guv,' she faltered, 'but I had to check on something.'

'So I believe,' Ansell said, his tone brittle. 'I have just had my ear bent by the DCI at Bridgwater, complaining about our interference in his investigation. Our last acrimonious conversation was over the blast at the block of flats on his manor, so he's not a particularly happy man.'

Kate reddened. 'If I hadn't *interfered* this time, the whole Naomi Betjeman thing would have been cuffed as a bloody accident,' she blurted angrily, forgetting for a moment who she was talking to, 'and it's pretty obvious that it was anything but.'

'Is that so?' Ansell rasped. 'Well, maybe you'd like to share this new found information with us. After all, we only happen to be running the inquiry.'

So Kate did just that and by the time she had finished, the atmosphere in the room had noticeably changed.

'I'll get a plod over to the hospital straightaway,' Roscoe growled and headed out into the incident-room.

Ansell sat back in his chair, for the first time the anxiety that was weighing him down clearly visible in his pale haunted expression. Kate found herself feeling almost sorry for him. 'It gets worse and worse,' he murmured wearily, then, biting his lip, raised his head to study her for a moment. 'And I have something else to put to you, too.'

Kate made a face. 'Sounds a bit ominous, Guv,' she said.

His elbows were on the table again, fingers steepled under his chin in a characteristically thoughtful pose. 'Doctor Norton has come up with an idea, Kate,' he said. 'I don't like it and I've told him so, but …' and he waved an arm towards the psychologist. 'Perhaps you'll explain, Doctor.'

Roscoe returned to the room as Norton began and he scowled his own disapproval as he caught the drift of what was going on.

'I've come to a conclusion, Kate,' Norton said, 'and not a very nice one either.'

Kate raised an eyebrow, but said nothing and he went on slowly and deliberately. 'It suddenly dawned on me, looking at the original Operation Firetrap files last night, that the murder of the two police officers in the surveillance van took place exactly two years ago tomorrow night. I don't know why it's never occurred to us before.' He paused for a moment to let the effect of his words sink in and when he spoke again, his face wore a much more sober expression. 'Which means that tomorrow night will be the anniversary of their deaths *and* of your own miraculous escape.'

Kate was already ahead of him and she felt the muscles knotting in her stomach. 'You're saying Twister plans to waste me tomorrow night?' she said in a voice that did not sound like her own.

Norton shrugged. 'His so-called game must end sometime and it is significant that he returned here just days before the infamous night in question.'

'So why didn't he come back last year then?' Roscoe cut in. 'Why leave it two years?'

Norton smiled, as if addressing a tiresome child. 'That would have been stupid, with the police manhunt still in full swing – and anyway, if he was suffering from a serious stab wound, perhaps it was quite a few months before he achieved full recovery.'

'So you're saying I have to stay under lock and key until after the anniversary?' Kate said.

Norton quickly shook his head. 'Anything but. That would only delay the inevitable. He would still come after you, whether it was on the night of the anniversary or days or weeks later. You would be forever at risk, not knowing when he might strike. We need to bring this thing to a close now – to be in control of events.'

'He wants to use you as bait,' Roscoe put in. 'Set up a sting, with you as the prize.'

'*Thank you*, Inspector,' Norton snapped and it was plain that he was furious at the interruption.

He got no support from Ansell, however. 'Thing is, Kate,' the DCI said, 'how would you feel about being put in that sort of risky position?'

Kate smiled faintly. 'Not exactly overjoyed,' she replied, 'but how would it work? After all, Doctor Norton's theory could be wrong.'

Norton nodded. 'Quite so, but it's all we've got at present and it's a little bit too much of a coincidence that our killer embarked on his murderous campaign at this particular time. It is also logical and fully in line with the profile I have drawn up on him that he would arrange things this way. Remember, I've already said that he is a meticulous planner. He doesn't rush into things – OK, so a bit of improvisation along the way when absolutely necessary, like the murder of PC Taylor, for instance – but overall, he is someone who doesn't leave things to chance and who knows exactly when and where the endgame will be.'

'Which could be at any time tomorrow then?' Kate responded.

Norton shook his head. 'If I know our adversary, he will want to make his hit on you as close as possible to the time of the original murder of your two colleagues two years ago, otherwise it will lose its significance. I am quite certain you will be safe until then.'

'So you're saying he will have planned it for around midnight tomorrow?' Kate summarized. 'Assuming you are right, what's our next move?'

Norton smiled again. 'We offer you up to him on a plate,' he replied, 'and see if he bites!'

'Are you crazy?' Hayden Lewis was angrier than Kate had ever seen him before – more so even than he had been with Phil Sharp – although he did look faintly ridiculous dressed in his striped apron, with the frying pan in one hand and the egg spatula in the other.

En route to see the president of a local bird-watching group, armed with a SOCO photograph of the flask she had found in the hide, Kate had suggested they first stopped off at home for a snack, having already missed lunch and while they ate, she had broached the subject of Norton's plan there.

'It's the only way,' she said defensively. 'At least we will be in control and the troops will be right there, watching my back.'

Lewis returned the frying pan to the unlit hob and slammed the spatula down on the work-surface. 'Out of the question,' he exclaimed. 'I won't hear of it!'

Her eyes blazed. '*You* won't hear of it? It's not about you, Hayden, it's about me and I do as I please.'

Lewis just stared at her for a moment, his face red and his mouth compressed into a familiar truculent line. 'Then you're a bloody fool!' he shouted.

She gaped at him. Lewis was so old school that he was regarded as comically eccentric by most of his colleagues and she had never heard him use abusive language in all the time that she had known him – especially not in front of a woman.

'So what's the alternative, eh?' she demanded with equal passion. 'Wait until he catches me on my own? And when is that likely to be – in two days, three days, a month? Are we going to spend our lives looking over our shoulders, just in case he is out there, waiting?'

The flush started to leave his face and he studied her for a moment, the logic of what she was saying obviously getting through to him in spite of his instinctive opposition.

'So tell me in detail,' he said, 'what lunatic scheme you have signed up to. All you've told me so far is that you are going to be used as the bait in a trap.'

She sighed and leaned back against a tall kitchen cupboard. 'We going to eat those eggs raw?' she queried.

He hesitated, then abruptly turned back to the cooker, switched it on and broke the four eggs on the side of the pan before carefully dropping them into the sunflower oil he had already poured into it. 'I'm listening,' he said tightly, still with his back towards her.

She filled the kettle and switched it on before loading the toaster with four slices of white bread. 'Quite simple really,' she said, snapping the lever down on the toaster. 'HQ Press Office will be leaking a story to the local media later tonight to say that I have been over the side with Clement Norton—'

He swung round quickly again, dripping oil from the spatula on to the kitchen floor. 'You what?'

'Well, everyone in the nick knows he has been trying to get into my knickers—'

'Do you have to be so crude?' he interjected.

'Watch the eggs,' she warned and continued as he returned to the pan. 'And there was that incident with Phil Sharp over the chocolates too – a pretty public thing – which means the story will be easily believed.'

The kettle boiled and switched off and, as she crossed the room to fill the pot, the buzzer went on the toaster.

'So far as everyone is concerned,' she continued, 'you and I will have had a monumental row over the issue, resulting in you belting me in a jealous rage, being arrested for ABH and detained in custody.' She finished filling the tea pot and crossed to the toaster, removing the toast and starting to butter it. 'No one except the top team and those directly involved, such as the firearms unit, must know what's going on. Guv'nor obviously doesn't want any leaks getting to the ears of the press or being picked up by Twister, which would scupper the whole thing.'

He snorted. 'Thanks a lot,' he retorted, dumping rather than easing the eggs on to the toast and ripping off his apron and tossing it into a corner as Kate took the plates over to the breakfast bar. 'This will do wonders for my reputation.'

She ignored his indignation and sat down at the table, tucking into her meal. 'The story will obviously hit local radio first and be broadcast tonight, and this will be followed by gleeful reports in the newspapers in the morning. With the coverage expected, it is almost certain that Twister will hear about it.'

'The crucial thing,' she emphasized, 'is to create a situation where our man is encouraged to believe I will be left on my own in your cottage when I return here tomorrow night, providing him with the very opportunity he needs. Armed teams will be deployed all round the place, using hi-tech surveillance kit, and I will be wearing a wire, so the risk will be minimal.'

'I don't like it,' he said after swallowing a mouthful of egg. 'I wasn't even consulted before this thing went ahead.'

'You don't have to like it,' she replied. 'Just cooperate – and that means staying at the nick throughout the operation. If you're seen near the cottage, it will blow the whole thing apart.'

'I'll think about it,' he replied sullenly.

'Just don't think too long,' she finished. 'Now it's time to hit the road again – we'll leave the dishes for you to wash up before you beat me up tonight. OK?'

CHAPTER 27

Phil Sharp stood for a long time in the shower, feeling the hot water streaming down his body and trying to relax his tense muscles. He needed time to think. Already in the cart for drink-driving and with his job right on the line, he couldn't afford any indiscreet revelations by Naomi Betjeman while she was semi-conscious in the CCU. OK, so she might not make it – and that was a pleasing thought in itself as far as he was concerned – or she could be in a coma without the ability to communicate to anyone, but he couldn't afford to chance it. He had to get to her somehow to see what the state of play was and, if she was conscious, impress on her the need to keep shtum before Ansell or one of his minions got to her.

He could still drive – at least he could until the drink driving court case, but with his own car in a terminal condition at the garage pound, he could do nothing until he got hold of a replacement motor, so that had to be his first move.

Dressing in a neat, dark suit – people tended to be swayed by someone who was smartly turned out – he headed for the nearest bus stop and took a local service to a garage just out of town. As a CID man, he knew this crowd – they tended to be less than particular about hiring out vehicles, and within half an hour he was pulling away from their forecourt in a six-year-old Peugeot with around 80,000 miles on the clock.

So far so good then, but deep down he knew that, while hiring the car might have been relatively easy, getting into the hospital's critical care unit was likely to be a lot more difficult and, when he finally left the Peugeot in the large car park and headed for the main building, he did so with more than a little trepidation.

Surprisingly enough, however, he attracted little interest from hospital staff all the way up to the top floor where the CCU was located – maybe his luck was changing – and gaining entry to the unit itself, with its security coded access control box, proved to be just as much of a breeze. The young man in the white coat, wearing a name tag and a badge labelled 'Red Cell Serology', was coming out through the double doors, carrying a cardboard box lid containing a number of glass phials, as he approached and even he made no attempt to challenge him.

'Allow me,' he said cheerfully, letting Sharp through, then walking away humming to himself.

The detective was astounded at the ease with which he had managed to get into the place. Didn't they know anything about security? He could have been anyone. But his luck did not last.

'And who the hell are you?' a voice snapped rudely from an open doorway. 'And how did you get in here?'

He quickly flashed his warrant card at the young staff nurse standing there – although he didn't know it, she was the same nurse who had confronted Kate not long before. 'Police,' he said, without giving his name.

She frowned. 'You must be the police guard they said they'd be sending,' she surmised. 'At least they've had the good sense to send someone in civvies.'

Sharp was careful not to enlighten her and she nodded towards the window of the small room behind him. 'She's in there, conscious now fortunately, but still very fragile. I'll get someone to put a chair outside the door for you.'

Sharp gave her his best smile. 'Thanks. Any chance of speaking to her?'

The Staff snorted angrily. 'No way. You keep out of there, do you understand? She's far too ill to be interviewed.'

Her bleep sounded stridently and she muttered an oath. 'Got to go. I'll get you that chair in a minute.'

Then she was off down the corridor with a brisk tap of her shoes, shortly disappearing through double doors at the end.

Sharp waited a couple of minutes before entering the small room and, as he approached the bed, his eyes took in the tubes and wires connected to the pale-faced woman lying there. Her eyes were open and they seemed to jerk when she saw him.

'Hi, Nom,' he said. 'Only just heard what happened. Didn't have time for any grapes.'

He hesitated, feeling uncomfortable about his reasons for being there, then abruptly took the plunge. 'Ansell's on the warpath,' he blurted clumsily. 'You will keep shtum if he comes to see you, won't you? I'm in enough shit already – you can forget the four hundred, OK?'

To his surprise, Naomi reached up and pulled away the mask covering the lower part of her face, then beckoned him closer. Her breathing was rough and her lips were trembling as she tried to say something. Curious, he bent closer and her hand grabbed his arm and pulled him down towards her pillow. Her voice was just a crackle and he shook his head. 'Can't understand you, Nom,' he said.

He felt her take a deep breath and bent his ear to within a couple of inches of her mouth to listen. And it was at this point that she finally got through to him, the words jerked out in a halting rasping whisper that carried with it not only a sense of the terrible pain she was suffering, but revelations that pumped such a rush of adrenalin through his veins that he almost lost his balance and would have fallen on top of her if he had not staggered backwards.

'Are you serious?' he gasped, staring at her in a state of shock. 'This is dynamite!'

He thought he detected a faint, grim smile, but that soon faded and then there was a dramatic change in her expression – a look of acute distress. As her hand fumbled to replace the mask over her face, her body arched and went into a series of violent spasms, her eyes swivelling upward to disappear beneath the lids and a choking gasp issuing through tightly clenched teeth.

He should have tried to help her – replaced the mask or done something – but instead, he simply shrank away from the bed and, as a high-pitched alarm sounded and footsteps hammered down the corridor, he stumbled out of the room in a panic.

The portly nurse slammed him aside as she raced into the room, followed by a doctor, with his white coat flapping around him. Staring with a sort of horrible fascination through the window into the room, Sharp saw them bend over the bed as Naomi continued to writhe and arch her body in the throes of some sort of seizure. Another nurse appeared, with the staff nurse in their wake and the look she gave the white-faced DS was vicious as he stood there helplessly watching the proceedings.

It was over almost as suddenly as it had begun. The team tried everything they could, including, Sharp thought, the use of a defibrillator and an injection of some kind, but in the end, the machine on the stand beside her bed changed its beeping note to a chilling continuous whine as it flatlined.

The staff nurse looked drawn and haggard as she came back out into the passage and gently closed the door behind her. 'What the hell did you do?' she almost snarled at him.

He shook his head several times, backing away from her. 'I … I didn't do anything,' he lied. 'She had some kind of fit and I went in there to see if I could help, then you lot arrived.' He swallowed hard. 'Is she … is she…?'

The staff nurse moved out of the way as the doctor left the room and strode off along the corridor with a sad shake of his head. 'Let's just say, you won't be needed anymore,' she said, watching as the two nurses remaining in the room started to disconnect the apparatus from the now motionless patient. 'She's beyond the reach of any assassin now.'

Toby Pomeroy lived in a big pseudo-Georgian detached house in the village of Wedmore and when Kate and Lewis arrived, a beautiful red Austin Healey 3000 was drawn up to one side of the front door. 'Very nice,' said an appreciative Lewis, 'but I think I'll stick to my Mk II Jag.'

The shining brass doorbell rang inside the house for ages before the door was opened by a diminutive dark-haired woman in her sixties. Her eyes widened when Kate produced her warrant card. 'Nothing to worry about – er – Mrs Pomeroy?' she queried and when the lady of the house nodded with a quick relieved sigh, Kate went on, 'Mr Pomeroy at home?'

Mrs Pomeroy shook her head. 'No, I'm afraid he's out at present – board meeting at his company's headquarters in London.'

She smiled to see Lewis walking slowly around the Austin Healey, studying it with obvious admiration.

'My son's,' she called out. 'He's on holiday with his fiancée at present.'

Kate glared at Lewis. 'Any idea when your husband will be back?'

'Not until very late tonight – they have a board dinner after the meeting, you see, and it can go on a bit. Can you tell me what this is all about?'

Lewis concluded his examination of the Austin Healey and turned back to the front door. 'We understand Mr Pomeroy is a twitcher?' he said.

Kate winced, but Mrs Pomeroy just chuckled. 'Don't let him hear you call him that,' she said. 'Actually he's the president of the Somerset Levels Avian Society.'

Kate nodded and, explaining the reason for their visit, but excluding reference to the discovery of the body on the wildlife reserve, she produced the photograph of the flask with its inscribed initials clearly visible.

Mrs Pomeroy peered at the photograph. 'Can't help you there, I'm afraid, but if you can leave the photograph with me, I'll get Toby to contact you tomorrow. If it belongs to one of his flock—' and she chuckled suddenly at her pun, 'I'm sure he'll know.'

Kate handed the photograph and one of her business cards to her. 'Thanks for your help,' she said. 'He can get hold of me at Highbridge police station.'

'You might also ask your son if he fancies selling that Austin Healey too,' Lewis said brightly, then hurriedly turned to follow Kate as she stalked back to the CID car after a courteous nod in Mrs Pomeroy's direction.

'Dipstick!' Kate blazed at him through clenched teeth as they drove away.

'What did I do?' Lewis replied. 'I was going to buy it for you.'

'What with?' Kate snapped back. 'Buttons or confidence?'

CHAPTER 28

Phil Sharp tapped one foot repeatedly on the floor in an agitated rhythm as he sat in the worn armchair by the window of his flat, staring at nothing in particular. Downing the remains of the coffee he had made himself fifteen minutes before, he automatically reached for his packet of cigarettes, only to remember that he had smoked the last one when he had been released from Bridgwater police station that morning.

Seeing someone you know dying in front of you is never pleasant and he also felt more than a little responsible for Naomi Betjeman's tragic end. He had done nothing at the crucial moment, just stood there – not even tried to replace her oxygen mask. He felt even more guilty at his sense of relief over her death, knowing that maybe his lack of action had been motivated by self-interest, bearing in mind that she could have given evidence against him in any police inquiry.

Anyway, at least now, provided he kept his cool, he was in the clear. No one at the hospital was aware of his identity and luckily he had caught early sight of the uniformed policeman – almost certainly the plod sent to guard Naomi – climbing the stairs as he'd headed back down, which had given him just enough time to duck into an adjacent ward until the other had passed.

Although he felt relieved at his lucky escape, he was unable to relax, for his head was still spinning over the reporter's last painful, gasped disclosures. He could hardly believe what she had told him; it was too fantastic for words. Yet, when he thought about it, it all fitted, just like the last pieces of a complicated jigsaw. But what to do with the information, that was the point? Running to Ansell with it was the proper thing to do, for, if Naomi's allegations were true, it would bring the inquiry to a very speedy end and maybe save Kate Hamblin's life.

He scowled to himself. Problem was, did he *want* Kate Hamblin to survive – any more than he'd wanted Naomi Betjeman to survive? She had always been an irritant to him and now it seemed very likely that she would be given his job if, as he suspected, he got the push or was thrown off CID when he was finally done for drink-driving. Could be that this guy, Twister, would be inadvertently doing him a favour by wasting her? He might still lose his job, but at least he would have the satisfaction of knowing Hamblin would not benefit from it.

Yeah, and then there was the question of Ansell. If he *did* spill the beans to the cold clinical DCI, would it make any difference to his own precarious position? Ansell wouldn't be able to do a touch of the quid pro quos and get him off his drink-driving charge in any case; it wasn't within the DCI's power. So the best thing he could hope for from his boss was a word in the right ear at the top to stop him being sacked. But even if Ansell was prepared to do that, and he doubted it with all the other baggage he was already carrying, it would still mean the humiliation of being put back in uniform – maybe even reduced to the rank of constable. And it would also mean having to admit to being in cahoots with Naomi Betjeman, which would land him in an even worse predicament over any subsequent inquiry into the leak of information to the Clarion. Shit, he couldn't risk that!

So what then? Forget what Naomi had said? Let the psycho get on with his stuff regardless? Make out he knew nothing? Tempting, very tempting. But he knew deep down that that would not be enough for him. Knowledge was power, and, like most CID officers, he loved having information about something that no one else had access to.

Then he frowned as another option occurred to him, one so obvious that he was surprised he hadn't considered it before, for it had the potential of not only solving his present dilemma, but his financial problems as well. It was risky, but there again, if he took the right precautions, there was no reason why it shouldn't succeed. Then Ansell could stick the bloody job right up his trim little jacksie!

Feeling nervous, but excited, he slipped into his bedroom and bent down to pull open the bottom drawer of a small chest of drawers. Feeling beneath a pile of sweaters, he extracted a bulky object bound up in an old oily cloth. Carrying it gingerly through to the living room, he unwrapped it on the dining table and stood for a moment staring at the old snub-nosed Smith & Wesson revolver, his stomach twisting as he looked at it.

He had had the gun ever since the drugs raid on the house in Bristol several years before. He'd been on uniform at the time – part of a detail supplying mutual aid from his own district – and he'd found the gun hidden in an external waste pipe. Should have handed it in as evidence, of course, but he'd decided to keep it as a souvenir instead, hiding it in the plastic lunchbox of the rucksack that he'd taken with him on the operation. No one had suspected a thing and none of the low-life they'd arrested at the place were going to come forward and report the gun missing, were they? Yeah, unbeknown to his colleagues, he'd been a bad boy throughout his short service, but he'd always managed to avoid getting caught – until the drink-driving thing came along anyway.

Weighing the gun carefully in his hand, he felt a thrill run through him. He had once fancied himself as a member of the force's armed unit and had actually applied for a vacancy earlier in his service, but his application hadn't got beyond the 'in' tray of his wily old sergeant, so he'd gone for CID instead. Now that job looked like heading for the buffers, maybe, just maybe, this little souvenir would help him to get him some compensation for the way he had been treated.

Opening the cylinder, he inserted the three .38 calibre shells, with which the gun had originally been loaded, into three of its chambers, wondering, with a sense of perverse excitement, why the weapon had not been fully loaded when he'd found it and whether it might have been fired by the previous owner in the commission of some serious crime, maybe even murder. Finally closing it, he held the revolver in the two-handed grip he imagined to be the combat stance of a member of the firearms team – and which he had so far only seen demonstrated in television dramas – swinging around the room and aiming at nothing in particular, while grinning inanely.

Then, abruptly straightening, he returned the revolver to the table before crossing to his drinks cabinet to pour himself a whisky. Slumped in his armchair again, he sat there, sipping his drink and going over the haphazard plan that was forming bit by bit in his mind. It could work, but did he have the balls for it, that was the point? Once he slipped that gun into his pocket and went through his front door into the street, it was the point of no return for him; he had crossed the line for good. 'Don't be a fool,' a voice in his brain warned. 'Put the thing back in the drawer.' But there was another voice chiming in too. 'It's your big chance,' it urged. 'You'll never get one like this again.'

Plagued by nail-biting indecision, it was late in the afternoon before he finally made up his mind. Then, slipping the revolver into his coat pocket, he jerked open the front door and stepped out into the communal hallway, slamming the door shut behind him with an air of finality. Doctor Jekyll had become Mr Hyde; he had decided to cross the line. But, as he headed out of the building and over the road towards his parked car, he was unaware of the fact that police colleagues were already on their way to see him and that, had he decided to leave minutes later, he would have been prevented from heading into yet another personal disaster.

Kate and Lewis had received the radio call as they were heading back to Highbridge police station and they were at the hospital within twenty minutes.

The staff nurse Kate had had words with before was still on duty and she gave a faint bitter smile of recognition the moment she clapped eyes on the detective. Naomi had been moved from the critical care unit to the mortuary, but the uniformed police constable who had been sent to the hospital had used his common sense, after telephoning the police control-room, and stayed with the body.

'This is now a suspected murder,' Kate commented, 'and we will need the Home Office pathologist to examine the body before anything else is done. We will also be needing a statement from you and the doctor who certified death.'

The staff nurse nodded, obviously anxious to get back to her duties in the CCU. 'No problem,' she said, 'but your officer was actually at the deceased's bedside moments before she died, so he could obviously tell you more about her last moments.'

Kate raised an eyebrow and nodded toward the uniformed man standing to one side of her. 'You mean this officer?' she queried, while the young bobby shook his head several times in absolute denial.

The staff nurse hissed impatiently. 'No, not him – he arrived afterwards – I am talking about the plainclothes officer you sent.'

'Plainclothes officer?' Lewis chimed in. 'What plainclothes officer?'

The Staff shrugged. 'He flashed his ID card, but didn't leave his name.'

'And you let him in here just like that?' Kate exclaimed, adding before the nurse could respond, 'You seem to make a habit of this, don't you? Like the woman visitor you admitted earlier.'

The nurse seemed to shrink into her uniform. 'I … I'm a staff nurse, not … not a security officer,' she blurted. 'I have other seriously ill patients and—'

Lewis interjected with an impatient wave of his hand. 'This is getting us nowhere,' he said. 'What did this officer look like?'

The nurse swallowed several times, plainly very worried now, but she was able to give a very clear description, so clear, in fact, that Lewis interrupted her again halfway through. 'Phil Sharp,' he exclaimed. 'That's him down to a tee.'

Kate threw him a penetrating glance. 'Sharp? But why would he be here?'

Lewis grunted. 'Speak to you in the car,' he muttered, then turned to the nurse. 'Sounds like one of our CID sergeants, dear,' he patronized. 'So, don't worry about it. But we'll leave this officer here to prevent any other visitors dropping in before we can get the pathologist out. OK?'

The nurse left quickly then, seemingly much relieved, but Kate was in a completely different frame of mind when they got back to the car. 'Bloody hell!' she exploded. 'Why was that little shit here?'

Lewis winced at her language. 'Maybe trying to make sure she kept quiet about their little arrangement,' he replied grimly.

'Arrangement? You mean he's been the leak?'

'Guv'nor seems to think so. Heard him talking about it. Point is, did he just *talk* to the poor woman or do something more.'

Kate's eyes widened. 'What are you saying?'

Lewis avoided her gaze, looking embarrassed. 'Well, maybe he pulled out a few wires or something.'

She snorted heavily. 'Oh come on, Hayden, Sharp may be a slimy little prat, but I don't see him as a murderer.'

Lewis started the engine. 'No, neither do I,' he admitted, 'but he didn't call in to give her some grapes, did he? Maybe we should pay him a quick visit.'

Kate nodded. 'Good idea – that's if he's still at home.'

But he wasn't and Kate's brain was almost on fire as they headed back to the police station in thoughtful silence. First ex-DCI Roz Callow showing an interest in Naomi Betjeman and now Phil Sharp. What the hell was going on? Suddenly Kate felt things were getting far too complicated. But she had no idea just how complicated they were yet to become.

CHAPTER 29

Whether Kate was more embarrassed by the fake bruising on her cheekbone and the plaster across her temple or by Lewis being wheeled into the number 2 cell in Highbridge police station after his staged interview with Roscoe, was a moot point. But in any event the deception had so far gone extremely well.

Kate's distressed call to the nick that evening had brought the troops to the cottage in record time and a raging Lewis had had to be held down by two officers before being handcuffed and put in the back of the police car. What an Oscar-winning performance, Kate thought. After all his blatant opposition to the sting, she was full of admiration for him. It had certainly convinced their colleagues too and they had been none to gentle with him when they had dumped him in his allotted cell.

Sitting trembling in the incident-room, with a mug of coffee between clasped hands, Kate looked every bit the traumatized victim and she received bucket-loads of sympathy from her colleagues. The trembling was not manufactured either; the thought of returning to the cottage on her own to face heaven alone knew what was a daunting prospect. There was no going back now, though, and she just prayed that the armed surveillance team would be in place when she needed them.

To give even more credence to the staged assault, she spent over an hour afterwards in the incident-room commander's office with DI Roscoe, ostensibly writing up her statement of complaint and, after some convincing scribbling, which the rest of the incident-room team were able to witness through the internal window, they both adjourned to the DCI's office in CID downstairs for a full meeting with Detective Superintendent Willoughby and DCI Ansell.

Willoughby was plainly on tenterhooks as he sat down carefully on the very edge of one of three chairs lined up against the wall, while Ansell took centre stage, sitting, as he seemed to prefer, on a corner of the desk. Roscoe, chewing furiously as usual, selected the window sill and leaned against it, glowering at everyone in turn.

'So, I gather Naomi Betjeman is now dead and Master Philip Sharp was found at her bedside at the very moment of extremis?' Ansell almost purred.

Kate nodded, but said nothing, so Ansell continued speaking. 'And Sharp is now on his toes, I believe?' he added.

'Don't know where the little toad has got to,' Roscoe growled. 'Sent the heavy mob round to his flat, but there was no sign of him inside and we've no idea where he's gone.'

'At least we can now safely assume he was our leak,' Willoughby put in. 'By visiting the reporter, he's shot himself in the foot.'

Roscoe chewed furiously for a moment. 'Talking of shooting himself in the foot,' he went on,' that now seems like a real possibility too.'

Ansell frowned heavily. Once again his DI was feeding him information in dribs and drabs instead of in the form of a concise report and it was getting to him. 'Meaning?' he said tightly.

Roscoe shrugged. 'Well, it's not definite, but the search team found an oily rag spread out on his dining-room table and the skipper reckons the oil was gun oil. He said he could also pick out the impression of what looked like some kind of pistol in the stiffish material which the rag was made of, suggesting a weapon had been wrapped in it. Forensics are examining it as we speak.'

Ansell ran the palm of his hand across his forehead, while Willoughby just stared at the far wall, as if frozen to his seat. 'So you're suggesting he's tooled-up?'

'Could be, though I can't think why. Or where he would have got his piece from.'

Ansell released his breath in an exasperated hiss. 'I think I'll emigrate when this damned case is over,' he said. 'Become a hermit somewhere.'

'Has Sharp been circulated?' Willoughby queried in a strangled voice.

Roscoe shook his head. 'Bit difficult, Guv. We could be wrong about the shooter and he might just be out shopping.'

Ansell treated him to a withering stare. 'And, in his present state of mind, he could also be out to kill someone – or himself,' he said, 'so just do it!'

As a disgruntled muttering Roscoe left the office, the DCI sat back, studying Kate fixedly. 'You're very quiet, young lady,' he observed. 'All set for your big debut, are you?'

Kate took a deep breath. 'As ready as I'll ever be, Guv,' she replied.

Ansell pursed his lips for a second. 'Then I think it's time we briefed the firearms team who will be staking out your place and sort out your wire,' he said.

'I just hope our man bites,' Kate commented.

A grimace from the DCI which served as a smile. 'As long as it's not too hard,' he said, which did not exactly provide Kate with the reassurance she needed.

Twister completed the finishing touches to the Transit van in the derelict barn at just after nine and packed his tools away. Everything was now ready for his elaborate 'production' and he could not have felt more pleased with himself. Easing the Mercedes out of the barn, he closed and locked the double doors behind him and drove slowly out of the field. He bedded down several times prior to reaching the gate, but finally pulled on to the road in the moonlight to head back towards Wedmore and a half-hour sit-down with a wee dram in his borrowed study before embarking on the first part of his two-stage, dramatic endgame.

He had become quite used to living in the big house he had purloined from the unfortunate twitcher as his bolt-hole. There was still plenty of food in the freezer and he had enjoyed raiding his victim's well-stocked drinks cabinet for a whisky or three before settling into the comfortable armchair he always favoured. Then there was this nice Mercedes car; he liked that a lot. In fact, he had been living the life of the man he had killed for so long, that when the game was finally over, he felt it would be quite difficult to be himself again.

But the pretence would have to end soon and he smiled as he thought about the news flash he had picked up on his car radio earlier in the evening, which had reported with detectable relish the arrest and detention of Hayden Lewis. No doubt the papers would be full of the story in the morning and the whatnot would really hit the fan when the big boss at police headquarters got to read about it over his cornflakes. Things could not have worked out better – especially for yours truly. With Lewis now detained in custody and Kate deprived of her champion and protector, Twister could look forward to this being a real anniversary to remember. He could already feel his skin tingling again at the thought of what was to come. Pity about having to abandon the twitcher's soft bed and the rest of his excellent whisky, but sacrifices always had to be made for the greater good, didn't they?

Phil Sharp had never been that lucky. There had been occasions in his life when things had happened that seemed like imminent good fortune, but they'd invariably turned sour in the end – and now it was happening all over again. It wasn't as though he hadn't been given a gipsies warning either. Buying some cigarettes from a local store, he had been almost overwhelmed by a serious touch of the seconds about his night's escapade and had spent a couple of hours walking up and down Burnham's near-deserted esplanade, smoking one cigarette after another in a state of nervous agitation – acutely conscious of the revolver's unfamiliar bulge in his pocket and wondering if he would have the guts to use the thing if it came to it.

Perhaps inevitably, he ended up in one of the little resort's pubs and, after a sausage and chips meal, which he forced down with difficulty, he stayed until closing time, knocking back a lot more whiskies than was advisable and apparently conveniently forgetting the earlier debacle that had resulted from excessive alcohol. But if the alcohol did one thing for him, it was to raise his confidence levels and when the licensee finally kicked him out and he climbed back into his car, he was imbued with a new sense of optimism, convinced that the plan he had come up with this time just could not fail. But optimism can sometimes be cruelly premature.

The old Peugeot had been running OK until shortly after he left the pub, but on the straight, regally named The Queen's Drive, between Burnham and the Edith Mead roundabout, the oil starved engine lost the will to live and came to a shuddering stop with an enormous bang, as one of the pistons seemed to ram itself through the steaming head.

The police traffic car just happened to be heading for Burnham when the crew spotted the broken down vehicle on the other side of the road – the awkward position of the car, stopped at an acute angle almost over the crown of the road, leaving them with no alternative but to pull in and offer assistance.

Sharp's first mistake had been to hire a car that was already on its last gasp, his second was to approach one of the traffic officers with his warrant card extended and say, 'DS Sharp, CID Highbridge.' Unfortunately for him, his details had been circulated just minutes before and the traffic man was most grateful for the unintentional cough.

'You carrying a firearm?' he queried, eyeing him warily as his colleague moved up closer to the detective from behind.

'Don't be daft,' Sharp retorted in a strangled voice. 'Why would I be doing that?'

It was a futile denial and Sharp should have known that he would be searched, but he wasn't thinking straight and when he was relieved of his revolver, while adopting what the American cops would have called 'the position' up against the side of the car – with his arms stretched out along the roof and his legs kicked wide apart – he knew that luck had deserted him yet again.

Bundled into the back of the police car, handcuffed and humiliated, he was forced to sit there while the two uniformed policemen and a couple of passing motorists pushed the Peugeot into the kerb and switched on the four-way flashers before swinging their patrol car round and carting him back to Highbridge police station.

His one consolation when he arrived was the royal welcome he received from DCI Ansell, but he could have done without that.

CHAPTER 30

'So,' Ansell said very quietly, 'what have you got to tell us, Philip?'

Sitting across the table from the DCI and Detective Superintendent Willoughby, Sharp moistened dry lips, his eyes darting around interview room number one like those of a cornered animal, lingering in particular on the tape machine in the corner.

'I'm saying nothing without a solicitor present,' Sharp muttered.

'You might at least want to tell us where you got the revolver?' Willoughby suggested.

Sharp shrugged his shoulders. 'Found it,' he said.

'Where?'

'In a bus shelter in Bridgwater, after I was thrown out the nick.'

'And what were you doing in a bus shelter.'

There was a sneer on Sharp's face when he replied. 'Catching a bus.'

'Very funny,' Ansell cut in. 'But, as you can see, we're not laughing.'

Sharp leaned forward and glared at him. 'It wasn't meant to be a joke,' he said. 'See, I was waiting for a bus. I found the thing wrapped in a rag under the seat when I went to sit down. I was on my way here tonight to hand it in when I was stopped.'

'Took you long enough to do that, though, didn't it?' the DCI commented. 'Why didn't you just hand it in at Bridgwater nick the moment you found it?'

There was a brief tell-tale flicker of uncertainty in Sharp's eyes, then abruptly he recovered and sat back, shrugging again.

'I was tired, grubby and hungry,' he said, 'so I went home to change, have a shower and a bite to eat first.'

'Didn't catch your bus, though, did you?' Roscoe put in from across the room. 'I've been speaking to Jimmy Noble. He says he picked you up from the roadside and dropped you off at home – so why didn't you give him the revolver then to hand in?'

'I was curious about it and wanted to do the job myself.'

'That's bollocks and you know it,' Ansell went on. 'Why don't you spare us all this crap and tell the truth? Your job is already out the window and you are going to face criminal charges anyway. What have you got to lose?'

Sharp's mouth tightened. 'No further comment without my solicitor.'

Ansell nodded and, placing his hand palms downwards on the table top, started to lever himself to his feet. 'Fine,' he said. 'Then we'll just charge you with unlawful possession of a prohibited firearm – maybe much more later when we finally trace where the weapon came from and what it's been used for in the past.' He snapped his fingers, pausing halfway to his feet. 'Oh yes, and then there's the possibility of a murder charge re Naomi Betjeman.'

'Murder?' The colour drained from Sharp's face. 'I never touched her,' he gasped.

Ansell straightened with a sigh. 'You were seen bending over her when she died,' he pointed out. 'Maybe you didn't mean to kill her, but funny how her oxygen mask had been pulled off.'

'She did that herself.'

'Oh, right,' Willoughby commented with heavy sarcasm. 'Just the sort of thing you'd do when you're on the critical list in the CCU.'

Sharp's gaze darted across the room to DI Roscoe sitting by the tape machine, but he saw no hint of sympathy or understanding in the DI's bleak expression, just a brief bubble of gum erupting from between his lips before being licked back in.

'This is all crap, and you know it,' he blurted. 'I had nothing to do with that bitch's death. Why would I want to kill her anyway? It doesn't make sense.'

Satisfied that he had at least got him talking once more, Ansell sat back down with a faint humourless smile. 'It makes perfect sense to me,' he said. 'She could have dropped you in it if she had survived, told us all about the confidential info you had been selling to her.'

Immediately Sharp clammed up again. 'I want a solicitor,' he repeated. 'It's my right.'

'Your right?' Ansell emitted a hollow laugh. 'Don't make me laugh. You're in so deep, your so-called rights won't matter a jot when you go up the steps to Crown Court. Excess alcohol, unlawful possession of a firearm, bribery and maybe even manslaughter at the very least – a pretty formidable list.'

'Exactly,' Willoughby put in. 'You could be looking at a lengthy stretch inside with the baggage you're carrying.'

'And it's no fun for an ex-copper in stir,' Roscoe added. 'Especially when the nonces get hold of you—'

Sharp turned like the cornered rat he was. 'Listen,' he snarled. 'I know things – things that would fix this murder inquiry for good.'

'What *things*?' Ansell said softly.

Sharp snorted. 'Wouldn't you like to know?' he threw back.

'Just more bollocks, is it?' the DCI suggested.

Sharp shook his head vigorously. 'I know where you can find Twister,' he said. 'That's what the Betjeman bitch told me before she died.'

'I don't believe you.'

Yet another shrug and Sharp, obviously feeling he had the upper hand now and starting to enjoy himself, studied his fingernails with a cultivated disinterest. 'Suit yourself,' he said, then looked up quickly to meet Ansell's gaze. 'But if you want what I've got, you're going to have to agree to a deal.'

'What sort of deal?' Willoughby joined in, his eagerness a little too apparent.

Sharp pursed his lips reflectively. 'You lose the charge of unlawful possession of a firearm and accept that I had nothing to do with Naomi Betjeman's death.'

'No dice,' Ansell grated.

Sharp smirked. 'Then you can go whistle for the info,' he said, 'and when Kate Hamblin gets wasted, you can try and explain to everyone why you kicked a gift horse in the mouth.'

'More like kicked an arsehole,' Roscoe growled.

Sharp giggled inanely. 'Yeah,' he sneered, 'but this is one arsehole that's got you lot over a barrel. Now, get me my solicitor.'

Hayden Lewis felt that he was going stir-crazy. Banged up in the tiny cell, completely in the dark as to what was going on in the world outside and desperately worried about Kate, he had spent sleepless hours pacing the hard bare floor, with just the shouts of a drunk further down the passageway and the occasional burst of raucous laughter from the custody office itself for company.

He had no means of knowing exactly what time it was when he heard the footsteps approaching, as his wrist-watch had been taken off him. He guessed it had to be pretty late, however, because it was ages since he had heard the familiar clamour of doors banging and cars leaving the rear yard outside the cell block, indicating the change of shift from late to night turn.

There seemed to be two pairs of feet and, as they drew closer, he recognized the voice of the night turn's Geordie custody officer, barking out an instruction, 'Next, but one. Right beside your mate, Lewis.'

Springing to the open hatch in the cell door, Lewis bent his head to peer through and met the arrogant stare of a dishevelled Philip Sharp.

The former DS stopped short and treated him to a characteristic sneer. 'Well, well, well,' he mocked, 'if it isn't good ol' Hayden Lewis – my, how the mighty have fallen.'

'Not as far as you, it would seem,' Lewis retorted. 'I wondered what hole you'd slid into when we came looking for you.'

'Move it,' the custody officer growled, tapping Sharp on the shoulder. 'I said the *next* one.'

But Sharp stood his ground for a moment. 'Heard you were in here, Hayden,' he went on and grinned. 'They told me you belted that stupid cow, Hamblin? 'Bout time someone did.'

Lewis's fists clenched involuntarily, but he controlled himself with an effort and didn't dignify the insults with a reply. The next instant the custody officer gave Sharp a hard shove. '*Next one*, I said,' he repeated.

Darting the tough little Geordie a venomous glance, Sharp grudgingly obeyed and, shortly after he had disappeared from view, Lewis heard a heavy iron door close with a reverberating crash. The noise woke not only a dozen echoes, but the drunk too, who shouted a string of obscenities before lapsing into silence again.

'Hey, Hayden,' Sharp shouted from his cell after the custody officer had gone. 'Bet Kate's new boyfriend's got a real surprise planned for her tonight while you're in here – a real hot surprise. Hope she's brushed her teeth and got clean knickers on.'

Lewis had meant to keep his cool and ignore whatever his disreputable colleague's vicious tongue came out with next, but, already deeply sensitive to the fabricated story that was being circulated by the police propaganda machine about Kate's bogus affair, he could not stop himself jumping to her defence.

'That's all you know,' he shouted back. 'You haven't got a clue what's going on.'

For a few seconds there was a pregnant silence and Lewis inwardly cursed himself for a fool. If Sharp got even an inkling of things, it would wreck the whole operation, for he would be certain to shout the odds from his cell, which was bound to get to the ears of the custody crew and then be relayed all around the station. But he was in luck, for his tormentor appeared not to have picked up on his Freudian slip; he was too wrapped up in himself and in his determination to get one over on Lewis.

'I know a lot more than you think,' he boasted. 'That reporter bitch – Naomi Betjeman – the one who snuffed it in the hospital? She'd been doing a lot of digging on the Twister case and had sussed everything out just before she hit the concrete. She gave me the whole SP on it before her lights went out.'

'The whole SP?' Lewis threw back. 'You are the gen kiddie then, aren't you?'

The contemptuous disbelief in his tone was very evident and it certainly rankled with Sharp. 'OK, sneer away,' he snarled, 'but I'll tell you this – I know exactly where Twister is *and* how he's managed to avoid being nicked for so long.'

'So you say,' Lewis retorted, trying to sound disinterested, but suddenly starting to feel uneasy, in spite of his contempt for Sharp.

'Yeah, so I say,' Sharp agreed. 'See, I really can finger him and unless that creep, Ansell, starts playing ball with me, the next time you'll see your girlfriend will be when she's lying naked on a slab, with a label tied to her toe.'

Sharp had always been a bull-shitter – professing to have inside information on everything when he hadn't, but for some reason this time his claim carried absolute conviction and Lewis was touched by the cold finger of fear. Ignoring Sharp's further jibes, he pressed the buzzer to the custody sergeant's office and kept his finger on the button.

CHAPTER 31

Lewis was almost beside himself with anxiety and frustration.

He had been pressing the bell for a good fifteen minutes without getting a response, but at last he could hear measured footsteps approaching.

Seconds later, Sergeant Bill Weymouth, the night custody sergeant, unlocked the cell door and he didn't look best pleased.

'Come on, Hayden, what's all this about?' he snapped. 'We'll be changing over shifts in a couple of hours and I can do without this sort of crap.'

Lewis took a deep breath. 'Listen to me, Bill,' he said, having made up his mind to reveal all, even if it did mean jeopardizing the sting. 'My arrest, the assault – everything – was just a put-up job. It's all part of an operation to nail the killer, but I think we could have made a big mistake.'

Weymouth sighed heavily. 'Hayden, why don't you just get your head down for a while, eh? You'll need to look your best if they decide to charge you and put you before the court.'

Lewis shook his head frantically. 'You don't understand,' he exclaimed. 'Kate's in danger, I can feel it.'

Weymouth grunted. 'You should have thought about that before you clocked her one,' he growled.

'But … but I didn't touch her, damn you! It was all a con. Ask Ansell – look, get him down here – or Roscoe – they'll vouch for what I say. You must let me out.'

But Weymouth was already back in the cell passage and, in the act of closing the door. 'You have a good kip, mate,' he said. 'I'll get one of the lads to bring you a cuppa a bit later.'

In desperation, Lewis hurled himself at the slowly closing gap, but he was too late and simply rebounded off the door. 'Bill,' he almost shrieked, 'tell Ansell Sharp can finger Twister. Tell him – please – for the sake of Kate!'

But Weymouth's footsteps were already fading back along the cell passage.

'So it was all a fix, was it?' Sharp chortled from his cell. 'Now that *is* worth knowing. Pity it will be for nothing, eh?'

Lewis put his head on one side in a futile attempt to thrust it through the open hatch. 'If you know something, man, for heaven's sake tell Ansell,' he shouted hoarsely.

'Tried that,' Sharp said with a loud sigh, 'but he wouldn't do a deal, so there you are, his funeral – or rather Kate's.'

'So hit your buzzer and call him down here.'

'Nah,' Sharp replied, 'think I'll just let it ride,' and he chuckled. 'Pity about ol' Kate, though, isn't it? She hasn't a clue what she's walking into.'

For reply, Lewis pressed his own buzzer again and, for a second time, kept his finger on the button.

Kate left the police station in the morning, just as it was getting light. The briefing to finalize the details of the impending sting operation had been interrupted by Sharp's arrest. Once by his initial interview and then, an hour later, a further interview in the presence of his solicitor. They'd both been a complete waste of time, as he had revealed nothing of value to the inquiry anyway and, perversely, just seemed to be enjoying the experience. When the briefing had once more resumed behind the closed door of the vacant office of the territorial DCI, it had been long and painstaking, involving just a small select team, comprising Kate, Willoughby,

Ansell, Roscoe, Norton and the sergeant heading the armed surveillance unit.

Kate had been surprised to find Norton there under the circumstances. Seen by the rest of the station as being the one primarily responsible for the violent break-up of Kate and Lewis, the psychologist had already been given the cold shoulder by a number of the incident-room team. Norton was plainly under a lot of strain and anxious to keep out of sight, but as the operation was his brainchild and he seemed to have such a keen insight into the psyche of the killer, he was obviously essential to the planning process and could not avoid being there. He had used his head though and delayed his arrival for the briefing until after ten when the bulk of the night shift were out on patrol.

For several hours the six of them had pored over Ordnance Survey maps of Burtle, drawing up detailed plans of the cottage and its garden. Only when Ansell was satisfied that all exigencies had been covered, did he allow them – with Willoughby's implied approval, of course – to stand down for coffee and chocolate bars, rustled up by Roscoe from the vending machines in the unmanned night kitchen. Even then, however, he'd insisted on a thorough recap of everything agreed upon before letting the exhausted team go home to bed.

Kate was one of the last to leave, downing an extra cup of coffee with Roscoe before she managed to tear herself away from the security of the office. She felt strangely sick and light-headed as she headed for the rear door of the station, the wire snaking between her breasts, connected to the small transmitter taped to her stomach just below her navel, rubbing against her skin as she walked.

She was quite upset about not being allowed to see Lewis before leaving – even though she had had to accept the logic of Ansell's argument. It *would* have looked mighty suspicious to her colleagues if she had visited him in his cell after making such a damning complaint of assault against him. She had also had to accept that in such circumstances it would have been so easy for one of them to have slipped up with some unguarded comment within the hearing of the custody staff, thereby jeopardizing the whole operation.

Nevertheless, logic aside, she would have felt a lot happier if she had been given the opportunity of just two minutes alone with Hayden and the certainty of a reassuring hug from him before leaving. As it was, she was plagued by a strong sense of unease, which she found impossible to shake off. Her feminine intuition told her that something was terribly wrong – something that had been missed from the start and which should have been obvious to all – and, although she couldn't put her finger on it, she knew instinctively that she was in much greater peril than she or anyone else associated with the operation had anticipated.

OK, so the wire she was wearing – currently switched off to conserve the battery power – was a lifeline, but she had no illusions about her own vulnerability. Even with armed police officers all around the cottage when she got home, she knew she would still be very much on her own if Twister managed to get close to her.

The rear yard of the police station looked strangely sinister as she stepped out of the back door, spooky fingers of white mist curling round the high-level security lights, and distorted shadows crowding around her like abnormalities from another world, as she headed for her car parked in the corner. Two uniformed officers passed her on the way, grunting curtly as they went by, no doubt anxious to complete any paperwork before signing off at the end of their shift, and, as the back door banged behind them, she shivered, feeling alone and vulnerable.

She saw the figure hunched over the open bonnet of the car parked next to hers as she flicked her remote to unlock the Mazda's doors, and frowned as she recognized Doctor Norton's distinctive figure. Something was obviously amiss with the vehicle, for he should have been gone long ago, having left the station at least twenty minutes before her.

'Problems?' she queried and walked over to him.

He straightened with a short unamused laugh. 'Damned thing won't start,' he said. 'I've been trying to get it going for at least fifteen minutes. Flat battery, I reckon.'

'Didn't the two officers I just saw offer to help you?'

Another grim laugh. 'I did ask, but they said they were too busy.'

'That's awful.'

He sighed. 'Not really. With the story that's going around the station about you and me and Hayden Lewis's arrest, I'm not exactly flavour of the week at the moment – your fiancé is a pretty popular guy.'

She thought for a second. 'I can soon instruct one of the lads to take a look, whether they want to or not? I'm pretty useless with cars myself, I'm afraid.'

He shook his head. 'No, no, I don't want to be a pain at shift changeover time and it would be best for me to keep a low profile at present.' He closed the bonnet with a bang. 'I'll just walk into the town and see if I can find a taxi.'

She stared at him. 'What at this time of the morning? You'll be lucky.'

He shrugged. 'Then I'll just have to wait until the next shift settles in and try to cadge a lift off the early turn.'

'You can't wait around that long. You've been up all night, like the rest of us.'

He yawned. 'Must admit, I am a bit shagged.'

'Look,' and she hesitated, thinking of his past history of making unwelcome advances towards her, but feeling sorry for his situation nevertheless, 'I can drop you off at your home, if you like.'

'No, no, no,' he said sharply. 'It'll be right out of your way. Honestly, I'll be fine.'

Aiming his remote at the car, he locked up and turned away from her. 'I'll be fine, really I will.'

He was halfway to the yard exit before she called him back. 'Doctor Norton, don't be stupid. I'm taking you and that's all there is to it, so please get in.'

He appeared embarrassed, standing there in the pool of light cast by one of the yard lights – looking for all like a little lost boy, with his toes turned in slightly and his hands clasped in front of him – and she smiled to herself in spite of her reservations about the man. He was certainly an oddball, but no one was perfect, and he was hardly likely to try anything on her while she was driving anyway. The only thing that really bothered her was his damned perfume. Yes, windows open, she thought, in spite of the cold.

'You – er – don't drive fast, do you?' he queried nervously as he lowered himself into the passenger seat. 'I'm not a great lover of speed.'

She smiled again to herself. So that was it: women drivers, the bugger didn't like women drivers. 'No, Doctor,' she said, revving the engine and pulling away with a screech of tyres. 'Except when I'm in a hurry.'

Her smile had broadened into a mischievous grin by the time they reached the main road and out of the corner of her eye she saw him shrink into his seat as she accelerated away. This will serve as a punishment for coming on to me in the first place, she thought, and hit the pedal hard, determined to enjoy this particular journey to the full. In fact, she was so busy revelling in the discomfort of her passenger that she failed to notice the powerful black saloon car which pulled out of a side turning behind her the moment she flashed by, then accelerated ahead of the early morning traffic to keep her in sight – and it wasn't a police mobile either.

CHAPTER 32

Kate's sense of mischief quickly evaporated once she had left Highbridge behind and was back on the Levels. The mist that had greeted her in the police station yard seemed to be thickening every few hundred yards and she was forced to cut her speed right down to avoid repeating the experience she had suffered during the original Firetrap inquiry two years before by ploughing into one of the rhynes.

These man-made drains formed a lattice-work of silver across the flat waterlogged fields and marshes that made up this incredibly beautiful, yet potentially deadly part of Somerset's heartland. They had swallowed many a careless motorist speeding along the broken uneven roads eroded by the treacherous peat beds over which they had been constructed. She had no desire to join them.

With negative thoughts already crowding her mind, the gloomy morning only served to add to her melancholic mood and it occurred to her that, while she might avoid becoming another fatal accident statistic, the odds on her achieving a similar outcome in relation to homicide figures might soon prove to be a lot lower.

Whether Norton – sitting in silence for much of the journey – sensed her change in mood was not absolutely clear. The more her speed came down, however, the more he seemed to relax and, when they finally pulled up in the grounds of the detached house he had directed her to, he actually seemed in a lot less of a hurry to get out of the car than she would have expected.

'Well, I'll be off then,' she encouraged, fearing that he might be about to invite her inside for a drink – and, with his track record, she dreaded to think what else.

At first he seemed not to have heard her, but simply stared straight ahead as if his gaze was rigidly fixed on something, while she impatiently tapped the steering wheel with both hands. Then suddenly he seemed to sag in his seat, one hand gripping his chest as he uttered a low agonized moan.

'Doctor?' She bent over him. 'What is it?'

His face seemed unnaturally pale and he had screwed his eyes tightly shut. 'Ticker,' he whispered through clenched teeth. 'Tab-tablets in my study.'

She reached for her police radio lying on the central consol, but he waved her hand away. 'No,' he gasped, 'no ambulance. Angina. Know what it is. Already having treatment.'

Inwardly cursing her luck, Kate scrambled out of the car and ran round to his door, jerking it wide. He had already released his seat belt and he waved her back almost irritably as he grabbed hold of the top of the door to hoist himself out of the bucket seat. Steadying him by the elbow, she helped him up the two stone steps to the front door of the house. 'Keys, coat pocket,' he breathed, falling against one of the stone pillars of the porch with another sharp cry.

She found the keys and helped him through the front door into the brightly lit hallway. The study turned out to be at the far end, past another open doorway, possibly to a lounge or sitting-room.

'You should have told us about your medical problem before, Doctor,' she admonished.

Fumbling for the light switch just inside the room, she flicked it on and stepped back as he shook her hand off his elbow to grab the door frame and pull himself through the doorway. There was a swivel chair in front of a leather-topped desk and he collapsed into it, his head lolling forward on to his chest.

'Tablets, Doctor,' Kate exclaimed, concern etched into her face as she knelt beside him. 'Where are your tablets?'

To her astonishment, he suddenly straightened up, with a big grin on his face, and carefully removed his glasses. 'I think I deserve an Oscar for that performance, don't you, Kate,' he said, his voice suddenly changing and losing its effeminate lisp. She felt her blood congeal and her limbs lock in a state of paralytic shock as she found herself staring, with a sense of horror and disbelief, into Twister's dead soulless eyes.

The powerful black saloon car which had followed Kate from the police station swung quickly into a convenient open gateway when the Mazda's right-hand indicator came on to indicate it was turning off the main Wedmore to Glastonbury road, but as soon as the sports car had disappeared, the black saloon car pulled out again and crept to the junction with its lights extinguished.

Nosing slowly into the mouth of the lane, the driver was just in time to see the Mazda turn off again into the entrance to the twitcher's house a few hundred yards further on. For a moment the driver of the car sat there, as if waiting to see if the Mazda would come out again. When it didn't, the big black saloon drove right into the lane, still with its lights out and mist curling around the windscreen like streamers at a mediaeval tournament.

The car made no effort to turn into the entrance to the house, but drove very slowly past, the figure behind the wheel casting a keen eye over the open gates and along the perimeter hedge. A few yards further on the lane took a sharp left and the driver seemed to hesitate before swinging into the mouth of a drove just beyond the bend. Making very little engine noise, the car reversed out again, turning in the direction from which it had come, then reversed back into the drove until it was concealed behind a low hedge. A moment later the engine was cut and the driver, muffled in a woollen coat and carrying something in a long canvas bag, climbed awkwardly out of the vehicle and pushed the door closed.

A crane – one of the new arrivals on the Levels – rose from the adjoining rhyne with a weird cry and a flapping of giant wings. The figure started, then relaxed, watching the bird disappear into the mist like a wraith. From the adjoining field a cow released a loud choking cough and, in the stillness which then descended, it could be heard tugging at the long grass with its tongue. On the main road lights heralded the approach of a heavy-goods lorry which thundered past in the direction of Wedmore.

Seemingly satisfied that the Mazda's headlights were not about to emerge from the grounds of the property, the figure moved off very slowly, heading back up the lane, but keeping close to the nearside hedge. At the gated entrance it paused to listen, but, hearing nothing, stepped through and picked its way with great care along the gravel driveway towards the house. Twister was about to have company.

Kate's reflexes had always been quicker than most, and her recovery this time was only fractionally slower than usual, but she was still not quick enough. Even as she stumbled back from the chair, falling over on to her behind in the process, Twister was on his feet and standing over her.

'You bastard,' she jerked out through clenched teeth, 'you filthy bastard!'

He smiled and held a finger up to his lips, motioning her to silence. Then, kneeling on one knee beside her, he undid the buttons on the short woollen coat she was wearing, followed by the buttons on her blouse. Mentally recoiling from his touch, she felt his fingers release the studs on her front-fastening bra and a second later winced as he tore the electronic wire free, brutally parting the tapes holding it in place. At the same time he snapped the connection to the tiny transmitter and removed it with similar brute force, drawing a sharp cry from her as the tapes were ripped from her stomach.

'That's better,' he said and stood up again, dropping the transmitter on the floor at his feet and crushing it under his heel. 'After all, we don't want anyone eavesdropping on our little tête-á-tête, do we?' He smiled. 'At least your police radio is still in your car. It's all worked out quite well really, hasn't it?'

Kate said nothing, but simply stared up at him, breathing heavily, her eyes burning with hatred as she forgot even to refasten her bra and blouse.

With a heavy manufactured sigh, he leaned over her again and, almost tenderly, did the job for her, making no attempt to caress her breasts, but acting like a doctor concluding the examination of a mentally retarded patient. 'There, there,' he said, 'all done now. Can't have you catching cold, can we?'

Reaching down, he offered her his hand. 'May I?' he said in the manner of a gentleman assisting a lady to her feet after she has accidentally tripped over at a society ball.

Without taking her eyes off him, she obediently accepted the offer, but the moment she was on her feet, she suddenly went for him, bringing her knee up savagely towards his crutch.

But she was out of her league. His knee deflected hers with bruising force and, bending her wrist downwards and sideways, he spun her round and forced her back on to the floor on her knees, with her arm now twisted up behind her back. 'Well, that *was* stupid, wasn't it?' he murmured, bending close to her ear, heedless of her moans at the stabbing pain in her constricted muscles. 'Now, I'm going to let you up. Try that again and I'll actually break your arm, OK?'

She nodded quickly, knowing full well that he would do precisely what he had threatened. At once his grip slackened and she allowed herself to be helped back on her feet.

'Sit down, Kate,' he said softly and indicated a two-seater settee opposite the desk. 'Then we can have our little chat in comfort.'

She sat down carefully, rubbing the circulation back in to her arm. 'So you've been leading us by the nose right from the start?' she said.

He dropped into the swivel chair again with a soft chuckle and poured himself a large whisky from a half-empty bottle of Talisker single malt. 'All the way,' he gloated, 'and it has been really ace.' He shook his head with another sigh. 'I *am* surprised that you didn't see through me, though, Kate – you of all people. But I did go to a lot of trouble to change my appearance – shaved off the beard, changed the colour and style of my hair and everything. Nature helped too. I lost a couple of stone after I was stabbed all that time ago and I made sure I kept the weight off for the part I had to play.'

'And I suppose the body at the reserve will turn out to be Norton's?' she went on bitterly. 'Another innocent victim.'

He nodded several times. 'Been watching him for weeks,' he explained. 'Knew where he lived, what he looked like, what car he drove – even his twitching habits. *Had* to be him, you see. As a notable criminal psychologist and profiler, he was my "in" as far as the police murder inquiry was concerned, so I couldn't afford any mistakes. Presenting myself as an arty effeminate wasn't easy, but I made sure I adopted all the right mannerisms – even down to that awful lisp he had—'

'But you couldn't hide your smell,' she cut in viciously, 'and you certainly stink!'

He tutted. 'Now that isn't very nice, Kate,' he said and smiled again. 'But, yes, I do have a personal problem, which made the strong perfume essential and, of course, my rather unique eyes are a real giveaway, so I was pleased that poor old Norton wore those fancy specs. All I had to do was snuff him out, take over his identity and ring your gullible boss to offer my expert services. Simple really. Just a pity I left that flask of his behind in the hide – nearly scuppered me, that did.'

'And all those killings, just to get at me,' Kate choked, her sudden surge of distress quite genuine.

He shook his head. 'Oh you mustn't think that,' he corrected. 'It wasn't done to get at you. It was just part of a little game I'd put together and I had hoped you would accept it for what it was and get into the spirit of things. See, I always regarded you as a bit of unfinished business, and it hurt my pride to think that I hadn't tidied up properly after Operation Firetrap.'

'So now you're going to murder me, like the others?' she said, but, even as she spoke, her eyes were flicking round the room, looking for an escape route.

'Oh no,' he said, almost beaming at her. 'Nothing so mundane. I have a much more spectacular demise reserved for you.'

'So why go to all the trouble of setting up the sting operation if you were going to snatch me like this anyway?' she queried.

There was a smug expression on his face now. 'An essential part of the game, Kate,' he said. 'You see, I knew I would have to get your boyfriend out of the way on the big day in order to isolate you. Wasting him would simply have sent the balloon up and resulted in an even tighter protective net being put around you, so I hit on the idea of making a series of passes at you. The intention was to provoke an angry and very public reaction from him, which would plant the idea in everyone's mind that you and I could be having an affair and enable me to suggest at the crucial time that this be used as the foundation for the sting operation, with Hayden banged up to give it authenticity—'

'And we all fell for it,' she cut in, deliberately pandering to his ego in an effort to distract him – and for a very good reason.

With a sudden rush of adrenalin, she had glimpsed the figure at the window peering in at them. She couldn't tell whether it was a man or a woman from where she sat – the face was just a blob inside a hood – but for the first time she felt a stab of hope.

He chuckled. 'It worked even better than I had expected too,' he went on, seemingly oblivious to the intruder just feet away from him on the other side of the thin pane of glass. 'Poor old Hayden gave an excellent demonstration of jealous rage in front of half of his colleagues by thumping

Phil Sharp. Then, as the expert criminal psychologist, it was easy to convince Ansell and Co not only to go along with my plan, but to assume nothing would happen to you until tonight. So, lulled into a false sense of security, the twats forgot all about the risk to you in the meantime. Pure genius on my part.'

The figure at the window had disappeared. Kate gnawed at her lip. Who the hell was it? What were they doing wandering about the garden? More importantly, how would they know she was being held captive by a homicidal maniac? And would they actually care anyway if they were up to no good? She had to keep him talking a bit longer to give the intruder the opportunity of taking another look, so she could attract their attention in some way.

'But why snatch me from the nick like this?' she blurted, casting another quick glance at the window. 'You could have lain in wait for me at home.'

He emitted a hard laugh. 'What, and risk the prospect of running into your tooled-up colleagues staking out your place? That would have been stupid. No, I had to do it before you got home and when everyone's guard was down. Trouble is, this has presented me with a slight problem.'

To her alarm, he was on his feet again, draining his whisky glass as he did so. 'Get up,' he said. 'I want to show you something.'

She hesitated and his eyes narrowed. 'I'll say it one more time, Kate,' he warned. 'Up!'

Reluctantly, she obeyed, glancing once more at the window, but seeing no one. Damn!

He nodded towards the door. 'You first,' he ordered.

She could actually feel his breath on her neck as he nudged her out into the hallway and towards a small door under the stairs. 'Open it,' he said.

She obeyed and saw steps leading down. He prodded her forward and flicked a switch, flooding the stairway with light. There was a cellar at the bottom, glistening with moisture, and Kate saw racks of wine bottles stacked along one wall and an assortment of decrepit looking furniture in a corner, including a stained mattress.

'Some good years down here,' Twister joked, nodding towards the wine, and Kate flinched as he grabbed her right arm and snapped a handcuff over her wrist. 'But don't knock back too much, will you?'

Pushing her in the direction of the furniture, he told her to sit on the mattress and, when she had done so, he trailed a long steel chain looped around one of the thick iron legs of the wine rack across the floor and snapped the other half of the handcuffs to one of the links, preventing her moving more than four feet in any direction. Then he straightened up again. 'Sorry about this,' he said, 'but my problem is that we are left with a few hours to kill before the big event and I can't chance moving you until after dark. Still, you're nice and comfy down here and you can always have a little snooze.'

'When my colleagues sus you out, this house will be the first place they'll look,' she threw back at him. 'That will bugger up your so-called event, won't it?'

He laughed again. 'I doubt that very much, Kate,' he said. 'After the long night they've had, they'll all be safely tucked up in bed until at least lunchtime and anyway, how can they possibly have worked out that their quarry is actually their own brilliant psychologist? After all, they've been clueless throughout the whole inquiry so far.'

Then she saw him climbing the stairs back up to the hallway and seconds later the lights went out and she was alone in the darkness, listening to the faint trickle of water down the walls.

CHAPTER 33

Twister's first job after dumping Kate in the cellar was to head for the shower and he spent a good twenty minutes washing away the last traces of Doctor Norton's identity, including the dyed blond hair, and dumping the hated clothes and shoes into a dirty linen basket. What did it matter if the police found them later? He felt sure he would be long gone before they managed to put two and two together anyway.

He nearly forgot the earring with its attached crucifix and made a face when he saw it in the mirror. 'That's certainly not you, my friend,' he commented, unclipping it and dropping it down the toilet, but still, it had served its purpose and he was well satisfied with the way he had managed to impersonate Norton over such a protracted period.

Dressing in his own crepe shoes, brown corduroy trousers and thick winter shirt, he headed downstairs with a spring in his step, checking Kate on the way and blowing her a kiss before shutting her in darkness again. His hooded woollen coat was hanging on a peg by the front door and, pulling it on, he left the house and crunched his way to Kate's Mazda. Opening the garage doors wide, he drove the little sports car inside, parking next to the battered green Land Rover with the canvas hood that Norton had been using for his twitcher activities.

He smiled as he got out of the Mazda. The Land Rover was a crappy motor, as he had found out when he had driven it back from the wildlife reserve after killing Norton, but it had proved very useful to him and it had at least removed the need for him to hire – or steal – another vehicle for the final part of his little operation. All he had to do now was to finish up at Norton's house, then collect Kate and be on his way – game, set and match. Couldn't be easier – or so he thought – but unbeknown to him at that precise moment, a rather sticky problem was about to descend on him, which had the capacity to derail everything he had worked for, and it materialized with the crunch of feet in the gravel in front of the garage as he slammed the Mazda's door shut.

Jerking his head in the direction of the sound, he found himself staring down the twin barrels of a twelve-bore shotgun, which was levelled at his stomach by another hooded figure standing in the open doorway.

'Larry Wadman,' Roz Callow gloated, shaking the hood off her head. 'I knew if I kept on Hamblin's tail, she'd lead me to you eventually.'

Twister treated her to a mirthless smile, seemingly unfazed by the formidable weapon in her grip, almost as if the whole thing was part of the same sort of perverse game he himself liked to play.

'Well, well, well,' he murmured, propping himself on the rear offside wing of the sports car. 'The inimitable Rozalind Callow. How nice to see you again. Quite nostalgic actually.'

'You think so, do you?' Callow grated, leaning heavily on her stick with her other hand. 'Maybe you'll change your mind in a few minutes.'

'Come to arrest me then, have you?' Twister queried. 'Bit late for that, isn't it? After all, you're no longer in the force, are you? No power of arrest and all that?'

Callow emitted a harsh laugh. 'Arrest?' she echoed. 'I'm not here to arrest you, you bastard, I'm here to kill you.'

Twister tutted. 'Kill me? That's a bit out of order for an ex-DCI, isn't it? Still smarting over the death of your girlfriend two years ago, are you?'

At first it seemed that he had lost his senses. It was patently obvious that Callow had become seriously deranged and winding up a deranged woman armed with a shotgun is never the most sensible thing to do. As it was, Callow seemed to go rigid at the jibe and the shotgun jerked upwards, wandered slightly then steadied, with the stock pressed against her hip and the barrels levelled at his chest. She was obviously having difficulty holding the heavy weapon in one hand and for a second Twister really thought there was a danger of it going off involuntarily.

'The pair of you ruined my life,' she said, her voice trembling with emotion. 'Once I had a career and a future.' She tapped her leg awkwardly with the stick, swaying slightly. 'But, thanks to you and that bitch, Pauline, I ended up a bloody cripple with nothing. So now it's payback time.'

And before Twister could say anything else, the twin barrels of the shotgun erupted with a deafening roar.

DCI Ansell dragged himself out of bed at just after one in the afternoon – feeling a bit like death warmed up after barely five hours fitful sleep – and snatched a quick bite to eat and a shower before returning to Highbridge police station to prepare for the night's 'fun and games'. It was close on three before he finally pushed through the back door of the nick and he muttered an oath when he almost collided with the duty inspector, Taff Holland, who had come on late-turn duty at 2.00 pm.

Holland looked even more haggard than he did and his face wore an anxious frown as he acknowledged Ansell with a brief 'Afternoon, sir,' and a polite nod.

The DCI was actually halfway to the stairs when he called out after him. 'Couldn't have a word, could I, sir?' he blurted.

Ansell turned with a characteristic frown. 'If you must,' he responded tightly.

Holland hesitated. 'It's Hayden Lewis, sir,' he said. 'Couldn't bail him now, could we?'

Ansell raised an eyebrow. 'Why?'

'Well, sir, by rights we shouldn't be holding him on just an ABH charge anyway and the custody sergeant says the charge sheet has an endorsement on it, saying he cannot be released – er – without the expressed authority of yourself.'

'Quite right and that still stands. Is that all?'

Holland fidgeted for a moment. 'Point is, sir, he's been a bloody nuisance ever since he was nicked apparently – ringing the buzzer, denying he hit Kate Hamblin and saying his arrest and detention was all a put-up job—'

Ansell cut in like a whiplash. 'He said what?'

Holland gave a nervous laugh. ''Course, we know that's crap, sir – he's obviously lost the plot somehow – but with Phil Sharp winding him up from the next cell, it's bedlam down there.'

Ansell leaned back against the wall for a moment and studied him narrowly. 'Exactly what has he said?'

Holland took a deep breath. 'Well, I haven't seen him myself, sir, but both the night turn and early turn custody sergeants have said he's been going on about DC Hamblin being in some sort of danger and demanding to see you before it's too late. We reckon Sharp said something to him that set all this off. Now the late turn skipper wants rid of him before he drives everyone crackers.'

Ansell came off the wall, his face ashen. 'I see,' he said curtly. 'Leave it with me.' And before Holland could say anything more, he was heading back to the stairs.

Roscoe was already in the main incident-room, talking to one of the operators when he strode through the door and he indicated to the DI with a nod of his head to join him in the SIO's office.

'Lewis has been spilling the beans all night,' he grated, shutting the door carefully behind him. 'Wound up by that prick, Sharp, apparently. This could wreck everything if it gets to the ears of the press.'

Roscoe nodded grimly. 'With respect, Guv,' he said, 'we've got a lot more to worry about than the press.'

For the first time Ansell read the anxiety in his eyes.

'Meaning?'

Roscoe shrugged unhappily. 'Kate Hamblin's disappeared.'

'What?'

'Sergeant Mills on the firearms team has just rung in. He says he's been trying to contact Kate for an hour, on both her home line and her mobile, to touch base with her before deploying his team and he hasn't been able to get an answer. So he took a chance and checked the house. She's not there – and, worse still, the wire she's wearing is dead.'

Ansell felt a sharp stabbing pain in his chest and carefully sat down on the edge of the desk as the room swayed briefly around him. 'Shit!' he said slowly and distinctly. 'Has Mr Willoughby been told about this?'

Roscoe shook his head. 'Not in yet,' he said. 'Probably still in bed.'

'That's one saving grace anyway,' Ansell murmured uncharitably. 'You'd better get over to the house. Tear it apart if you have to. Yes, and get Lewis out of the cells and take him with you.'

'You know that will blow the whole operation, Guv?' Roscoe warned.

Ansell emitted a cracked laugh. 'With Lewis shouting his mouth off and our key player missing, I think it is already blown, don't you, Ted? And if anything has happened to Kate Hamblin, our careers will be blown with it.'

Detective Superintendent Willoughby strolled into the incident-room at four o'clock to find the place in sombre mood and Ansell talking in an agitated manner to a detective sergeant on one of the workstations.

'Problems?' he queried, sensing the atmosphere around him.

'You could say that,' Ansell retorted, and had the satisfaction of seeing his boss quail when he told him the news. 'I've just had a full circulation put out on her,' the DCI went on, 'and I've asked for flight operations assistance.'

'The helicopter?' Willoughby's eyes widened and he swallowed hard. 'But that will let the whole force know we've cocked up. The Chief will—'

'Can't be helped,' Ansell cut in. 'This is an officer's life we're talking about,' and he broke off as someone shouted his name.

Turning, he saw one of his operators on the other side of the room holding up a telephone receiver.

'Toby Pomeroy, Somerset Levels Avian Society, Guv,' the call-handler shouted.

'So?' Ansell threw back at him.

The operator shrugged. 'Wanted to speak to Kate Hamblin, but I said she wasn't here. Tried to speak to her this morning apparently without success and he's not very happy about being given the run around.'

'So why would he want me instead?'

'Says he has some information for us and insists on speaking to a supervisor – something about a flask.'

Ansell felt his heartbeat quicken and he threw Willoughby a quick sideways glance. 'A flask, you say? Better put him through.'

The voice at the other end of the extension phone sounded irritable when Ansell announced himself. Then, as the DCI listened to what the caller had to say, his jaw dropped and he threw another glance at Willoughby. 'You're sure about this, Mr Pomeroy?' he exclaimed. 'Have you got an address?'

Ansell snapped his fingers and a uniformed officer sitting at the workstation beside him handed him a pen. For a second he scribbled furiously on the back of a used message form, then nodded quickly. 'Got all that,' he said. 'Right, thank you for ringing, sir.'

Setting the phone down, he held on to the receiver in its cradle for a few seconds, staring at Willoughby with a look of disbelief. 'Remember the flask Hamblin found in the hide?' he said.

'Of course, I do. So we have an owner at last, do we?'

'You could say that. The man I've just spoken to is president of some bird-watching group or other Kate Hamblin went to see and he reckons he knows who the flask belongs to.'

'Well, that's good news at least. We could have an ID for our stiff then?'

Ansell nodded. 'It's a lot more complicated than that,' he said. 'Pomeroy has apparently seen the flask several times before and he reckons that the initials RCJN engraved on the thing stand for Richard Clement John Norton.'

Willoughby gaped. 'What? There must be some mistake?'

'Maybe,' Ansell said grimly, 'but if Pomeroy's right, I would very much like to know how our Doctor Norton's flask came to be left in the hide and why he didn't tell us about it.'

'So let's get him in here and ask him.'

Ansell's eyes gleamed. 'Which is what I intend doing right now,' he replied, nodding to the policeman sitting beside him. 'And while my man here is fixing that up for me, I think we should have another word with Master Philip Sharp – and this time there will be no more games.'

CHAPTER 34

Hayden Lewis was shivering and he wasn't in the least bit cold. Released from his cell to be told that Kate had disappeared, he was still in a state of shock and his empty cottage, once so warm and cosy, had seemed like an alien place, greeting him with a bleak indifferent shrug.

'Well, she's not here anyway,' Roscoe said, stating the obvious and scowling as he looked around him.

'She never got back here in the first place,' Lewis retorted as he returned to the room from the kitchen. 'The fire's not cleared out and there are dirty dishes on the draining-board from last night. She would never have left the place like this if she'd come back first.' He clenched his fists in a sudden spasm. 'She must have been snatched en route, that's the only explanation.'

As he spoke, the control-room's observation message regarding Kate's disappearance blasted from Roscoe's radio and at the same time they heard the thud of rotor blades approaching. Dashing out of the cottage, they saw the police helicopter almost skimming the tops of the hedgerows as it sped towards them, like some giant flying bug. Seconds later it was hovering over them.

'I've got to get up in that,' Lewis exclaimed.

Roscoe shook his head. 'No way headquarters ops will allow it,' he said. 'They'll have their own trained observer on board.'

Lewis took a deep breath. 'Listen,' he said earnestly, 'I know Kate's car. I'd recognize it straightaway – even without the number. I've got to *do something*, for goodness sake!'

Roscoe studied him for a moment, chewing furiously, then moved away to speak into his radio. As he'd expected, he received an immediate refusal to the request, but the next instant Ansell's hard clinical voice cut through the radio traffic, overturning the decision. The formidable DCI had no intention of allowing anything to interfere with the search for Kate Hamblin and no one was prepared to argue with him.

Fixing a rendezvous in a nearby field, Lewis found himself airborne within half an hour of the argument, and as the machine banked sharply towards Glastonbury Tor's phallic-like spire and the vast expanse of the Levels spread out far below, it suddenly dawned on him just how much the odds were stacked against them. It would be dark before long and he knew instinctively that if they didn't find Kate before then, they were likely to be doomed to failure – and the consequences of that didn't even bear thinking about.

Phil Sharp was fast losing his bottle – and his bravado with it. Sitting once again in the police interview room, across the table from Ansell and a grim-faced Roscoe, who had only just got back from the negative search of Kate's house, he continually licked his lips and darted frequent glances at his two ashen-faced interrogators with mounting apprehension.

The news that Kate Hamblin had disappeared – almost certainly snatched by the killer – should have pleased him, but it didn't, despite his earlier desire to see her written off. He sensed he was in even bigger trouble now than he had been before and he was desperately racking his brains for a way out.

'I want my solicitor back here,' he blurted out eventually.

Ansell leaned forward, his eyes like gimlets. 'Sod your solicitor,' he grated. 'I need some answers and you're going to give me them now.'

'I don't have to tell you anything,' Sharp prevaricated.'

'Listen to me, you little shit,' Ansell continued, 'we've got a police officer missing and there's every chance of her turning up dead if we don't find her soon. I've got enough on you already to have you sent down for three to five and, if she dies, I'll make damned sure you get life as an accessory.'

Sharp's jaw dropped. 'You can't do that. I've had nothing to do with her disappearance,' he protested. 'I was in here anyway when she went AWOL.'

'You could still have planned it with Twister,' Roscoe cut in. 'Don't forget what we said before. Naomi Betjeman snuffed it after a visit from you – maybe you've been helping Twister out with Kate, the same as you did with Naomi?'

'That's bloody ridiculous.'

'Is it?' Ansell resumed. 'I reckon we'll have little difficulty convincing a jury of the fact. It all dovetails neatly. Why otherwise would you withhold vital information?'

'Yeah,' Roscoe added, 'and why would any self-respecting copper be driving around late at night carrying a loaded shooter? You were obviously up to no good.'

Sharp shook his head desperately. 'You've got it all wrong. I had the gun for protection.'

'Protection against whom?'

The former DS hesitated, gnawing at his lip. Then abruptly he took a deep breath and blurted, 'I was going to bring Twister in.'

'Bring Twister in?' Roscoe echoed. 'Don't make me laugh. You wouldn't have the guts to bring in a one-legged nun.'

'It's the truth,' Sharp insisted hotly, even beginning to believe the lie himself and conveniently forgetting that it had been his intention to blackmail Twister rather than to arrest him. 'If I hadn't been stopped, he would be in the pokey by now.'

Ansell silenced Roscoe's next disparaging remark with a wave of his hand. 'We've wasted enough time on this already, Sharp,' he rapped. 'So, game over; tell us what we need to know right now.'

'Deal first,' Sharp said, still sticking to his stubborn line, even though he was now quaking in his shoes.

Ansell shot to his feet so quickly – almost knocking over his chair in the process – that even Roscoe jumped. 'I'll tell you what the deal is,' he hissed, thrusting his face so close to Sharp that the latter drew back from him with a sharp cry. 'You either open up or when you are sent down, I'll make sure every con in stir knows you were a copper. Be interesting to see how long it will be before someone sticks something sharp between your shoulder-blades while you're taking a shower.'

'All right, *all right*!' Sharp almost shrieked, cracking at last. 'It's Norton, Doctor bloody Norton – Twister is Norton.'

'What?' For a few moments Ansell seemed to freeze where he stood. 'That's not possible,' he breathed and he dropped back heavily into his chair, as if his legs were no longer able to support him. Even Roscoe looked transfixed, his mouth hanging open and the bubble from his gum collapsed over his lip like a deflated parachute.

Sharp's arrogance surfaced again for a moment. 'Oh it's not only possible, it's fact,' he sneered. 'Bloody good detectives you were – the bastard has been running the whole thing from inside the inquiry team itself and you didn't have a clue.'

Roscoe lunged forward and grabbed Sharp by his shirt collar, hauling him out of his seat and halfway across the table. His closed meat-hook of a fist would have practically taken Sharp's head off his shoulders if Ansell had not grabbed his wrist.

'Enough!' the DCI rasped, forcing the DI to release his grip and let the other slump back in his chair. 'Get on with it, Sharp or by heaven, I'll leave Roscoe in here with you!'

Sharp was visibly shaking now and he rubbed his neck tenderly where Roscoe's knuckles had grazed the skin. 'OK, OK,' he muttered hastily, 'I'm telling you, aren't I?' He swallowed hard and, scowling at the DI, rubbed some saliva from his lips on to the back of his hand. 'Before she snuffed it, Betjeman told me she had sussed that Twister and Norton were both the same person. Twister's bloody awful perfume was the first thing that had given him away apparently, although she hadn't twigged the connection between the stuff Norton had had on and the scent the man who had attacked her was wearing until later. Twister's second mistake was to take his glasses off during the interview to clean the lenses, exposing those weird eyes of his.

'When she did some research on a follow-up story at The Tribune's archives that night, she saw a mug-shot of Twister in an old newspaper report and not only made the visual connection, but remembered the perfume as well. I … I was able to find out Norton's address and was on my way there when I was stopped.'

'We've really been had, haven't we?' Roscoe commented savagely. 'The stiff at the reserve was obviously Norton's work – which explains the abandoned flask – so Twister must have taken on the doctor's identity completely. He has probably even been holed up in the poor sod's house ever since.'

Ansell shot to his feet again. 'Get a team over to Norton's house pronto,' he exclaimed, then, glaring at Sharp, he added, 'And in the meantime, this *thing* can be stuck back in the cell where it belongs.'

Calling in the uniformed constable who had been left standing outside the door of the interview room, the DCI headed for the stairs at an uncharacteristic trot, but he was only halfway up before he ran straight into a flustered Willoughby coming down.

'No reply from Doctor Norton's house,' Willoughby exclaimed breathlessly, 'but one of the late turn has just been upstairs in response to the circulation about Kate Hamblin. He says he was on nights last night and, just before he went off, he saw Kate talking to Doctor Norton in the yard. He thinks they must have gone off together in Kate's Mazda, as they were both gone when he nipped out to his car again and Norton's Merc was still parked there. What the hell's going on?'

Ansell pushed past him. 'That figures,' he snapped. 'Tell you about it after I've grabbed my car keys.'

Willoughby gaped after him. 'Your car keys?' he echoed. 'So where on earth are we going?'

'To try to prevent another murder,' the DCI said, 'but I think we may already be too late.'

CHAPTER 35

The police helicopter was running out of options. The mist, which had been clearing steadily for a couple of hours, was once more drifting back in spectral patches, joining with the dusk to blot out large tracts of countryside, and, despite sweep after sweep of the Levels, there had been no sign of Kate's Mazda.

'Be zero visibility soon,' the pilot observed. 'Might as well pack this in now.'

'Just one more sweep,' Lewis pleaded, 'please, just one more.'

And it was as the helicopter banked sharply to swing back towards Glastonbury Tor's fading sentinel that they saw the Land Rover – a green canvas topped vehicle – bumping through the mist along a narrow drove in the direction of Burtle.

'Take us down to check that out,' Lewis said sharply.

'Thought you were looking for a Mazda MX5?' the official observer snapped, obviously still feeling peeved over the detective's usurpation of his role.

'Just a hunch,' Lewis retorted, leaning forward to peer through the nose of the helicopter's glass cockpit. 'Maybe Twister has changed vehicles.'

'Yeah,' the observer retorted. 'Then maybe we should also have checked out the couple of dozen buses, rigids and artics we clocked earlier?'

The sarcasm was lost on Lewis. He was too engrossed in his scrutiny of the Land Rover, now just feet below them.

'Obviously a farm wagon,' the pilot commented, switching on the helicopter's powerful Nite Sun searchlight and grinning as the Land Rover swerved slightly under the downdraught of the machine and a hand appeared out of the driver's window, giving them an obscene sign. 'But I don't think we've made any new friends by checking him out.'

'Something suspicious here, I can feel it in my water,' Lewis commented.

'Feel what you like,' the pilot replied, switching off the searchlight, 'but I'm taking her up anyway.'

The machine had only just begun its ascent when the radio call came through from the police control room with the stunning news about Norton and directing the chopper to the deceased's home near Wedmore, just a stone's throw from their present position.

'I'll put you down in that field behind the house,' the pilot told Lewis seconds later. 'Hope you're good at climbing gates.'

The convoy of flashing blue lights was already converging on the house as the helicopter began its descent and Lewis had only just sprinted across the field to the five-barred gate, when the first of the police cars raced past and swung into the driveway of Norton's isolated property on the opposite side of the adjacent lane.

Lewis trotted into a cacophony of slamming doors, blasting radios and barking dogs – temporarily blinded by a surreal blaze of pulsing red and blue strobes – as he pushed through the confusion of uniformed bodies and parked patrol cars to the front door of the house.

He heard the door go in under the swing of the police ram before he got there and he followed the armed team into the now lighted hallway, brushing aside a couple of his colleagues who tried to stop him. But it was all too late; after a thorough search of the house and grounds, the place proved to be completely empty.

It was only when he was stumbling back out into the driveway that he heard the loud yell. 'Hayden, over here.' The doors to the garage stood wide open and the interior lights came on even before he got to them.

'Is this hers?' Roscoe demanded, his pork-pie hat askew on his bullet head and his heavy jowls working hard on his chewing gum.

Lewis clutched at the door frame for support. The blue Mazda was parked inside – nose first – and he recognized the number immediately.

'It's OK,' Ansell rapped from the other end of the garage, 'Kate's not here. ' He paused. 'But unfortunately something else is.'

Lewis walked slowly, hesitantly towards his boss, dreading what he might find, then froze just a few feet from him.

The woman was obviously dead, and her body had been strung up by the ankles from a cross member of the roof frame like a stuck pig, a savage gash in her throat and the pool of blood beneath indicating that her throat had been cut. Just feet away, a discarded shotgun lay beside a bale of straw, broken open like a snapped leg, sinister, but useless. Roz Callow may have had the upper hand when she had confronted Twister, but she had still ended up dead!

Twister had seen the police helicopter seconds before it zoomed in on him, shaking the Land Rover violently and causing him to over-steer briefly. He was not that concerned about being spotted. He knew the crew wouldn't be able to identify him from overhead and Kate was well out of sight already trussed up and insensible in the back.

He had employed his usual pressure point technique on her straight after killing Roz Callow and a quick injection while she was unconscious had made sure she would stay that way – at least for a few hours anyway. He couldn't have felt more confident about passing police scrutiny and it was in a surge of exuberance that he had made his obscene gesture to the chopper overhead, reasoning that they would not expect a fugitive to be so brazen as to do that.

It worked too and, as the helicopter rose into the darkening heavens again before thudding away across the Levels, he grinned to himself. Everything was going so well, despite Roz Callow's brief intervention, and he relived her last moments in his mind with a deep sense of satisfaction, while he negotiated the labyrinth of droves and tracks towards his ultimate destination just a few miles away.

The silly cow had obviously not known much about shotguns. Fancy trying to fire the thing using one arm and with the stock resting against her hip of all places. The recoil itself must have done her some real mischief. It had literally blown her off her feet, piling the shot into the roof of the barn instead of into him. He hadn't given her the opportunity to reload, but had been on to her even before she could regain her feet, snapping her neck in a second. He had only slit her throat and strung her up from the roof of the barn for effect – she was already dead by then.

Yeah, he was on course for a really brilliant finale to his endgame. Nothing could stop him now and by the early hours he would be en route to the safe house in Manchester that he had already organized, with the prospect of a flight out of the country to look forward to in a month. OK, so it was tempting to blow immediately after the job, but that would have been stupid. Patience was always his watchword. People got nicked because they rushed into things. The trick was to lie low and wait for the heat of the police hunt to dissipate and the imposition of the inevitable 'all ports' warning to be relaxed. Then it was a case of 'Rio, here I come', he mused. Brilliant.

'So now what?' Lewis said bitterly, watching two uniformed police officers fixing the blue and white 'police crime scene' tapes across the garage doorway as he digested Roscoe's information about Norton. He was trembling slightly and his eyes had the wide-eyed look of someone very close to the edge.

Roscoe made a face. 'We've called out SOCO, so they should be here within the hour—' he began.

'SOCO?' Lewis stormed. 'I don't give a damn about SOCO. What about Kate? She's out there somewhere in the clutches of a madman.'

'We're doing everything we can,' Willoughby joined in hesitantly. 'Half the district is out looking for her. She's bound to be located before long.'

Lewis laughed, a cracked unnatural sound. 'Yes, but in what condition?' he retorted. 'She's probably already lying dead in a ditch somewhere.'

'I doubt that very much,' Ansell spoke at his elbow. 'Midnight is several hours away yet.'

'Midnight?' Lewis exclaimed. 'You don't seriously believe all that the nonsense Twister fed us in his guise as Doctor Norton is still relevant, do you? It was all a con to put us off the scent.'

Ansell shook his head. 'I disagree. Twister may have been leading us up the garden path as our so-called adviser throughout much of the inquiry, but I reckon his claim that Kate will be executed at midnight – the exact moment when the surveillance van was blown apart two years ago – was legit.'

'And why the devil would he reveal something so critical to his own sick plan?'

Ansell studied him fixedly in the light streaming out of the garage. 'For the same reason that he was so keen to provide us with what I think was such a candid profile of himself,' he said. 'He sees all this as a contest – and it bolsters his ego to drip-feed us with the necessary information all the way through, with the intention of pulling the rug out from under us at the final moment, thus proving his superiority. But, as he himself revealed at one of the briefings in a rather stupid Freudian slip, arrogance is his Achilles heel and that's what we will use against him now.'

Lewis snorted. 'And exactly how will that work?' he blazed, heedless of rank or anything else in his impotent fury. 'We don't have the slightest idea where he has taken Kate or even what vehicle he is using.'

'I might be able to help there, Hayden,' another voice cut in. Jimmy Noble had obviously overheard what Lewis was saying – along with half the officers at the scene, in fact – and he steered the detective by the elbow to the garage doors.

'See that,' he said and pointed. Two wheels with thick heavy tyres stood against one wall, alongside a badly dented metal wing. 'Norton had two vehicles – the Merc that Twister left at the nick, and another motor, which was obviously parked there,' and he pointed at a heavy oil stain on the concrete floor. 'And, looking at those wheels and the shape and colour of that damaged wing, I'm willing to bet that the other vehicle was an old green Land Rover.'

For a moment Lewis simply stared at the oil stain as if Noble had drawn his attention to another corpse, his mind in shocked paralysis, as he remembered the green Land Rover he had spotted from the police helicopter. 'Hell's bells!' he choked, finally shaking off his numbing mental blanket, 'I let it go – I let the damned thing go!'

Grabbing Noble by the shoulders, he shook him fiercely. 'Where's your car?' he shouted. 'We must get after them. There may still be time.'

Noble looked bewildered. 'I … I'm boxed in,' he said, his gaze roving quickly around the jam of police cars, 'I can't go anywhere.'

'What's all this about?' Ansell demanded, striding over to them.

But Lewis was in no mood for explanations. Pushing his boss roughly aside, he sprinted between the vehicles to a traffic car, parked, with its engine running, in the mouth of the driveway. Flinging the driver's door wide and ignoring the shouts of the crew as they ran back towards him from the house, he engaged gear and reversed at speed out through the gateway of the property, clipped the far verge, then pulled away like a madman along the lane towards the main road, fish-tailing dangerously as he went.

Behind him he left pandemonium as other police cars, one with Roscoe and Ansell aboard, tried to extricate themselves from the mêlée of vehicles with a blaring of horns and the crunch of metal. Even when Roscoe finally found a way through and raced towards the open gateway into the lane, a big SOCO van swung in through the entrance, followed closely by a police dog van, blocking them in again. Roscoe was still remonstrating with the SOCO driver as the deep, misty dusk of the Levels swallowed Lewis whole.

CHAPTER 36

Kate surfaced through a clammy mist, conscious of a raging thirst, a splitting headache and an inability to see anything, save distorted white blobs that constantly expanded and shrank in front of her, like spectral amoeba. As the waves of nausea that had accompanied her awakening began to subside and her vision steadied, she began to focus on her surroundings – and immediately to doubt her own sanity.

She was in a small room, held in the glare of powerful spotlights placed at one end, which prevented her seeing beyond their blazing orbs. Her wrists were secured by sticky black tape to the arms of what appeared to be a leather swivel chair, which was bolted to the floor. She frowned. No, it wasn't a room, but the rear of some kind of van or lorry – she could now see that the walls, roof and floor were made of spray-painted grey steel and there were double doors at the opposite end to the spotlights, which were tightly closed, plus a further side door a few feet to the left of her chair. Directly in front of her, a laptop computer, fitted with an external camera pointing directly at her and linked to what looked like a DVR, occupied a square pedestal and there were two more swivel chairs, one fixed to the floor to the left of the pedestal and the other to the right – both just a few feet away. Each of the other two chairs was occupied by a sinister looking figure wearing a woollen coat and she had actually opened her mouth to speak to one of them before she realized that neither of them were people at all, but clothed shop mannequins.

Then something else, something crazy and totally unbelievable, dawned on her. She was in the back of a Ford Transit van and she had been here before – not in this particular vehicle, but in one very much like it; one that had been similarly furnished and fitted with electronic equipment, much like the kit in front of her. The next moment her gaze focused on one of the mannequins, seated like some grotesque Frankenstein creation, to her right. 'Strewth, it had long blond hair, just like …

She tried to get a grip on herself. What sort of sick joke was this? Someone had deliberately recreated the interior of the police surveillance van that had been blasted apart two years before – and that someone could only be one person.

'Hello, Kate? Comfy then?' The mocking voice issued from the computer and, staring at the screen, she suddenly saw it had illuminated under some form of remote activation and Twister's cold expressionless face was staring straight at her. Meeting the gaze of those corpse-like fish eyes, she felt a chill spread through her body that deadened her limbs and seeped into her brain.

'Bring back a few memories in there, does it?' Twister went on and his chuckle had about as much warmth as that of a Dalek. 'I have gone to an awful lot of trouble to try to set it up as you'd remember it – and I must admit, the old crime file I was given access to was a lot of help in that respect.'

'What *is* all this?' Kate said, her voice strangely hoarse. 'It doesn't make sense.'

He shook his head and tutted. 'Oh, but I think it makes perfect sense,' he went on. 'You see, you should have died in the incendiary blast all that time ago. It's not right that your two colleagues, Detective Sergeant Andy Seldon and Detective Constable Alf Cross, should have been incinerated while you got off scot-free, not right at all. So I decided to rectify my previous *faux pas* by recreating the original scenario on the two year anniversary of the event – couldn't get back here before, I'm afraid – to give you the opportunity of joining your old chums.'

'You're totally out of your tree,' she blurted incredulously, desperately trying to control her shakes. 'A … a complete nutter.'

Twister smiled. 'Depends what you mean by the term nutter, Kate,' he said. 'If you are suggesting that I am insane, I beg to disagree, for that description conjures up visions of a dribbling imbecile paddling in the toilet or eating his own faeces, and I do none of those things. I do accept, however, that I have a personality disorder – I have been told that by the best psychiatrists around, so it must be true. This gives rise to certain psychopathic tendencies, but such traits merely make me different to the normal run of society and insanity doesn't enter into it.'

'You're going to *blow me up* in here?' Kate said, her voice now little above a whisper.

Another series of tuts. 'Oh, that's a rather crude way of putting it, my dear, but, in essence, I suppose you're right. Just like before, I have assembled a powerful incendiary device to precipitate you into oblivion, although I have simplified things this time so that it can be inserted into the petrol filler pipe itself, rather than being magnetically attached to the vehicle – bit like a pipe bomb, actually. This one, though, is much more sophisticated and will be detonated by a remote wireless signal, which I can despatch myself from a safe distance by means of a micro transmitter.'

He held up a narrow cylindrical object in front of the screen, which was about eight inches in length, with a wired attachment at one end, then put it down carefully and held up another item, not unlike an electronic pager.

'Clever, isn't it?' he said. 'And soon we will drive out to the very same drove you used two years ago. It will be quite a nostalgic experience for us both and the best part about it all is that, due to the technical expertise I gained in the army, I have been able to set up an equally sophisticated surveillance system that will allow me to watch the whole thing as it is actually happening inside the vehicle from my own ringside seat out here.'

Kate raised her head and tried to swivel the chair, guessing that there were other cameras trained on her from the shadows, but the chair would not budge – it seemed to be fixed in some way – so she was unable to pick them out.

'At least you'll have some company in your final moments,' Twister gloated, 'and I did try to make my mannequins look as much like your old colleagues as possible. Detective Sergeant Seldon's long fair hair was a particular characteristic and I went to a lot of trouble to obtain the right sort of wig. Good, isn't it?'

'You grotesque, sick bastard,' she said in reply.

He sighed, but ignored her insults and carried on with his summary. 'Alf Cross? Well, I had to make do there with the same sort of silly woollen hat I gather he liked to wear, as he had no real distinguishing features like Seldon's nice fair hair.'

He smiled again. 'You can see that I've dressed them both in woollen coats over the smart suits the mannequins had on when I stole them from a certain local warehouse and I hope that's how you remember their being dressed at the time. You should be impressed by my attention to detail anyway. I did do a lot of research on your team and on the interior layout of the Transit.

'For instance, you can't see it, but the van's even got the same sign, "Water Monitoring Agency", on the side. So, although I couldn't swear that everything is one hundred percent accurate, I think it's as near as damn it. Only thing I didn't bother with was the surveillance camera you had on the roof, but, I think you'll agree, there's no point in wasting money when everything is soon going to go up in smoke anyway.'

'They'll hunt you down for this, you know that, don't you?'

She saw him shrug. 'They will probably do their best, but they tried that before, didn't they? Got them nowhere then either—' He broke off. 'Oh, I nearly forgot, you'll see a nice digital clock on the pedestal. Thought you might like to keep abreast of the time. Not long until it all happens now. Exciting, isn't it?'

Before she could think of anything else to say, the monitor went blank and his face disappeared. It was 8.00 pm.

The blonde SOCO officer found Ansell in Norton's study, watching one of the fingerprint officers dusting a glass and a nearby empty bottle of Talisker whisky and brooding over the futility of it all.

The DCI was tired, hungry and frustrated after several long hours hanging around the house while the search and technical units did their stuff. At least Willoughby had managed to find an excuse to return to the comfort of the nick, on the pretext of directing the search operation from the control-room, he mused. As DCI, he seemed to have drawn the short straw – yet again.

The daft thing was everyone knew full well who they were looking for and Twister wouldn't care whether they found his dabs at the scene or not. He still had Kate Hamblin and they had absolutely no idea where he could have gone to ground – they didn't even know where Hayden Lewis had disappeared to in the borrowed traffic car. What a bloody awful mess, and to think that the whole inquiry team had actually been hoodwinked into allowing the very psychopath they were looking for to lead them in the hunt for the man himself.

'Yes?' he snapped, sensing the SOCO officer hovering.

'We … er … found a pair of handcuffs attached to a chain in a cellar under the stairs,' she said. 'There's also a mattress down there. Looks like that's where he might have held her.'

The DCI nodded curtly. 'Fat lot of use that information is to us now,' he threw back uncharitably. 'Unless it can tell us where the bastard has gone to ground.' He scowled. 'What I can't understand is why he would bring Kate back here then shoot off somewhere else. Why not go there straight away?'

'I think I might be able to help on that score, Guv,' Roscoe growled, stomping into the room. 'One of the lads found a bundle of clothes in a dirty linen basket upstairs, including,' he added, 'a pair of blue suede shoes.'

'So he came back here to rid himself of Norton's ID,' Ansell said, 'which means we're not looking for a Norton look-alike any more, but possibly Twister as he really is – minus the beard.'

'Plus a green Land Rover with a canvas top, according to Lewis,' Roscoe reminded him. 'Don't forget that.'

Ansell glared at him. 'Which is where exactly? None of the patrols have so far turned it up. And while we ponce about here, Twister just sits it out in his bolt-hole, waiting for midnight.'

'We can only keep looking, Guv,' Roscoe said lamely. 'We've still got several hours to go and I've got every available unit out on the Levels, plus the chopper again, equipped with a searchlight and night vision bins.'

Ansell gave a disparaging snort. 'Great,' he said, 'so all we need now then is a clairvoyant or a bloody miracle!'

As he spoke, he glanced at his wristwatch. It was 9.30 pm.

CHAPTER 37

Lewis was not an advanced driver, neither had he been on one of the force's specialist traffic driving courses, but he was used to tasty vehicles after years of Jaguar ownership and the high performance car he had borrowed was certainly tasty. The trouble was, he had no real idea where he was going. He was sure the green Land Rover he had seen from the police helicopter was the key, but finding the right drove was another story and, even if he did manage to find it, where did he go from there? He could hardly search every house, barn and shed he came across in the hope of striking lucky. But he had to do something and time was fast running out for Kate.

As it was, he drove backwards and forwards along a veritable labyrinth of droves and tracks for what seemed like an eternity, before he found what might have been the right one, catching the front wing of the traffic car on a stony bank and scraping the front and rear passenger doors along a barbed wire fence in the process.

'Slow down,' a voice in his brain warned as he churned along the drove between the silvery lines of twin rhynes like a dragster. He did slow once when a large barn loomed up above the hedgerow on his left and he peered at the tumble-down structure for a brief moment in the light of the newly risen moon before deciding it did not merit closer inspection. A group of isolated farm buildings attracted his attention shortly afterwards and, seeing a Land Rover parked in front of one of them, he went to investigate, but a search of the buildings revealed nothing more than cattle feed and farm machinery and the Land Rover turned out to be an abandoned wreck, tenanted by rats, which fled in the blaze of his torch.

The drove then met a main road, and he braked hard just in time as a Tesco delivery van flashed past, blasting its horn as he almost shot out in front of it. He was starting to hyperventilate, feeling the panic welling up inside him as the futility of what he was doing hit him. Which way did he go now? Treacherous mist clouded the moon and dimmed his headlights. If it got any thicker, he knew he would be stuffed.

In desperation, he turned left towards Mark village and headed back to Highbridge, determined to check the derelict funeral parlour where the police investigation had ended two years ago. He knew it was unlikely that Twister would have chosen somewhere so obvious for his bolt-hole, but he had to make sure anyway. As it transpired, his assumption was spot on: the place was totally deserted, not even the sign of a police presence – just blue and white crime-scene tapes across the entrances stirring creepily in a faint breeze. A complete waste of time.

Returning to the traffic car and heading back to the Levels, he switched on the vehicle's radio again, listening briefly to the transmissions as he drove. Control had been calling him incessantly ever since he had roared away from Norton's house, ordering him to return there at once, and in the end he had turned the radio off. But he realized now that this had been a stupid thing to do. It was vital for him to know what was going on, just in case something turned up. But his change of heart altered nothing. In quick succession he heard the units responding to Control's location checks with negative after negative result. It seemed Kate had vanished off the face of the earth. It was 10.15 pm.

Kate had intended ignoring the digital clock, trying to concentrate her mind instead on coming up with an escape plan, but for some reason her mind seemed sluggish and unresponsive and her gaze was continually drawn to the red numerals grinning at her in silent mockery.

She had already tried to tear herself free from the black tape which bound her wrists to the arms of the chair, but Twister had done too good a job and it didn't give a centimetre. She'd even tried to free the swivel chair from its fixings by a forceful rocking, with the intention of walking it to the rear doors of the Transit, but the legs were bolted too securely to the steel floor of the vehicle and wouldn't budge.

Twister's face appeared on the screen – obviously by means of some remote activation again – in the midst of her futile struggles, deriding her attempts and letting her know that he was keeping a close eye on her. She refused to let him see that she was rattled by his taunts and made a conscious effort not to respond to them. In the end, he seemed to lose interest, but before the screen went blank again, he made sure she was aware of the time displayed by the digital clock. It was 10.28 pm.

Sergeant Daniel Brown – nicknamed Da Vinci, after his famous namesake's best-selling novel, *The Da Vinci Code* – was tired and losing his focus. They had been aloft again in the Eurocopter 135 for close on three hours now without spotting anything of interest and the pilot, Ed Cole, was getting more and more twitchy about the poor visibility and the fact that his fuel was getting low. It was bad enough flying at night, but the ever thickening mist was making things increasingly difficult – as well as a lot more hazardous. The thought of running out of fuel was the sort of thing that nightmares were made of.

'One more sweep, then home,' Cole snapped into his headphones mic. 'Sod what your headquarters wants. I'm not risking our necks any more in this.'

'Sounds good to me,' Brown replied, knocking his own mic with his hand as he stifled a yawn. 'I'm about done anyway.'

In fact, as it turned out, they didn't complete the sweep and ironically, just ten minutes later, it was the pilot who spotted the faint chinks of light in the roof of the building directly below them, not his so-called observer, and he nudged his colleague quickly. 'What's that?'

Brown peered in the direction the pilot had indicated and shrugged. 'Some sort of barn. It may have escaped your notice, but there're quite a few of them dotted around the Levels.'

Cole zoomed in closer, switching on the chopper's powerful searchlight. 'Yeah, maybe,' he said, ignoring the sarcasm, 'but lit up inside? That seems a bit strange.'

Brown took another look. 'No lights as far as I can see,' he retorted. 'Place looks derelict – like the farmhouse next to it.'

Cole frowned, seeing that the place was now in complete darkness. 'Well, there were lights on just now. I'm sure of it.'

Brown chuckled. 'You're losing it, Ed. The old eyes are going. Anyway, I don't see a Land Rover parked there – or any other vehicle for that matter. Place looks deserted. Probably just ghosts.'

Cole shrugged, switched off the spotlight and took them up again. 'Ghosts or not, better report it anyway,' he said, 'just in case.'

'Do that when we get back,' his colleague replied. 'I'm bloody starving and if we tell them over the air, we'll be kept here for the next hour till the troops can check it out. Waste of bloody time anyway, if you ask me.'

As the helicopter's flashing navigation light disappeared in the swirls of mist, Twister, standing motionless in the darkness of the barn, got up to switch on his portable spotlights again. Then, returning to the box in front of his computer, which served as a makeshift seat, he sat down and drank some more coffee from his mug. In the Transit van parked just feet away from him, Kate heard the fading sound of the machine with a sense of despair. It was 11.06 pm.

Lewis was in the process of negotiating a sharp bend in the mist-shrouded road he was following when he saw the helicopter swoop in overhead and train its searchlight on something to his right. Pulling into a gateway, he peered through gaps in the swirling moonlit tinged clouds to try and catch a glimpse of what could have attracted their attention. But after dropping to within what must have been just a hundred feet of the ground, the searchlight was extinguished and the machine's flashing navigation light faded into the murk as it thudded away across the desolate farmland in the direction of Bristol.

What the hell had they seen? It couldn't have been a positive sighting of anything, otherwise there would have been an alert over the air on the police radio, but they had spent several minutes hovering above a particular spot, obviously scrutinizing something, so it must have been worth a look in the first place.

Frowning, he pulled out again, keeping his speed right down this time and throwing frequent glances over the low skeletal hedgerows as he carefully steered the car between the treacherous rhynes bordering the road on each side.

He saw the flicker of light a few minutes later – a ghostly iridescence which showed itself only briefly in the murk before being swallowed up again. Veering across the road up on to the grass verge, he slithered to a stop and clambered out on to the verge, where he stood for a moment, waiting for the clouds of vapour to clear. He didn't have to wait long and he stiffened when the farmhouse suddenly materialized several hundred yards away across an open field, chinks of light showing through the roof of a large barn at its rear.

The place was supposed to be derelict – and he knew that for a fact, because it had suddenly dawned on him exactly where he had ended up, and he felt his body chill as his mind peeled back the years. He remembered with horrible clarity the burned out police surveillance van; the sweet stench of cremated flesh thrusting its way through the smell of burned rubber and fabric and scorched steel. He knew without investigating further that the drove, which had seen the incineration of his colleagues two years before, cut through the field on the other side of the buildings he was looking at. This had been the very property the police surveillance crew had been targeting when they had been murdered: the home of serial arsonist, Terry Duval.

Duval was long since dead, of course – wasted by police marksmen who had believed him to be armed when they had confronted him – and, as far as Lewis was aware, the farm had been empty ever since. Yet the spectral glow hovering over the roof of the barn was unmistakable and even when the mist swirled back in front of him to repair its tattered skeins, he stood there motionless and disbelieving.

Surely Twister wouldn't have had the nerve to haul Kate back to the scene of his original crime? Like the funeral parlour Lewis had just visited, that would have been much too obvious a move. Yet when Ansell had initiated his area search, it did not seem to have occurred to him to prioritize the Duval place. Maybe he hadn't considered it, *because* it was so obvious. Knowing Twister, however, this was exactly the sort of brazen thing he would do – and it made sense for the psychopath to want to finish his so-called game on the anniversary of Operation Firetrap at the very spot where the whole awful business had begun.

The detective's throat was dry and his hands were shaking as he grabbed his torch and scrambled out of the car.

Not even bothering to shut his car door, he trotted down the road a few yards until he found a gap in the hedge, with wooden planks bridging the rhyne to a chained-up gate.

He realized he could be wasting more valuable time checking the property out. There could be any number of reasons why the barn was lit up the way it was and Twister could be holding Kate somewhere miles away, but he had to find out for certain and there was a familiar cold twist in his gut that he knew he dare not ignore. It was only after he had clambered over the gate and was heading diagonally across the field that he remembered he had left his police radio in the car and had no means of calling for assistance. But there was no way he could go back, for time was already running out for Kate – and it was then that he came face to face with the massive black bull! It was 11.15 pm.

CHAPTER 38

'Time to go, Kate.' Twister's face was back on the screen, his expression bleak.'

Kate simply stared at him, her eyes vacant and seemingly lacking in comprehension and her vocal chords frozen with the kind of shock-induced paralysis that comes with the approach of imminent death. She had expended so much energy trying to free herself from the swivel chair, that she had reached exhaustion point and an almost fatalistic acceptance of the inevitable. Her wrists were raw and bloodied and she had cut her thigh through her trousers on a sharp piece of plastic packing material still attached to the underside of her seat. Although her wounds had now dried a little, blood had spattered all around her chair and she had vomited on the floor on one side.

'I've never actually witnessed a live cremation,' Twister went on with brutal indifference. 'Not even poor old Pauline's. It should be quite interesting, though I would think the initial blast and resultant dismemberment might spoil the ultimate action of the flames.' He gave a brief smile. 'Still, we shall have to see, shan't we?'

Then the screen went blank and, as if from afar, Kate heard what sounded like the heavy wooden doors of a barn scrape open. Moments later the Transit shook as a door slammed at the front of the van and a heavy engine burst into life. They were moving, slowly at first, but gathering speed over a rough bumpy surface that sent stones clanging up under the vehicle.

The tears were rolling down Kate's face now. She had tried so hard to be brave and resolute; tried so hard not to give Twister any satisfaction, but the pretence was over now. She was going to die – at 28 years of age – going to be ripped to pieces by a powerful explosive charge and shards of torn metal and all she could hope for was that her end would be quick. Unable to stop herself, she raised her head to look at the digital clock and saw that it was 11.22 pm.

Lewis had never been so close to a bull before and, distorted by the action of the mist, it seemed even bigger and more ferocious than it probably was in reality. Either way, it was big enough for him and he turned and fled from the thing, heading in the direction of the now barely visible derelict farmhouse as fast as he could manage, his feet sinking deep into the sodden ground and making loud sucking noises with each extraction. Once he looked behind him and saw that the animal was coming after him, not in a charge, but more in the form of a lumbering gait, its curiosity obviously aroused and its aggression no doubt mounting by the second.

He reached the far side of the field within a few yards – only to find further progress blocked by another four to five foot wide rhyne, separating the field from the derelict property on the other side. When he turned to glance behind him, he saw that the bull was right there too, some three to four yards behind him, snorting, tossing its head and pawing the ground.

Then the mist came to his aid, swirling in between them, drowning everything in a clammy white sea. He veered sharply to his left, hoping the bull would lose track of him, but there it was again, a sinister black shadow emerging from the gloom directly in front of him. He backtracked, as he thought – although it was difficult to tell in the gloom – but seconds later the animal was lumbering towards him from his right, forcing him to duck back into the mist.

For several anxious minutes, he played a spooky game of hide-and-seek with the animal, which, despite constant changes in his direction, always seemed to sense where he was heading and block his path.

At one stage he thought he heard a vehicle making its way through the mist a few hundred yards away, its wheels churning into a loose gravelly surface, but he couldn't see a thing. What if it was Twister, leaving the barn? Maybe the helicopter had spooked him or he had glimpsed Lewis's own approach in the patrol car? On the other hand, what if the ruthless psychopath had not been using the barn at all and, while Lewis was playing silly games with the bull, he was actually somewhere else, waiting for the appointed hour to snap poor little Kate's neck? The detective felt panic welling up inside him. It had to be nearly midnight.

Then he saw the gate – standing there on the edge of the rhyne – looking incongruous, unattached as it was to adjoining fences, but obviously giving access to a bridge of some sort linking the two fields. In desperation he went for it, but so did the bull, just feet away now to his right. The darned thing had to be telepathic.

He reached the gate seconds before the now enraged creature and, without checking to see if the gate was locked or not, he leaped for it, fingers scrabbling at the wooden bars as he literally threw himself over, the torch flying from his hand ahead of him and pitching into the rhyne with a dull 'plop'.

He almost made it too, although not entirely, and one wicked curved horn caught his left trouser leg ripping the material apart and gouging his calf. But then he was on the other side, stumbling to his knees, jerking upright almost immediately and limping away from the gate across a grass bridge, teeth gritted against the pain in his torn calf as something wet and sticky streamed down his leg into his sock.

Throwing one final glance behind him, he caught a brief glimpse of the bull, snorting and stamping its feet on the other side of the gate as it raked its lethal horns against the frail rotten wood. Then the mist closed in again, blotting it out completely – at which point the spookily lit barn loomed up in front of him. It was now 11.26 pm.

PC Noble was feeling the strain. He had been behind the wheel of his patrol car in the hunt for Kate and her ruthless kidnapper for several hours without a break; eyes glued to the windscreen as he peered through the swirling mist, looking for anything and everything, yet not absolutely clear what that thing was. He had checked any number of wayside barns and other buildings during his lengthy patrol, but had found nothing, save farm machinery and rotting, evil-smelling straw. He had also pulled over three canvas topped Land Rovers and a couple of closed vans, but with a similar negative result. Now, tired and disillusioned, he was on the verge of admitting defeat and returning to Highbridge police station for a much needed break.

It was at that moment that the big traffic car, with its roof strobe and blue and yellow checked bodywork gleaming with moisture in his headlamps, appeared directly ahead of him, parked at an angle on the right-hand grass verge.

Frowning, he swung in behind it and climbed out of his patrol car. The traffic car was unlocked, the driver's door not properly shut, but there was no sign of anyone. He quickly checked the fleet number displayed inside and radioed the control-room with his location. After a brief pause, the message came back, advising him that the vehicle was the one Hayden Lewis had purloined from Norton's house and he felt his heart begin to race. 'Then you'd better get the troops out here pronto,' he radioed back. 'I think he might be in trouble.'

Almost immediately, over a dozen police vehicles, one containing Ansell and Roscoe, began converging on the scene, the firearms team had also been alerted and the force helicopter scrambled again. Lewis was about to receive all the back-up he could possibly need, but the problem was – would it arrive in time? It was 11.30 pm.

Moonlight. It came out suddenly and unexpectedly, bathing the scene in opalescent light and sending the mist streaking away into the night, as if it had been sucked back into the marshy ground. Lewis stopped short to throw a swift glance up into its eye-twisting brilliance, conscious of the fact that he was in the middle of the field and clearly visible from the barn. Lurching forward, he headed for the ramshackle building at a limping run, stopping only when he was in its shadow, panting heavily with the exertion and stifling the groan that rose to his lips from the pain in his still bleeding leg.

Silence. Not a sound from inside the barn, but, with a start, he noticed a Ford Transit van parked on the drove on the other side of the field. His mind flashed back to that time two years ago when another Transit had been parked there – burned out and reeking of cremated human flesh. He gritted his teeth and tore his gaze away from the vehicle. 'Keep focused, Hayden,' a voice in his brain rapped. 'Stay with it!'

He eased himself along the wall until he reached the barn doors. He was surprised to find them standing ajar and his heart took a dive. It was hardly likely Twister would be so careless. He was on the wrong track; he had to be – this was just a wild goose chase.

He peered through the gap, expecting to see nothing more sinister than a tractor or stacked bales of hay, but he got a big surprise. He was presented instead with something that resembled a professional workshop – with a workbench at the end, littered with a variety of tools and other materials. Of even more interest, was a portable table set against the left-hand wall, carrying a laptop computer, fitted with two external cameras – one pointing into the room and the other at a small square hole that had been cut into the adjacent wall – and connected to a DVR and other electronic kit. Unusual equipment for a derelict barn, but the thing that really held his attention was the green canvas-topped Land Rover parked nose in to his right and for a moment he just stared at the vehicle, as if mesmerized. Eureka, he had struck oil!

Pulling one of the doors open a little further, he pushed through, standing there for a few moments, scanning the interior in the light of four free-standing spotlights. So far so good, but where was Twister and, even more importantly, where the hell was Kate?

Then he noticed that the computer screen was illuminated, suggesting someone had been using it not so long ago. Curious, he took a closer look and that was when – in an agonizing heart-stopping moment – he saw Kate. She was sitting in a swivel chair of some sort, facing the screen, her wrists apparently lashed to the arms of the chair and her body sagging forward, allowing her shoulder-length auburn hair to tumble over her face.

'Kate,' he gasped hoarsely even though he knew she couldn't hear him. 'Hang in there, old girl – just hang in there!'

Straightening up, he threw wild panic-stricken glances around the barn, searching for a further door, giving access to another room, but it was patently obvious that there wasn't one; there wasn't even a loft. So where the devil was Kate being held then? The derelict house maybe? It had to be. But even as he turned towards the barn doors, he skidded to an abrupt halt, his attention drawn to the other camera which had been set up with its lens directed at the small square hole in the wall. In spite of his panic to find Kate, the presence and position of the camera jarred on his senses and he bent down to peer through the eyepiece.

To his surprise, the Transit van he had spotted on the nearby drove earlier practically filled the view-finder. In fact, the camera's tele-photo lens brought the vehicle up so close that it appeared to be actually parked on the other side of the barn wall. It revealed something else too – an oblong sign attached to the side of the vehicle, bearing the words 'Water Monitoring Agency'.

Something stirred in his memory, something critical, but for a few seconds he just couldn't draw it out. He straightened up, frowning. Why was that sign so significant? What had a water monitoring agency to do with Kate? Bending down again, he adjusted the focus and noticed that the flap of the petrol filler cap on the Transit was wide open and that there was a strange looking tubular object projecting from the pipe. Abruptly realization dawned with a sickening thud and, as icy fingernails trailed down his backbone, he swung for the doors.

Water Monitoring Agency. That had been the cover for the crew in Operation Firetrap. Now he knew exactly what Twister intended to do with Kate. Not for her the usual method of execution – the bastard had planned a repeat performance of the horrendous crime he had committed in that same spot two years before and, quickly glancing at his watch, Lewis saw that his beloved Kate had just minutes left to live!

And that was when things got even more complicated. Hearing a faint sound behind him, he turned quickly and came face to face with Twister. It was 11.52 pm.

CHAPTER 39

'How nice of you to join us,' Twister said, treating Lewis to a cold smile. 'And the show is just about to start too.'

He looked off-guard and relaxed, but Lewis was not deceived. He knew from past experience how quickly the ex-SAS man could move and how tough he was in a physical confrontation. He would stand little chance against him, yet he had to do something before it was too late.

'You're weighing up your chances, I think,' the psychopath went on. He tutted and shook his head. 'No contest, I'm afraid – as you found out once before, if I recall correctly.'

Twister's smile broadened and he produced a small oblong device from his pocket that resembled an electronic pager. 'And with this I hold all the aces anyway.'

Before Lewis could do anything, he flicked open a flap with his thumb and pressed something.

'It's been activated now, you see,' he said, holding the device up to display a flashing red light. 'All it needs is just one little press of a button and a signal will be sent to a receiver on the explosive charge I have only just finished inserting in the petrol filler pipe of the Transit. Then it's Guy Fawkes Night all over again, but, just in case your colleagues miss the show, I have ensured that the DVR here will capture everything in glorious colour, as it happens. Now, wasn't that thoughtful of me?'

'Let her go,' Lewis blurted hoarsely. 'She's done nothing to you.'

Twister sighed. 'I'm afraid it's too late for that, Hayden – may I call you that? I've invested too much in this little operation to abandon it now and besides, poor little Katie is a loose end from my past debacle and I don't like loose ends – so untidy.'

Lewis caught sight of the time registered in the corner of the computer screen. It was four minutes to midnight. He tensed his muscles, preparing to launch himself at his antagonist in a last ditch effort, knowing in his heart of hearts that it was pointless, but desperately hoping he could somehow gain the advantage.

'Your call, Hayden,' Twister said softly, sensing what Lewis had in mind, and giving him another cold smile. 'What have you got to lose?'

It was the thudding blades of the approaching helicopter that changed the dynamics of the situation, for the noise provided a brief distraction and that was just enough. Even though Twister must have known that he would not be able to see anything through the roof of the barn, his dead eyes instinctively flicked upwards and the next second Lewis cannoned into him.

The detective did not have the stature or muscular power of the psychopath, but his overweight body mass was still substantial and it carried them both forward several feet. They burst through the half-open barn doors, locked together in a grotesque embrace, the remote flying from Twister's hand and into the field's short stubby grass, as they ended up in a tangle of arms and legs on the sodden ground, with the detective on top.

But Lewis's advantage did not last long. Even as he hammered Twister's face and body with his fists, the killer simply shrugged him off like an irritating itchy blanket, seemingly impervious to the blows he was receiving, one huge powerful hand gripping the detective round the face and forcing his head back at an impossible angle.

Then suddenly there were flashing blue lights on the road beyond the field and the helicopter's blinding searchlight was fixing on them like the super trouper spot of a stage set. With a snarl of anger, Twister hurled Lewis away from him and scrambled to his feet, his eyes scanning the area around them for his remote.

He saw the flashing red light among the tufts of grass and went for the remote at the same time as Lewis – struggling weakly to his feet – made a dash for it. Twister got there first, but before he could grab his prize, he was bowled over for the second time by the detective, whose determination to save his beloved Kate imbued him with a renewed strength, born of desperation.

For just a moment Twister was taken aback by the unexpected ferocity of Lewis's attack, but, although the detective initially succeeded in gaining the upper hand, pinning the killer to the ground, the latter then recovered and hurled him sideways, kicking the policeman in the stomach before he could regain his feet.

Now the psychopath had the remote in his hand and, lashing out at Lewis's head with his foot when the detective tried to get back on his feet, he turned towards the target Transit as a convoy of police cars raced along the drove and skidded to a halt behind the doomed van.

'So the cavalry have arrived, have they?' he shouted above the roar of the helicopter still hovering overhead. 'Well, that's just more fuel for the fire, isn't it?'

And a fraction of a second later the night sky was blasted by a violent explosion, which seemed to light up the nearby drove from end to end and sent a tremor surging through the ground like the aftershock of a mini earthquake.

Twister was laughing inanely now, his usual dearth of emotion buried in an outpouring of psychotic glee, but it didn't last long. The owner of the field in which the black bull had been kept should have known that the gate between his property and that of the derelict farm was rotten and incapable of standing up to a determined onslaught by such a huge, aggressive animal; his negligence was Twister's downfall.

The creature, already wound up by Lewis's earlier escape, was maddened even more by the roar of the helicopter some two hundred feet above. Clocking Twister standing in its path, it saw the opportunity to satisfy its pent up fury, lowered its head and charged.

Alerted by some kind of uncanny sixth-sense, the psychopath swung round with remarkable speed, but, nimble as he was, he was much too late. The massive head of the bull slammed into him with the force of an articulated lorry, tossing him high in the air like an uprooted scarecrow. Then, even as Twister's screaming writhing body plummeted back to the ground, one vicious horn speared him in mid-spin, slicing through his abdomen and practically ripping him in two when the enraged beast shook its head violently to free itself before it finished the job by trampling and goring his already dismembered remains into the marshy ground.

The whole thing lasted just seconds, but for Lewis, lying there on the sodden ground – only half-conscious and bleeding heavily as a result of the injury he had received to his head from Twister's boot – time seemed to stand still.

It was Lewis's immobility that probably saved his life too, for the bull showed no interest whatsoever in his prostrate form and, immediately after wreaking its horrific carnage, it trotted off into the moonlight, bellowing its defiance and leaving the detective with just the psychopath's bloody, mutilated cadaver, glistening in the helicopter's searchlight, and the blazing torches of his colleagues bobbing across the field towards the scene.

It was all over, but at what price? And, staring up into the blazing orb of the searchlight, Lewis saw nothing of the helicopter or its spinning blades – only the face of a beautiful auburn-haired girl, whose blue eyes and mischievous smile would no longer light up his life.

AFTER THE FACT

Hayden Lewis climbed the narrow staircase with difficulty. His leg was heavily bandaged, but still hurting him after over a week of treatment. The hospital had told him that it was likely the injury from the bull's horn had become infected. 'No alcohol,' he had been warned, 'because of the antibiotics,' and he smiled ruefully as he pushed through the bedroom door with his breakfast tray.

The young woman was lying very still in the big double bed, her hair spread out over the pillow, framing her pale, freckled face. Setting the tray on the bedside table, he bent over and kissed her gently on the forehead.

She opened her eyes and smiled at him. 'Time to get up, is it?' Kate Hamblin asked.

He shook his head. 'Doctor said you were to rest for another couple of days.'

She made a face, then eased herself into a sitting position, staring with amused approval at the boiled egg and bread soldiers on the plate beside the bed. 'You're spoiling me,' she said, then added, 'Leg any better?'

He sighed. 'Still sore.' And he shook his head again, devouring her with his eyes. 'I still can't believe you survived that blast,' he said.

She nodded grimly. 'Neither can I. How's Roscoe?'

He grinned. 'Swearing his head off, with half his hair missing and his face still a nice two-tone colour. He wants to get back to work, but I think it'll be a while yet.'

She released her breath in a heavy sigh. 'That man saved my life,' she said for the umpteenth time since the incident.

'He certainly did,' Lewis agreed, 'and he's a lot brighter than we gave him credit for. Seeing the Transit parked on the drove with that damned sign on the side when he and Ansell arrived allowed him to make an immediate connection with what happened two years ago – it was nothing short of incredible.'

She snorted. 'Pulling the IED out of the filler pipe without even knowing if it was fitted with an anti-handling device and chucking it just before it went off was even more incredible – and it took real guts, too.'

Hayden sat on the end of the bed. 'It did that,' he acknowledged, and he chuckled, 'but the Chief wasn't very happy about his CID car, which caught the full blast instead.'

'What was it you said he told the ACC?' Kate put in and lowered her voice to a gruff: 'Slight miscalculation on my part, sir!'

And they both laughed uproariously.

Lewis leaned across to cut the top off her egg with a knife and pushed the tray towards her. 'Don't forget your breakfast.'

'Any other news?' she queried, taking the plate off the tray and dipping one bread soldier into the hardening yoke.

He pursed his lips for a second. 'Willoughby's going—'

'Going?'

'Yep. Retiring they say, though I reckon he's been given the big heave-ho after his latest performance. Ansell is tipped to succeed him.'

'Well, well. And what about Sharp?'

He shrugged. 'Still on his toes. They shouldn't have let the little blighter out on police bail in the first place. They had enough on him for a charge of unlawful possession of a firearm anyway, in my opinion, but they decided to await the result of inquiries into the origin of the gun and to seek CPS advice on the suspected bribery charge before going ahead on anything. They reckon he's scarpered abroad somewhere.'

Kate made another face and put her plate back on the tray. 'Sorry, Hayden, just can't eat it. Nice thought, though.'

He frowned. 'No problem, but what would you like instead?'

She stared at him, a familiar mischievous glint in her eye. 'There's only one thing I want at this moment, Detective Constable Lewis,' she said and threw back the bedclothes to reveal one shapely, bare thigh. 'And it isn't food.'

He raised an eyebrow as she pulled her nightdress up over her head. 'Well, in that case, Sergeant Hamblin,' he said, undoing his dressing-gown and letting it fall to the floor. 'I have no option but to do as instructed!'

THE END

ALSO BY DAVID HODGES

DETECTIVE KATE HAMBLIN MYSTERY SERIES

Book 1: MURDER ON THE LEVELS
Book 2: REVENGE ON THE LEVELS
Book 3: FEAR ON THE LEVELS
Book 4: KILLER ON THE LEVELS
Book 5: SECRETS ON THE LEVELS
Book 6: DEATH ON THE LEVELS
Book 7: POISON ON THE LEVELS
Book 8: WITCH FIRE ON THE LEVELS
Book 9: STALKER ON THE LEVELS
Book 10: VENOM ON THE LEVELS

Thank you for reading this book.

If you enjoyed it please leave feedback on Amazon or Goodreads, and if there is anything we missed or you have a question about, then please get in touch. We appreciate you choosing our book.

Founded in 2014 in Shoreditch, London, we at Joffe Books pride ourselves on our history of innovative publishing. We were thrilled to be shortlisted for Independent Publisher of the Year at the British Book Awards.

www.joffebooks.com

We're very grateful to eagle-eyed readers who take the time to contact us. Please send any errors you find to corrections@joffebooks.com. We'll get them fixed ASAP.

Printed in Great Britain
by Amazon

38653811R00153